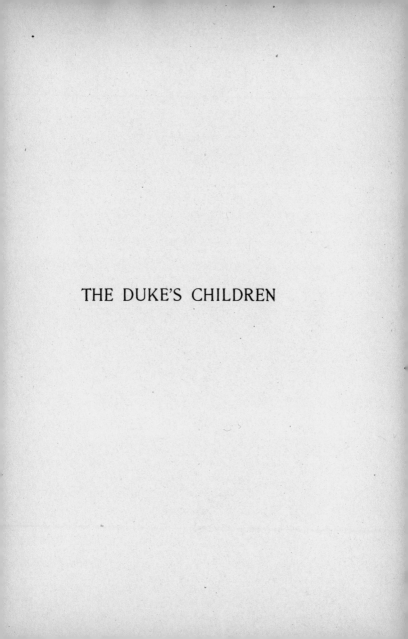

THE DUKE'S CHILDREN

THE DUKE'S CHILDREN

BY

ANTHONY TROLLOPE

VOL. II

NEW-YORK

DODD, MEAD & COMPANY

1925

Printed in U. S. A.

CONTENTS.

CONTENTS.

THE DUKE'S CHILDREN.

CHAPTER I.

MAJOR TIFTO AND THE DUKE.

" I BEG your pardon, Silverbridge," said the Major, entering the room, " but I was looking for Longstaff."

" He is n't here," said Silverbridge, who did not wish to be interrupted by his racing friend.

" Your father, I believe ? " said Tifto. He was red in the face, but was in other respects perhaps improved in appearance by his liquor. In his more sober moments he was not always able to assume that appearance of equality with his companions which it was the ambition of his soul to achieve. But a second glass of whiskey and water would always enable him to cock his tail and bark before the company with all the courage of my lady's pug. " Would you do me the great honour to introduce me to his Grace ? "

Silverbridge was not prone to turn his back upon a friend because he was low in the world. He had begun to understand that he had made a mistake by connecting himself with the Major, but at the club he always defended his partner. Though he not unfrequently found himself obliged to snub the Major

himself, he always countenanced the little master of
hounds, and was true to his own idea of "standing to
a fellow." Nevertheless he did not wish to introduce
his friend to his father. The Duke saw it all at a
glance, and felt that the introduction should be made.
"Perhaps," said he, getting up from his chair, "this is
Major Tifto."

"Yes;—my Lord Duke. I am Major Tifto."

The Duke bowed graciously. "My father and I
were engaged about private matters," said Silverbridge.

"I beg ten thousand pardons!" exclaimed the Major.
"I did not intend to intrude."

"I think we had done," said the Duke. "Pray sit
down, Major Tifto." The Major sat down. "Though
now I bethink myself, I have to beg your pardon;—
that I a stranger should ask you to sit down in your
own club."

"Don't mention it, my Lord Duke."

"I am so unused to clubs, that I forgot where I
was."

"Quite so, my Lord Duke. I hope you think that
Silverbridge is looking well?"

"Yes;—yes. I think so." Silverbridge bit his lips
and turned his face away to the door.

"We did n't make a very good thing of our Derby
nag the other day. Perhaps your Grace has heard all
that."

"I did hear that the horse in which you are both
interested had failed to win the race."

"Yes, he did. The Prime Minister, we call him,
your Grace,—out of compliment to a certain ministry
which I wish it was going on to-day instead of the
seedy lot we 've got in. I think, my Lord Duke, that

any one you may ask will tell you that I know what running is. Well;—I can assure you,—your Grace, that is,—that since I 've seen 'orses I 've never seen a 'orse fitter than him. When he got his canter that morning, it was nearly even betting. Not that I or Silverbridge were fools enough to put on anything at that rate. But I never saw a 'orse so bad ridden. I don't mean to say anything, my Lord Duke, against the man. But if that fellow had n't been squared, or else was n't drunk, or else was n't off his head, that 'orse must have won,—my Lord Duke."

"I do not know anything about racing, Major Tifto."

"I suppose not, your Grace. But as I and Silverbridge are together in this matter I thought I 'd just let your Grace know that we ought to have had a very good thing. I thought that perhaps your Grace might like to know that."

"Tifto, you are making an ass of yourself," said Silverbridge.

"Making an ass of myself!" exclaimed the Major.

"Yes ;—considerably."

"I think you are a little hard upon your friend," said the Duke, with an attempt at a laugh. "It is not to be supposed that he should know how utterly indifferent I am to everything connected with the turf."

"I thought, my Lord Duke, you might care about learning how Silverbridge was going on." This the poor little man said almost with a whine. His partner's roughness had knocked out of him nearly all the courage which Bacchus had given him.

"So I do; anything that interests him interests me. But perhaps of all his pursuits racing is the one to which I am least able to lend an attentive ear. That

every horse has a head, and that all did have tails
till they were ill-used is the extent of my stable knowledge."

"Very good indeed, my Lord Duke; very good indeed! Ha, ha, ha,—all horses have heads, and all
have tails! Heads and tails. Upon my word that is
the best thing I have heard for a long time. I will do
myself the honour of wishing your Grace good night.
By-bye, Silverbridge." Then he left the room, having
been made supremely happy by what he considered to
have been the Duke's joke. Nevertheless he would remember the snubbing and would be even with Silverbridge some day. Did Lord Silverbridge think that
he was going to look after his lordship's 'orses, and do
this always on the square, and then be snubbed for
doing it!

"I am very sorry that he should have come in to
trouble you," said the son.

"He has not troubled me much. I do not know
whether he has troubled you. If you are coming down
to the House again I will walk with you." Silverbridge of course had to go down to the House again,
and they started together. "That man did not trouble
me, Silverbridge; but the question is whether such an
acquaintance must not be troublesome to you."

"I'm not very proud of him, sir."

"But I think one ought to be proud of one's friends."

"He isn't my friend in that way at all."

"In what way then?"

"He understands racing."

"He is the partner of your pleasure then;—the man
in whose society you love to enjoy the recreation of
the racecourse."

"It is, sir, because he understands it."

"I thought that a gentleman on the turf would have a trainer for that purpose;—not a companion. You mean to imply that you can save money by leaguing yourself with Major Tifto."

"No, sir,—indeed."

"If you associate with him, not for pleasure, then it surely must be for profit. That you should do the former would be to me so surprising that I must regard it as impossible. That you should do the latter—is, I think, a reproach." This he said with no tone of anger in his voice,—so gently that Silverbridge at first hardly understood it. But gradually all that was meant came in upon him, and he felt himself to be ashamed of himself.

"He is bad," he said at last.

"Whether he be bad I will not say; but I am sure that you can gain nothing by his companionship."

"I will get rid of him," said Silverbridge, after a considerable pause. "I cannot do so all at once, but I will do it."

"It will be better, I think."

"Tregear has been telling me the same thing."

"Is he objectionable to Mr. Tregear?" asked the Duke.

"Oh yes. Tregear cannot bear him. You treated him a great deal better than Tregear ever does."

"I do not deny that he is entitled to be treated well; —but so also is your groom. Let us say no more about him. And so it is to be Mabel Grex?"

"I did not say so, sir. How can I answer for her? Only it was so pleasant for me to know that you would approve if it should come off."

"Yes;—I will approve.   When she has accepted
you——"

"But I don't think she will."

"If she should, tell her that I will go to her at once.
It will be much to have a new daughter;—very much
that you should have a wife.   Where would she like
to live?"

"Oh, sir, we have n't got as far as that yet."

"I dare say not; I dare say not," said the Duke.
"Gatherum is always thought to be dull."

"She would n't like Gatherum, I 'm sure."

"Have you asked her?"

"No, sir.   But nobody ever did like Gatherum."

"I suppose not.   And yet, Silverbridge, what a sum
of money it cost!"

"I believe it did."

"All vanity, and vexation of spirit!"   The Duke
no doubt was thinking of certain scenes passed at the
great house in question, which scenes had not been
delightful to him.   "No, I don't suppose she would
wish to live at Gatherum.   The Horns was given ex-
pressly by my uncle to your dear mother, and I should
like Mary to have the place."

"Certainly."

"You should live among your tenantry.   I don't
care so very much for Matching."

"It is the one place you do like, sir."

"However, we can manage all that.   Carlton Terrace I do not particularly like; but it is a good house,
and there you should hang up your hat when in London.   When it is settled let me know at once."

"But if it should never be settled!"

"I will ask no questions; but if it be settled, tell

me." Then in Palace Yard he was turning to go, but before he did so, he said another word, leaning on his son's shoulder. "I do not think that Mabel Grex and Major Tifto would do well together at all."

"There shall be an end to that, sir."

"God bless you, my boy!" said the Duke.

Lord Silverbridge sat in the House,—or to speak more accurately, in the smoking-room of the House,— for about an hour thinking over all that had passed between himself and his father. He certainly had not intended to say anything about Lady Mab, but on the spur of the moment it had all come out. Now at any rate it was decided for him that he must, in set terms, ask her to be his wife. The scene which had just occurred had made him thoroughly sick of Major Tifto. He must get rid of the Major, and there could be no way of doing this at once so easy and so little open to observation as marriage. If he were but once engaged to Mabel Grex the dismissal of Tifto would be quite a matter of course. He would see Lady Mabel again on the morrow and ask her in direct language to be his wife.

CHAPTER II.

It was known to all the world that Mrs. Montacute Jones's first great garden-party was to come off on Wednesday, 16th June, at Roehampton. Mrs. Montacute Jones, who lived in Grosvenor Place and had a country-house in Gloucestershire, and a place for young men to shoot at in Scotland, also kept a suburban Elysium at Roehampton, in order that she might give two garden-parties every year. When it is said that all these costly luxuries appertained to Mrs. Montacute Jones, it is to be understood that they did in truth belong to Mr. Jones, of whom nobody heard much. But of Mrs. Jones,—that is, Mrs. Montacute Jones,—everybody heard a great deal. She was an old lady who devoted her life to the amusement of—not only her friends, but very many who were not her friends. No doubt she was fond of lords and countesses, and worked very hard to get round her all the rank and fashion of the day. It must be acknowledged that she was a worldly old woman. But no more good-natured old woman lived in London, and everybody liked to be asked to her garden-parties. On this occasion there was to be a considerable infusion of royal blood,— German, Belgian, French, Spanish, and of native growth. Everybody who was asked would go, and everybody had been asked,—who was anybody. Lord Silverbridge had been asked, and Lord Silverbridge in-

tended to be there.   Lady Mary, his sister, could not
even be asked, because her mother was hardly more
than three months dead; but it is understood in the
world that women mourn longer than men.

Silverbridge had mounted a private hansom cab in
which he could be taken about rapidly,—and, as he
said himself, without being shut up in a coffin.   In this
vehicle he had himself taken to Roehampton, purport-
ing to kill two birds with one stone.   He had not as yet
seen his sister since she had been with Lady Cantrip.
He would on this day come back by The Horns.

He was well aware that Lady Mab would be at the
garden-party.   What place could be better for putting
the question he had to ask!   He was by no means so
confident as the heir to so many good things might
perhaps have been without overdue self-confidence.

Entering through the house into the lawn he encountered Mrs. Montacute Jones, who, with a seat behind her on the terrace, surrounded by flowers, was
going through the immense labour of receiving her
guests.

" How very good of you to come all this way, Lord
Silverbridge, to eat my strawberries."

" How very good of you to ask me !   I did not come
to eat your strawberries but to see your friends."

" You ought to have said you came to see me, you
know.   Have you met Miss Boncassen yet? "

" The American beauty?   No.   Is she here? "

" Yes ; and she particularly wants to be introduced
to you ; you won't betray me, will you? "

" Certainly not ; I am as true as steel."

" She wanted, she said, to see if the eldest son of the
Duke of Omnium really did look like any other man."

"Then I don't want to see her," said Silverbridge, with a look of vexation.

"There you are wrong, for there was real downright fun in the way she said it.   There they are, and I shall introduce you."   Then Mrs. Montacute Jones absolutely left her post for a minute or two, and taking the young lord down the steps of the terrace did introduce him to Mr. Boncassen, who was standing there amidst a crowd, and to Miss Boncassen the daughter.

Mr. Boncassen was an American who had lately arrived in England with the object of carrying out certain literary pursuits in which he was engaged within the British Museum.   He was an American who had nothing to do with politics and nothing to do with trade. He was a man of wealth and a man of letters.   And he had a daughter who was said to be the prettiest young woman either in Europe or in America at the present time.

Isabel Boncassen was certainly a very pretty girl. I wish that my reader would believe my simple assurance.   But no such simple assurance was ever believed, and I doubt even whether any description will procure for me from the reader that amount of faith which I desire to achieve.   But I must make the attempt. General opinion generally considered Miss Boncassen to be small, but she was in truth something above average height of English women.   She was slight, without that look of slimness which is common to girls, and especially to American girls.   That her figure was perfect the reader must believe on my word, as any detailed description of her arms, feet, bust, and waist would be altogether ineffective.   Her hair was dark brown and plentiful; but it added but little to her

charms, which depended on other matters. Perhaps
what struck the beholder first was the excessive brilliancy of her complexion. No pink was ever pinker, no
alabaster whiteness was ever more like alabaster; but
under and around and through it all there was a constantly changing hue which gave a vitality to her countenance which no fixed colours can produce. Her
eyes, too, were full of life and brilliancy, and even when
she was silent her mouth would speak. Nor was there
a fault within the oval of her face upon which the
hypercritics of mature age could set a finger. Her
teeth were excellent both in form and colour, but were
seen but seldom. Who does not know that look of
ubiquitous ivory produced by teeth which are too perfect in a face which is otherwise poor ? Her nose at
the base spread a little,—so that it was not purely
Grecian. But who has ever seen a nose to be elo-
quent and expressive which did not so spread ? It
was, I think, the vitality of her countenance,—the way
in which she could speak with every feature, the command which she had of pathos, of humour, of sympathy, of satire, the assurance which she gave by every
glance of her eye, every elevation of her brow, every
curl of her lip, that she was alive to all that was going
on,—it was all this rather than those feminine charms
which can be catalogued and labelled that made all acknowledge that she was beautiful.

"Lord Silverbridge," said Mr. Boncassen, speaking
a little through his nose, "I am proud to make your
acquaintance, sir. Your father is a man for whom we
in our country have a great respect. I think, sir, you
must be proud of such a father."

"Oh yes,—no doubt," said Silverbridge awkwardly.

Then Mr. Boncassen continued his discourse with the gentlemen around him. Upon this our friend turned to the young lady. " Have you been long in England, Miss Boncassen? "

" Long enough to have heard about you and your father," she said, speaking with no slightest twang.

" I hope you have not heard any evil of me."

" Well! "

" I 'm sure you can't have heard much good."

" I know you did n't win the Derby."

" You 've been long enough to hear that."

" Do you suppose we don't interest ourselves about the Derby in New York? Why, when we arrived at Queenstown I was leaning over the taffrail so that I might ask the first man on board the tender whether the Prime Minister had won."

"And he said he had n't."

" I can't conceive why you of all men should call your horse by such a name. If my father had been President of the United States I don't think I 'd call a horse President."

" I did n't name the horse."

" I 'd have changed it. But is it not very impudent in me to be finding fault with you the first time I have ever seen you! Shall you have a horse at Ascot ? "

" There will be something going, I suppose. Nothing that I care about." Lord Silverbridge had made up his mind that he would go to no races with Tifto before the Leger. The Leger would be an affair of such moment as to demand his presence. After that should come the complete rupture between him and Tifto.

Then there was a movement among the elders, and

Lord Silverbridge soon found himself walking alone with Miss Boncassen. It seemed to her to be quite natural to do so, and there certainly was no reason why he should decline anything so pleasant. It was thus that he had intended to walk with Mabel Grex;—only as yet he had not found her. "Oh yes," said Miss Boncassen, when they had been together about twenty minutes; "we shall be here all the summer, and all the fall, and all the winter. Indeed, father means to read every book in the British Museum before he goes back."

"He 'll have something to do."

"He reads by steam, and he has two or three young men with him to take it all down and make other books out of it;—just as you 'll see a lady take a lace shawl and turn it all about till she has trimmed a petti-coat with it. It is the same lace all through,—and so I tell father it 's the same knowledge."

"But he puts it where more people will find it."

"The lady endeavours to do the same with the lace. That depends on whether people look up or down. Father, however, is a very learned man. You must n't suppose that I am laughing at him. He is going to write a very learned book. Only everybody will be dead before it can be half finished." They still went on together, and then he gave her his arm and took her into the place where the strawberries and cream were prepared. As he was going in he saw Mabel Grex walking with Tregear, and she bowed to him pleasantly and playfully. "Is that lady a great friend of yours?" asked Miss Boncassen.

"A very great friend indeed."

"She is very beautiful."

"And clever as well,—and good as gold."

"Dear me!   Do tell me who it is that owns all these qualities."

"Lady Mabel Grex. She is daughter of Lord Grex. That man with her is my particular friend.   His name is Frank Tregear, and they are cousins."

"I am so glad they are cousins."

"Why glad?"

"Because his being with her won't make you un-happy."

"Supposing I was in love with her,—which I am not,—do you suppose it would make me jealous to see her with another man?"

"In our country it would not.   A young lady may walk about with a young gentleman just as she might with another young lady; but I thought it was differ-ent here.   Do you know, judging by English ways, I believe I am behaving very improperly in walking about with you so long.   Ought I not to tell you to go away?"

"Pray do not."

"As I am going to stay here so long I wish to be-have well to English eyes."

"People know who you are, and discount all that."

"If the difference be very marked they do.   For in-stance, I need n't wear a hideous long bit of cloth over my face in Constantinople because I am a woman.   But when the discrepancies are small then they have to be attended to.   So I shan't walk about with you any more."

"Oh yes, you will," said Silverbridge, who began to think that he liked walking about with Miss Boncassen.

"Certainly not.   There is Mr. Sprottle.   He is father's secretary.   He will take me back."

" Cannot I take you back as well as Mr. Sprottle? "

" Indeed no ;—I am not going to monopolise such a man as you. Do you think that I don't understand that everybody will be making remarks upon the American girl who won't leave the son of the Duke of Omnium alone? There is your particular friend Lady Mabel, and here is my particular friend Mr. Sprottle."

" May I come and call? "

" Certainly. Father will only be too proud,—and I shall be prouder. Mother will be the proudest of all. Mother very seldom goes out. Till we get a house we are at the Langham. Thank you, Mr. Sprottle. I think we 'll go and find father."

Lord Silverbridge found himself close to Lady Mabel and Tregear, and also to Miss Cassewary, who had now joined Lady Mabel. He had been much struck with the American beauty, but was not on that account the less anxious to carry out his great plan. It was essentially necessary that he should do so at once, because the matter had been settled between him and his father. He was anxious to assure her that if she would consent, then the Duke would be ready to pour out all kinds of paternal blessings on their heads. " Come and take a turn among the haycocks," he said.

" Frank declares," said Lady Mabel, " that the hay is hired for the occasion. I wonder whether that is true."

" Anybody can see," said Tregear, " that it has not been cut off the grass it stands upon."

" If I could find Mrs. Montacute Jones I 'd ask her where she got it," said Lady Mabel.

" Are you coming? " asked Silverbridge impatiently.

"I don't think I am. I have been walking round the haycocks till I am tired of them."

"Anywhere else then?"

"There is n't anywhere else. What have you done with your American beauty? The truth is, Lord Silverbridge, you ask me for my company when she won't give you hers any longer. Does n't it look like it, Miss Cassewary?"

"I don't think Lord Silverbridge is the man to forget an old friend for a new one."

"Not though the new friend be as lovely as Miss Boncassen?"

"I don't know that I ever saw a prettier girl," said Tregear.

"I quite admit it," said Lady Mabel. "But that is no salve for my injured feelings. I have heard so much about Miss Boncassen's beauty for the last week, that I mean to get up a company of British females, limited, for the express purpose of putting her down. Who is Miss Boncassen that we are all to be put on one side for her?"

Of course he knew that she was joking, but he hardly knew how to take her joke. There is a manner of joking which carries with it much serious intention. He did feel that Lady Mabel was not gracious to him because he had spent half an hour with this new beauty, and he was half inclined to be angry with her. Was it fitting that she should be cross with him seeing that he was resolved to throw at her feet all the good things that he had in the world? "Bother Miss Boncassen," he said; "you might as well come and take a turn with a fellow."

"Come along, Miss Cassewary," said she. "We

will go round the haycocks yet once again." So they turned and the two ladies accompanied Lord Silverbridge.

But this was not what he wanted. He could not say what he had to say in the presence of Miss Cassewary,—nor could he ask her to take herself off in another direction. Nor could he take himself off. Now that he had joined himself to these two ladies he must make with them the tour of the gardens. All this made him cross. "These kind of things are a great bore," he said.

"I dare say you would rather be in the House of Commons;—or, better still, at the Beargarden."

"You mean to be ill-natured when you say that, Lady Mab."

"You ask us to come and walk with you, and then you tell us that we are bores!"

"I did nothing of the kind."

"I should have thought that you would be particularly pleased with yourself for coming here to-day, seeing that you have made Miss Boncassen's acquaintance. To be allowed to walk half an hour alone with the acknowledged beauty of the two hemispheres ought to be enough even for Lord Silverbridge."

"That is nonsense, Lady Mab."

"Nothing gives so much zest to admiration as novelty. A republican charmer must be exciting after all the blasé habitués of the London drawing-rooms."

"How can you talk such nonsense, Mabel?" said Miss Cassewary.

"But it is so. I feel that people must be sick of seeing me. I know I am very often sick of seeing them. Here is something fresh,—and not only unlike.

but so much more lovely. I quite acknowledge that.
I may be jealous, but no one can say that I am spite-
ful. I wish that some republican Adonis or Apollo
would crop up,—so that we might have our turn. But
I don't think the republican gentlemen are equal to the
republican ladies. Do you, Lord Silverbridge ? "

" I have n't thought about it."

" Mr. Sprottle, for instance."

" I have not the pleasure of knowing Mr. Sprottle."

" Now we 've been round the haycocks, and really,
Lord Silverbridge, I don't think we have gained much
by it. Those forced marches never do any good."
And so they parted.

He was thinking with a bitter spirit of the ill result
of his morning's work when he again found himself
close to Miss Boncassen in the crowd of departing
people on the terrace. " Mind you keep your word,"
she said. And then she turned to her father. " Lord
Silverbridge has promised to call."

" Mrs. Boncassen will be delighted to make his acquaintance."

He got into his cab and was driven off towards
Richmond. As he went he began to think of the two
young women with whom he had passed his morning.
Mabel had certainly behaved badly to him. Even if
she suspected nothing of his object did she not owe it
to their friendship to be more courteous to him than
she had been ? And if she suspected that object,
should she not at any rate have given him the opportunity ?

Or could it be that she was really jealous of the
American girl ? No ;—that idea he rejected instantly.
It was not compatible with the innate modesty of his

disposition.   But no doubt the American girl was very lovely.   Merely as a thing to be looked at she was superior to Mabel.   He did feel that as to mere personal beauty she was in truth superior to anything he had ever seen before.   And she was clever too;—and good-humoured;—whereas Mabel had been both ill-natured and unpleasant.

CHAPTER III.

Lord Silverbridge found his sister alone. "I particularly want you," said he, "to come and call on Mabel Grex. She wishes to know you, and I am sure you would like her."

"But I have n't been out anywhere yet," she said. "I don't feel as though I wanted to go anywhere."

Nevertheless she was very anxious to know Lady Mabel Grex, of whom she had heard much. A girl, if she has had a former love passage, says nothing of it to her new lover; but a man is not so reticent. Frank Tregear had perhaps not told her everything, but he had told her something. "I was very fond of her;—very fond of her," he had said. "And so I am still," he had added. "As you are my love of loves, she is my friend of friends." Lady Mary had been satisfied by the assurance, but had become anxious to see the friend of friends. She resisted at first her brother's entreaties. She felt that her father in delivering her over to the seclusion of The Horns had intended to preclude her from showing herself in London. She was conscious that she was being treated with cruelty, and had a certain pride in her martyrdom. She would obey her father to the letter; she would give him no right to call her conduct in question; but he and any other to whom he might entrust the care of her should be made to know that she thought him cruel. He had

20

his power, to which she must submit. But she also had hers,—to which it was possible he might be made to submit. "I do not know that papa would wish me to go," she said.

"But it is just what he would wish. He thinks a good deal about Mabel."

"Why should be think about her at all?"

"I can't exactly explain," said Silverbridge, "but he does."

"If you mean to tell me that Mabel Grex is anything particular to you, and that papa approves of it, I will go all round the world to see her." But he had not meant to tell her this. The request had been made at Lady Mabel's instance. When his sister had spoken of her father's possible objection, then he had become eager in explaining the Duke's feeling, not remembering that such anxiety might betray himself. At that moment Lady Cantrip came in and the question was referred to her. She did not see any objection to such a visit, and expressed her opinion that it would be a good thing that Mary should be taken out. "She should begin to go somewhere," said Lady Cantrip. And so it was decided. On the next Friday he would come down early in his hansom and drive her up to Belgrave Square. Then he would take her to Carlton Terrace and Lady Cantrip's carriage should pick her up there and bring her home. He would arrange it all.

"What did you think of the American beauty?" asked Lady Cantrip when that was settled.

"I thought she was a beauty."

"So I perceived. You had eyes for nobody else," said Lady Cantrip, who had been at the garden-party.

"Somebody introduced her to me, and then I had

to walk about the grounds with her.   That 's the kind
of thing one always does in those places."

"Just so.   That is what ' those places' are meant for,
I suppose.   But it was not apparently a great infliction."   Lord Silverbridge had to explain that it was
not an infliction;—that it was a privilege, seeing that
Miss Boncassen was both clever and lovely; but that
it did not mean anything in particular.

When he took his leave he asked his sister to go out
into the grounds with him for a moment.   This she
did almost unwillingly, fearing that he was about to
speak to her of Tregear.   But he had no such purpose
on his mind.   "Of course you know," he began, "all
that was nonsense you were saying about Mabel."

"I did not know."

"I was afraid you might blurt out something before
her."

"I should not be so imprudent."

"Girls do make such fools of themselves sometimes.
They are always thinking about people being in love.
But it is the truth that my father said to me the other
day how very much he liked what he had heard of her,
and that he would like you to know her."

On that same evening Silverbridge wrote from the
Beargarden the shortest possible note to Lady Mabel,
telling her what he had arranged.   "I and Mary propose to call in B. Square on Friday at two.   I must
be early because of the House.   You will give us
lunch.   S."   There was no word of endearment,—
none even of those ordinary words which people who
hate each other use to one another.   But he received
the next day at home a much more kindly written note
from her:

" Dear Lord Silverbridge,—You are so good! You always do just what you think people will like best. Nothing could please me so much as seeing your sister, of whom of course I have heard *very*, *very* much. There shall be nobody here but Miss Cass.

"Yours most sincerely,

"M. G."

" How I do wish I were a man!" his sister said to him when they were in the hansom together.

" You 'd have a great deal more trouble."

" But I 'd have a hansom of my own, and go where I pleased. How would you like to be shut up at a place like The Horns? "

" You can go out if you like it."

" Not like you. Papa thinks it 's the proper place for me to live in, and so I must live there. I don't think a woman ever chooses how or where she shall live herself."

" You are not going to take up woman's rights, I hope."

" I think I shall if I stay at The Horns much longer. What would papa say if he heard that I was going to give a lecture at an institute ? "

" The governor has had so many things to bear that a trifle such as that would make but little difference."

" Poor papa! "

" He was dreadfully cut up about Gerald. And then he is so good! He said more to me about Gerald than he ever did about my own little misfortune at Oxford ; but to Gerald himself he said almost nothing. Now he has forgiven me because he thinks I am constant at the House."

" And are you ? "

" Not so much as he thinks.   I do go there,—for his
sake.   He has been so good about my changing sides."

" I think you were quite right there."

" I am beginning to think I was quite wrong.   What
did it matter to me ? "

" I suppose it did make papa unhappy."

" Of course it did ;—and then this affair of yours."
As soon as this was said Lady Mary at once hardened
her heart against her father.   Whether Silverbridge
was or was not entitled to his own political opinions,
—seeing that the Pallisers had for ages been known as
staunch whigs and liberals,—might be a matter for
question.   But that she had a right to her own lover
she thought that there could be no question.   As they
were sitting in the cab he could hardly see her face,
but he was aware that she was in some fashion arming
herself against opposition.   " I am sure that this makes
him very unhappy," continued Silverbridge.

" It cannot be altered," she said.

" It will have to be altered."

" Nothing can alter it.   He might die, indeed ;—or
so might I."

" Or he might see that it is no good,—and change
his mind," suggested Silverbridge.

" Of course that is possible," said Lady Mary very
curtly,—showing plainly by her manner that the subject was one which she did not choose to discuss any
further.

" It is very good of you to come to me," said Lady
Mabel, kissing her new acquaintance.   " I have heard
so much about you."

" And I also of you."

" I, you know, am one of your brother's stern Mentors. There are three or four of us determined to make him a pattern young legislator. Miss Cassewary is another. Only she is not quite so stern as I am."

" He ought to be very much obliged."

" But he is not;—not a bit. Are you, Lord Silverbridge? "

" Not so much as I ought to be, perhaps."

" Of course there is an opposing force. There are the race-horses, and the drag, and Major Tifto. No doubt you have heard of Major Tifto. The Major is the Mr. Worldly-Wiseman who won't let Christian go to the Straight Gate. I am afraid he has n't read his ' Pilgrim's Progress.' But we shall prevail, Lady Mary, and he will get to the Beautiful City at last."

" What is the beautiful city? " he asked.

" A seat in the Cabinet, I suppose ;—or that general respect which a young nobleman achieves when he has shown himself able to sit on a bench for six consecutive hours without appearing to go to sleep."

Then they went to lunch, and Lady Mary did find herself to be happy with her new acquaintance. Her life since her mother's death had been so sad that this short escape from it was a relief to her. Now for a while she found herself almost gay. There was an easy liveliness about Lady Mabel,—a grain of humour and playfulness conjoined,—which made her feel at home at once. And it seemed to her as though her brother was at home. He called the girl Lady Mab, and Queen Mab, and once plain Mabel, and the old woman he called Miss Cass. It surely, she thought, must be the case that Lady Mabel and her brother were engaged.

"Come upstairs into my own room,—it is nicer than this," said Lady Mabel, and they went from the dining-room into a pretty little sitting-room with which Silverbridge was very well acquainted. "Have you heard of Miss Boncassen?" Mary said she had heard something of Miss Boncassen's great beauty. "Everybody is talking about her. Your brother met her at Mrs. Montacute Jones's garden-party, and was made a conquest of instantly."

"I was n't made a conquest of at all," said Silverbridge.

"Then he ought to have been made a conquest of. I should be if I were a man. I think she is the loveliest person to look at and the nicest person to listen to that I ever came across. We all feel that, as far as this season is concerned, we are cut out. But we don't mind it so much because she is a foreigner." Then just as she said this the door was opened and Frank Tregear was announced.

Everybody there present knew as well as does the reader what was the connection between Tregear and Lady Mary Palliser. And each knew that the other knew it. It was therefore impossible for them not to feel themselves guilty among themselves. The two lovers had not seen each other since they had been together in Italy. Now they were brought face to face in this unexpected manner! And nobody except Tregear was at first quite sure whether somebody had not done something to arrange the meeting. Mary might naturally suspect that Lady Mabel had done this in the interest of her friend Tregear, and Silverbridge could not but suspect that it was so. Lady Mabel, who had never before met the other girl, could hardly

refrain from thinking that there had been some underhand communication,—and Miss Casseway was
clearly of opinion that there had been some understanding.

Silverbridge was the first to speak. " Halloo, Tregear, I did n't know that we were to see you."

" Nor I, that I should see you," said he. Then of
course there was a shaking of hands all round, in the
course of which ceremony he came to Mary the last.
She gave him her hand, but had not a word to say to
him. " If I had known that you were here," he said,
" I should not have come ; but I need hardly say how
glad I am to see you,—even in this way." Then the
two girls were convinced that the meeting was acci-
dental ; but Miss Cass still had her doubts.

Conversation became at once very difficult. Tregear
seated himself near but not very near to Lady Mary,
and made some attempt to talk to both the girls at
once. Lady Mabel plainly showed that she was not
at her ease ;—whereas Mary seemed to be stricken
dumb by the presence of her lover. Silverbridge was
so much annoyed by a feeling that this interview was
a treason to his father that he sat cudgelling his brain
to think how he should bring it to an end. Miss Cassewary was dumbfounded by the occasion. She was
the one elder in the company who ought to see that
no wrong was committed. She was not directly re-
sponsible to the Duke of Omnium, but she was thoroughly permeated by a feeling that it was her duty to
take care that there should be no clandestine love
meetings in Lord Grex's house. At last Silverbridge
jumped up from his chair. " Upon my word, Tregear,
I think you had better go," said he.

"So do I," said Miss Cassewary. "If it is an accident—— "

"Of course it is an accident," said Tregear, angrily, —looking round at Mary, who blushed up to her eyes.

"I did not mean to doubt it," said the old lady. "But as it has occurred, Mabel, don't you think that he had better go ? "

"He won't bite anybody, Miss Cass."

"She would not have come if she had expected it," said Silverbridge.

"Certainly not," said Mary, speaking for the first time. "But now he is here—— " Then she stopped herself, rose from the sofa, sat down, and then rising again, stepped up to her lover,—who rose at the same moment,—and threw herself into his arms and put up her lips to be kissed.

"This won't do at all," said Silverbridge. Miss Cassewary clasped her hands together and looked up to heaven. She probably had never seen such a thing done before. Lady Mabel's eyes were filled with tears, and though in all this there was much to cause her anguish, still in her heart of hearts she admired the brave girl who could thus show her truth to her lover.

"Now go," said Mary through her sobs.

"My own one," ejaculated Tregear.

"Yes, yes, yes; always your own. Go,—go; go." She was weeping and sobbing as she said this, and hiding her face with her handkerchief. He stood for a moment irresolute, and then left the room without a word of adieu to any one.

"You have behaved very badly," said the brother.

"She has behaved like an angel," said Mabel, throwing her arms round Mary as she spoke, "like an angel.

If there had been a girl whom you loved and who loved
you, would you not have wished it ?   Would you not
have worshipped her for showing that she was not
ashamed of her love? "

"I am not a bit ashamed," said Mary.

"And I say that you have no cause. No one
knows him as I do. How good he is, and how
worthy!" Immediately after that Silverbridge took
his sister away, and Lady Mabel, escaping from Miss
Cass, was alone. "She loves him almost as I have
loved him," she said to herself. "I wonder whether
he can love her as he did me ? "

CHAPTER IV.

WHAT CAME OF THE MEETING.

NOT a word was said in the cab as Lord Silverbridge took his sister to Carlton Terrace, and he was leaving her without any reference to the scene which had taken place, when an idea struck him that this would be cruel. "Mary," he said, "I was very sorry for all that."

"It was not my doing."

"I suppose it was nobody's doing. But I am very sorry that it occurred. I think that you should have controlled yourself."

"No!" she almost shouted.

"I think so."

"No;—if you mean by controlling myself, holding my tongue. He is the man I love,—whom I have promised to marry."

"But, Mary,—do ladies generally embrace their lovers in public?"

"No;—nor should I. I never did such a thing in my life before. But as he was there I had to show that I was not ashamed of him! Do you think I should have done it if you all had not been there?" Then again she burst into tears.

He did not quite know what to make of it. Mabel Grex had declared that she had behaved like an angel. But yet, as he thought of what he had seen, he shuddered with vexation. "I was thinking of the governor," he said.

"He shall be told everything."

"That you met Tregear ? "

"Certainly; and that I—kissed him. I will do nothing that I am ashamed to tell everybody."

"He will be very angry."

"I cannot help it. He should not treat me as he is doing. Mr. Tregear is a gentleman. Why did he let him come? Why did you bring him? But it is of no use. The thing is settled. Papa can break my heart, but he can't make me say that I am not engaged to Mr. Tregear."

On that night Mary told the whole of her story to Lady Cantrip. There was nothing that she tried to conceal. "I got up," she said, "and threw my arms round him. Is he not all the world to me ? "

"Had it been planned? " asked Lady Cantrip.

"No;—no! Nothing had been planned. They are cousins and very intimate and he goes there constantly. Now I want you to tell papa all about it."

Lady Cantrip began to think that it had been an evil day for her when she had agreed to take charge of this very determined young lady; but she consented at once to write to the Duke. As the girl was in her hands she must take care not to lay herself open to reproaches. As this objectionable lover had either contrived a meeting, or had met her without contriving, it was necessary that the Duke should be informed. "I would rather you wrote the letter," said Lady Mary. "But pray tell him that all along I have meant him to know all about it."

Till Lady Cantrip seated herself at her writing-table she did not know how great the difficulty would be. It cannot in any circumstance be easy to write to a father as to his daughter's love for an objectionable

lover; but the Duke's character added much to the
severity of the task. And then that embrace! She
knew that the Duke would be struck with horror as he
read of such a tale, and she found herself almost struck
with horror as she attempted to write it. When she
came to the point she found she could not write it. "I
fear there was a good deal of warmth shown on both
sides," she said, feeling that she was calumniating the
man, as to whose warmth she had heard nothing. "It
is quite clear," she added, "that this is not a passing
fancy on her part."

It was impossible that the Duke should be made to
understand exactly what had occurred. That Silverbridge had taken Mary he did understand, and that
they had together gone to Lord Grex's house. He understood also that the meeting had taken place in the
presence of Silverbridge and of Lady Mabel. "No
doubt it was all an accident," Lady Cantrip wrote.
How could it be an accident?

"You had Mary up in town on Friday," he said to
his son on the following Sunday morning.

"Yes, sir."

"And that friend of yours came in?"

"Yes, sir."

"Do you not know what my wishes are?"

"Certainly I do;—but I could not help his coming.
You do not suppose that anybody had planned it?"

"I hope not."

"It was simply an accident. Such an accident as
must occur over and over again,—unless Mary is to
be locked up."

"Who talks of locking anybody up? What right
have you to speak in that way?"

"I only meant that of course they will stumble across each other in London."

"I think I will go abroad," said the Duke. He was silent for a while, and then repeated his words. "I think I will go abroad."

"Not for long, I hope, sir."

"Yes;—to live there. Why should I stay here? What good can I do here? Everything I see and everything I hear is a pain to me." The young man of course could not but go back in his mind to the last interview which he had had with his father, when the Duke had been so gracious and apparently so well pleased.

"Is there anything else wrong,—except about Mary?" Silverbridge asked.

"I am told that Gerald owes about fifteen hundred pounds at Cambridge."

"So much as that! I knew he had a few horses there."

"It is not the money, but the absence of principle, —that a young man should have no feeling that he ought to live within certain prescribed means! Do you know what you have had from Mr. Morton?"

"Not exactly, sir."

"It is different with you. But a man, let him be who he may, should live within certain means. As for your sister, I think she will break my heart." Silverbridge found it to be quite impossible to say anything in answer to this. "Are you going to church?" asked the Duke.

"I was not thinking of doing so particularly."

"Do you not ever go?"

"Yes;—sometimes. I will go with you now, if you like it, sir."

"I had thought of going, but my mind is too much harassed. I do not see why you should not go."

But Silverbridge, though he had been willing to sacrifice his morning to his father,—for it was, I fear, in that way that he had looked at it,—did not see any reason for performing a duty which his father himself omitted. And there were various matters also which harassed him. On the previous evening, after dinner, he had allowed himself to back the Prime Minister for the Leger to a very serious amount. In fact, he had plunged, and now stood to lose some twenty thousand pounds on the doings of the last night. And he had made these bets under the influence of Major Tifto. It was the remembrance of this, after the promise made to his father, that annoyed him the most. He was imbued with a feeling that it behoved him as a man to "pull himself together" as he would have said himself, and to live in accordance with certain rules. He could make the rules easily enough, but he had never yet succeeded in keeping any one of them. He had determined to sever himself from Tifto; and, in doing that, had intended to sever himself from affairs of the turf generally. This resolution was not yet a week old. It was on that evening that he had resolved that Tifto should no longer be his companion; and now he had to confess to himself that because he had drunk three or four glasses of champagne he had been induced by Tifto to make those wretched bets.

And he had told his father that he intended to ask Mabel Grex to be his wife. He had so committed himself that the offer must now be made. He did not specially regret that, though he wished that he had been more reticent. "What a fool a man is to blurt out everything!" he said to himself.   A wife would be a good thing for him; and where could he possibly find a better wife than Mabel Grex?   In beauty she was no doubt inferior to Miss Boncassen.   There was something about Miss Boncassen which made it impossible to forget her.   But Miss Boncassen was an American, and on many accounts out of the question. It did not occur to him that he would fall in love with Miss Boncassen; but still it seemed hard to him that this intention of marriage should stand in his way of having a good time with Miss Boncassen for a few weeks.   No doubt there were objections to marriage. It clipped a fellow's wings.   But then, if he were married, he might be sure that Tifto would be laid aside. It was such a great thing to have got his father's assured consent to a marriage.   It meant complete independence in money matters.

Then his mind ran away to a review of his father's affairs.   It was a genuine trouble to him that his father should be so unhappy.   Of all the griefs which weighed upon the Duke's mind, that in reference to his sister was the heaviest.   The money which Gerald owed at Cambridge would be nothing if that other sorrow could be conquered.   Nor had Tifto and his own extravagance caused the Duke any incurable wounds.   If Tregear could be got out of the way his father, he thought, might be reconciled to other things.   He felt very tender-hearted about his father; but he had no remorse in regard to his sister as he made up his mind that he would speak very seriously to Tregear.

He had wandered into St. James's Park, and had lighted by this time half-a-dozen cigarettes one after another, as he sat on one of the benches.   He was a handsome youth, all but six feet high, with light hair, with round blue eyes, and with all that aristocratic look which had belonged so peculiarly to the late Duke but which was less conspicuous in the present head of the family. He was a young man whom you would hardly pass in a crowd without observing,—but of whom you would say, after due observation, that he had not as yet put off all his childish ways. He now sat with his legs stretched out, with his cane in his hands, looking down upon the water. He was trying to think. He worked hard at thinking. But the bench was hard, and, upon the whole, he was not satisfied with his position. He had just made up his mind that he would look up Tregear, when Tregear himself appeared on the path before him.

"Tregear!" exclaimed Silverbridge.

"Silverbridge!" exclaimed Tregear.

"What on earth makes you walk about here on a Sunday morning?"

"What on earth makes you sit there? That I should walk here, which I often do, does not seem to me odd. But that I should find you is marvellous. Do you often come?"

"Never was here in my life before. I strolled in because I had things to think of."

"Questions to be asked in Parliament? Notices of motions, amendments in committee, and that kind of thing?"

"Go on, old fellow."

"Or perhaps Major Tifto has made important revelations."

"D—— Major Tifto."

"With all my heart," said Tregear.

"Sit down here," said Silverbridge. "As it happened, at the moment when you came up I was thinking of you."

"That was kind."

"And I was determined to go to you. All this about my sister must be given up."

"Must be given up!"

"It can never lead to any good. I mean that there never can be a marriage." Then he paused, but Tregear was determined to hear him out. "It is making my father so miserable that you would pity him if you could see him."

"I dare say I should. When I see people unhappy I always pity them. What I would ask you to think of is this. If I were to commission you to tell your sister that everything between us should be given up, would not she be so unhappy that you would have to pity her? "

"She would get over it."

"And so will your father."

"He has a right to have his own opinion on such a matter."

"And so have I. And so has she. His rights in this matter are very clear and very potential. I am quite ready to admit that we cannot marry for many years to come, unless he will provide the money. You are quite at liberty to tell him that I say so. I have no right to ask your father for a penny, and I will never do so. The power is all in his hands. As far as I know my own purposes, I shall not make any immediate attempt even to see her. We did meet, as you saw, the other day, by the merest chance. After that do you think that your sister wishes me to give her up?"

"As for supposing that girls are to have what they wish, that is nonsense."

"For young men, I suppose, equally so. Life ought to be a life of self-denial, no doubt. Perhaps it might be my duty to retire from this affair, if by doing so I should sacrifice only myself. The one person of whom I am bound to think in this matter is the girl I love."

"That is just what she would say about you."

"I hope so."

"In that way you support each other. If it were any other man circumstanced just like you are, and any other girl placed like Mary, you would be the first to say that the man was behaving badly. I don't like to use hard language to you, but in such a case you would be the first to say of another man—that he was looking after the girl's money."

Silverbridge as he said this looked forward steadfastly on to the water, regretting much that cause for quarrel should have arisen, but thinking that Tregear would find himself obliged to quarrel. But Tregear, after a few moments' silence, having thought it out, determined that he would not quarrel. "I think I probably might," he said, laying his hand on Silverbridge's arm. "I think I perhaps might express such an opinion."

"Well, then!"

"I have to examine myself, and find out whether I am guilty of the meanness which I might perhaps be too ready to impute to another. I have done so, and I am quite sure that I am not drawn to your sister by any desire for her money. I did not seek her because she was a rich man's daughter, nor,—because she is a rich man's daughter will I give her up. She shall be mistress of the occasion. Nothing but a word from her shall induce me to leave her;—but a word from her, if it comes from her own lips,—shall do so." Then he took his friend's hand in his, and, having grasped it, walked away without saying another word.

CHAPTER V.

THRICE within the next three weeks did Lord Silver
bridge go forth to ask Mabel to be his wife, but thrice
in vain. On one occasion she would talk on other
things. On the second Miss Cassewary would not
leave her. On the third the conversation turned in a
very disagreeable way on Miss Boncassen, as to whom
Lord Silverbridge could not but think that Lady Mabel
said some very ill-natured things. It was no doubt
true that he, during the last three weeks, had often been
in Miss Boncassen's company, that he had danced with
her, ridden with her, taken her to the House of Lords
and to the House of Commons, and was now engaged
to attend upon her at a river-party up above Maidenhead. But Mabel had certainly no right to complain.
Had he not thrice during the same period come there
to lay his coronet at her feet;—and now, at this very
moment, was it not her fault that he was not going
through the ceremony?

"I suppose," she said, laughing, "that it is all settled."

"What is all settled?"

"About you and the American beauty."

"I am not aware that anything particular has been
settled."

"Then it ought to be,—ought n't it? For her sake,
I mean."

"That is so like an English woman," said Lord Sil-

verbridge.   " Because you cannot understand a manner
of life a little different from your own you will impute
evil."

" I have imputed no evil, Lord Silverbridge, and you
have no right to say so."

" If you mean to assert," said Miss Cass, " that the
manners of American young ladies are freer than those
of English young ladies, it is you that are taking away
their characters."

" I don't say it would be at all bad," continued Lady
Mabel.   " She is a beautiful girl, and very clever,
and would make a charming duchess.   And then it
would be such a delicious change to have an American
duchess."

" She would n't be a duchess."

" Well, countess, with duchess-ship before her in
the remote future.   Would n't it be a change, Miss
Cass? "

" Oh, decidedly! " said Miss Cass.

" And very much for the better.   Quite a case of
new blood, you know.   Pray don't suppose that I
mean to object.   Everybody who talks about it approves.   I have n't heard a dissentient voice.   Only
as it has gone so far, and as English people are too
stupid, you know, to understand all these new ways,——
don't you think perhaps——? "

" No, I don't think.   I don't think anything except
that you are very ill-natured."   Then he got up, and,
after making formal adieux to both the ladies, left the
house.

As soon as he was gone Lady Mabel began to
laugh, but the least apprehensive ears would have perceived that the laughter was affected.   Miss Cassewary

did not laugh at all, but sat bolt upright and looked very serious. "Upon my honour," said the younger lady, "he is the most beautifully simple-minded human being I ever knew in my life."

"Then I would n't laugh at him."

"How can one help it? But of course I do it with a purpose."

"What purpose?"

"I think he is making a fool of himself. If somebody does not interfere he will go so far that he will not be able to draw back without misbehaving."

"I thought," said Miss Cassewary, in a very low voice, almost whispering, "I thought that he was looking for a wife elsewhere."

"You need not think of that again," said Lady Mab, jumping up from her seat. "I had thought of it too. But as I told you before, I spared him. He did not really mean it with me;—nor does he mean it with this American girl. Such young men seldom mean. They drift into matrimony. But she will not spare him. It would be a national triumph. All the States would sing a pæan of glory. Fancy a New York belle having compassed a duke!"

"I don't think it possible. It would be too horrid."

"I think it quite possible. As for me, I could teach myself to think it best as it is, were I not so sure I should be better for him than so many others. But I should n't love him."

"Why not love him?"

"He is such a boy. I should always treat him like a boy,—spoiling him and petting him, but never respecting him. Don't run away with any idea that I should refuse him from conscientious motives, if he

were really to ask me. I too should like to be a
duchess. I should like to bring all this misery at home
to an end."

" But you did refuse him."

" Not exactly;—because he never asked me. For
the moment I was weak, and so I let him have another
chance. I shall not have been a good friend to him
if it ends in his marrying this Yankee."

Lord Silverbridge went out of the house in a very ill
humour,—which, however, left him when in the course
of the afternoon he found himself up at Maidenhead
with Miss Boncassen. Miss Boncassen at any rate did
not laugh at him. And then she was so pleasant, so
full of common sense, and so completely intelligent!
" I like you," she had said, " because I feel that you
will not think that you ought to make love to me.
There is nothing I hate so much as the idea that a
young man and a young woman can't be acquainted
with each other without some such tomfoolery as that."
This had exactly expressed his own feeling. Nothing
could be so pleasant as his intimacy with Isabel Boncassen.

Mrs. Boncassen seemed to be a homely person, with
no desire either to speak or to be spoken to. She
went out but seldom, and on those rare occasions did
not in any way interfere with her daughter. Mr. Boncassen filled a prouder situation. Everybody knew
that Miss Boncassen was in England, because it suited
Mr. Boncassen to spend many hours in the British
Museum. But still the daughter hardly seemed to be
under control from the father. She went alone where
she liked; talked to those she liked; and did what she
liked. Some of the young ladies of the day thought

that there was a good deal to be said in favour of the freedom which she enjoyed.

There is, however, a good deal to be said against it. All young ladies cannot be Miss Boncassens, with such an assurance of admirers as to be free from all fear of loneliness. There is a comfort for a young lady in having a pied-à-terre to which she may retreat in case of need. In American circles, where girls congregate without their mothers, there is a danger felt by young men that if a lady be once taken in hand, there will be no possibility of getting rid of her,—no mamma to whom she may be taken and under whose wings she may be dropped. "My dear," said an old gentleman the other day walking through an American ball-room, and addressing himself to a girl whom he knew well, —"My dear—— " But the girl bowed and passed on, still clinging to the arm of the young man who accompanied her. But the old gentleman was cruel, and possessed of a determined purpose. "My dear," said he again, catching the young man tight by the collar and holding him fast. "Don't be afraid; I've got him; he shan't desert you; I'll hold him here till you have told me how your father does." The young lady looked as if she did n't like it, and the sight of her misery gave rise to a feeling that, after all, mammas perhaps may be a comfort.

But in her present phase of life Miss Boncassen suffered no misfortune of this kind. It had become a privilege to be allowed to attend upon Miss Boncassen, and the feeling of this privilege had been enhanced by the manner in which Lord Silverbridge had devoted himself to her. Fashion of course makes fashion. Had not Lord Silverbridge been so very much struck by the

charm of the young lady, Lords Glasslough and Popplecourt would not perhaps have found it necessary to
run after her.   As it was, even that most unenergetic
of young men, Dolly Longstaff, was moved to profound
admiration.

On this occasion they were all up the river at Maidenhead.   Mr. Boncassen had looked about for some
means of returning the civilities offered to him, and had
been instigated by Mrs. Montacute Jones to do it after
this fashion.   There was a magnificent banquet spread
in a summer-house on the river-bank.   There were
boats, and there was a band, and there was a sward
for dancing.   There was lawn-tennis, and fishing-rods,
—which nobody used,—and better still, long shady
secluded walks in which gentlemen might stroll,—and
ladies too, if they were kind enough.   The whole thing
had been arranged by Mrs. Montacute Jones. . As the
day was fine, as many of the old people had abstained
from coming, as there were plenty of young men of the
best sort, and as nothing had been spared in reference
to external comforts, the party promised to be a success.
Every most lovely girl in London of course was there,
—except Lady Mabel Grex.   Lady Mabel was in the
habit of going everywhere, but on this occasion she had
refused Mrs. Boncassen's invitation.   " I don't want to
see her triumphs," she had said to Miss Cass.

Everybody went down by railway of course, and in-
numerable flies and carriages had been provided to take
them to the scene of action.   Some immediately got
into boats and rowed themselves up from the bridge,—
which, as the thermometer was standing at eighty in the
shade, was an inconsiderate proceeding.   " I don't
think I am quite up to that," said Dolly Longstaff,

when it was proposed to him to take an oar. " Miss Amazon will do it. She rows so well, and is so strong." Whereupon Miss Amazon, not at all abashed, did take the oar; and as Lord Silverbridge was on the seat be-hind her with the other oars he probably enjoyed her task.

" What a very nice sort of person Lady Cantrip is." This was said to Silverbridge by that generally silent young nobleman Lord Popplecourt. The remark was the more singular because Lady Cantrip was not at the party,—and the more so again because, as Silverbridge thought, there could be but little in common between the countess who had his sister in charge and the young lord beside him, who was not fast only because he did not like to risk his money.

" Well,—yes ; I dare say she is."

" I thought so, peculiarly. I was up at that place at Richmond yesterday."

" The devil you were! What were you doing at The Horns ? "

" Lady Cantrip's grandmother was,—I don't quite know what she was, but something to us. I know I 've got a picture of her at Popplecourt. Lady Can-trip wanted to ask me something about it, and so I went down. I was so glad to make acquaintance with your sister."

" You saw Mary, did you ? "

" Oh yes ; I lunched there. I 'm to go down and meet the Duke some day."

" Meet the Duke!"

" Why not ? "

" No reason on earth,—only I can't imagine the gov-

ernor going to Richmond for his dinner.   Well! I am
very glad to hear it.   I hope you 'll get on well with
him."

"I was so much struck with your sister."

"Yes; I dare say," said Silverbridge, turning away
into the path where he saw Miss Boncassen standing
with some other ladies.   It certainly did not occur to
him that Popplecourt was to be brought forward as
a suitor for his sister's hand.

"I believe this is the most lovely place in the world,"
Miss Boncassen said to him.

"We are so much the more obliged to you for bringing us here."

"We don't bring you.   You allow us to come with
you and see all that is pretty and lovely."

"Is it not your party?"

"Father will pay the bill, I suppose,—as far as that
goes.   And mother's name was put on the cards.   But
of course we know what that means.   It is because
you and a few others like you have been so kind to us,
that we are able to be here at all."

"Everybody, I should think, must be kind to you."

"I do have a good time pretty much; but nowhere
so good as here.   I fear that when I get back I shall
not like New York."

"I have heard you say, Miss Boncassen, that Americans were more likeable than the English."

"Have you?   Well, yes; I think I have said so.
And I think it is so.   I 'd sooner have to dance with
a bank clerk in New York, than with a bank clerk here."

"Do you ever dance with bank clerks?"

"Oh dear, yes.   At least I suppose so.   I dance

with whoever comes up. We have n't got lords in
America, you know."

"You have got gentlemen?"

"Plenty of them;—but they are not so easily defined
as lords. I do like lords."

"Do you?"

"Oh yes,—and ladies;—countesses, I mean, and
women of that sort. Your Lady Mabel Grex is not
here. Why would n't she come?"

"Perhaps you did n't ask her."

"Oh yes, I did;—especially, for your sake."

"She is not my Lady Mabel Grex," said Lord Silverbridge, with unnecessary energy.

"But she will be."

"What makes you think that?"

"You are devoted to her."

"Much more to you, Miss Boncassen."

"That is nonsense, Lord Silverbridge."

"Not at all."

"It is also—untrue."

"Surely I must be the best judge of that myself."

"Not a doubt; a judge not only whether it be true,
but if true whether expedient,—or even possible. What
did I say to you when we first began to know each
other?"

"What did you say?"

"That I liked knowing you;—that was frank enough;
—that I liked knowing you because I knew that there
would be no tomfoolery of love-making." Then she
paused; but he did not quite know how to go on with
the conversation at once, and she continued her speech.
"When you condescend to tell me that you are devoted to me, as though that were the kind of thing

that I expect to have said when I take a walk with a young man in a wood, is not that the tomfoolery of love-making?" She stopped and looked at him, so that he was obliged to answer.

"Then why do you ask me if I am devoted to Lady Mabel? Would not that be tomfoolery too?"

"No. If I thought so, I would not have asked the question. I did specially invite her to come here because I thought you would like it. You have got to marry somebody."

"Some day, perhaps."

"And why not her?"

"If you come to that, why not you?" He felt himself to be getting into deep waters as he said this,—but he had a meaning to express if only he could find the words to express it. "I don't say whether it is tomfoolery, as you call it, or not; but whatever it is, you began it."

"Yes;—yes. I see. You punish me for my unpremeditated impertinence in suggesting that you are devoted to Lady Mabel by the premeditated impertinence of pretending to be devoted to me."

"Stop a moment. I cannot follow that." Then she laughed. "I will swear that I did not intend to be impertinent."

"I hope not."

"I am devoted to you."

"Lord Silverbridge!"

"I think you are—— "

"Stop, stop. Do not say it."

"Well, I won't;—not now. But there has been no tomfoolery."

"May I ask a question, Lord Silverbridge? You

will not be angry ?   I would not have you angry with me."

"I will not be angry," he said.

"Are you not engaged to marry Lady Mabel Grex?"

"No."

"Then I beg your pardon.   I was told that you were engaged to her.   And I thought your choice was so fortunate, so happy !   I have seen no girl here that I admire half so much.   She almost comes up to my idea of what a young woman should be."

"Almost!"

"Now I am sure that if not engaged to her you must be in love with her, or my praise would have suffered."

"Though one knows a Lady Mabel Grex, one may become acquainted with a Miss Boncassen."

There are moments in which stupid people say clever things, obtuse people say sharp things, and good-natured people say ill-natured things.   "Lord Silverbridge," she said, "I did not expect that from you."

"Expect what?   I meant it simply."

"I have no doubt you meant it simply.   We Americans think ourselves sharp, but I have long since found out that we may meet more than our matches over here.   I think we will go back.   Mother means to try to get up a quadrille."

"You will dance with me?"

"I think not.   I have been walking with you, and I had better dance with some one else."

"You can let me have one dance."

"I think not.   There will not be many."

"Are you angry with me?"

"Yes, I am ; there."   But as she said this she smiled. "The truth is I thought I was getting the better of you, and you turned round and gave me a pat on the head to show me that you could be master when it pleased you. You have defended your intelligence at the expense of your good-nature."

"I 'll be shot if I know what it all means," he said, just as he was parting with her.

CHAPTER VI.

MISS BONCASSEN'S RIVER-PARTY.—NO. 2.

Lord Silverbridge made up his mind that as he could not dance with Miss Boncassen he would not dance at all. He was not angry at being rejected, and when he saw her stand up with Dolly Longstaff he felt no jealousy. She had refused to dance with him, not because she did not like him, but because she did not wish to show that she liked him. He could understand that, though he had not quite followed all the ins and outs of her little accusations against him. She had flattered him,—without any intention of flattery on her part. She had spoken of his intelligence and had complained that he had been too sharp to her. Mabel Grex when most sweet to him, when most loving, always made him feel that he was her inferior. She took no trouble to hide her conviction of his youthfulness. This was anything but flattering. Miss Boncassen, on the other hand, professed herself to be almost afraid of him.

"There shall be no tomfoolery of love-making," she had said. But what if it were not tomfoolery at all? What if it were good, genuine, earnest love-making? He certainly was not pledged to Lady Mabel. As regarded his father there would be a difficulty. In the first place he had been fool enough to tell his father that he was going to make an offer to Mabel Grex. And then his father would surely refuse his consent to

a marriage with an American stranger.   In such case
there would be no unlimited income, no immediate
pleasantness of magnificent life such as he knew would
be poured out upon him if he were to marry Mabel
Grex.   As he thought of this, however, he told himself
that he would not sell himself for money and magnifi-
cence.   He could afford to be independent, and to
gratify his own taste.   Just at this moment he was of
opinion that Isabel Boncassen would be the sweeter
companion of the two.

He had sauntered down to the place where they
were dancing and stood by, saying a few words to Mrs.
Boncassen.   "Why are you not dancing, my lord?"
she asked.

"There are enough without me."

"I guess you young aristocrats are never over-fond
of doing much with your own arms and legs."

"I don't know about that; polo, you know, for the
legs, and lawn-tennis for the arms, is hard work enough."

"But it must always be something new-fangled; and
after all it is n't of much account.   Our young men
like to have quite a time at dancing."

It all came through her nose!   And she looked so
common!   What would the Duke say to her, or Mary,
or even Gerald?   The father was by no means so objectionable.   He was a tall, straight, ungainly man,
who always wore black clothes.   He had dark, stiff,
short hair, a long nose, and a forehead that was both
high and broad.   Ezekiel Boncassen was the very man,
—from his appearance,—for a President of the United
States; and there were men who talked of him for that
high office.   That he had never attended to politics
was supposed to be in his favour.   He had the rep-

utation of being the most learned man in the States, and reputation itself often suffices to give a man dignity of manner. He, too, spoke through his nose, but the peculiar twang coming from a man would be supposed to be virile and incisive. From a woman, Lord Silver-bridge thought it to be unbearable. But as to Isabel, had she been born within the confines of some lordly park in Hertfordshire, she could not have been more completely free from the abomination.

"I am sorry that you should not be enjoying your-self," said Mr. Boncassen, coming to his wife's relief.

"Nothing could have been nicer. To tell the truth I am standing idle by way of showing my anger against your daughter who would not dance with me."

"I am sure she would have felt herself honoured," said Mr. Boncassen.

"Who is the gentleman with her?" asked the mother.

"A particular friend of mine,—Dolly Longstaff."

"Dolly!" ejaculated Mrs. Boncassen.

"Everybody calls him so. His real name I believe to be Adolphus."

"Is he,—is he—just anybody?" asked the anxious mother.

"He is a very great deal,—as people go here. Every-body knows him. He is asked everywhere, but he goes nowhere. The greatest compliment paid to you here is his presence."

"Nay, my lord, there are the Countess Montague, and the Marchioness of Capulet, and Lord Tybalt, and—— "

"They go everywhere. They are nobodies. It is a charity to even invite them. But to have had Dolly Longstaff once is a triumph for life."

"Laws!" said Mrs. Boncassen, looking hard at the young man who was dancing. "What has he done?"

"He never did anything in his life."

"I suppose he's very rich?"

"I don't know. I should think not. I don't know anything about his riches, but I can assure you that having had him down here will quite give a character to the day."

In the meantime Dolly Longstaff was in a state of great excitement. Some part of the character assigned to him by Lord Silverbridge was true. He very rarely did go anywhere, and yet was asked to a great many places. He was a young man,—though not a very young man,—with a fortune of his own and the expectation of a future fortune. Few men living could have done less for the world than Dolly Longstaff,— and yet he had a position of his own. Now he had taken it into his head to fall in love with Miss Boncassen. This was an accident which had probably never happened to him before, and which had disturbed him much. He had known Miss Boncassen a week or two before Lord Silverbridge had seen her, having by some chance dined out and sat next to her. From that moment he had become changed, and had gone hither and thither in pursuit of the American beauty. His passion having become suspected by his companions had excited their ridicule. Nevertheless he had persevered;—and now he was absolutely dancing with the lady out in the open air. "If this goes on, your friends will have to look after you and put you somewhere," Mr. Lupton had said to him in one of the intervals of the dance. Dolly had turned round and scowled, and suggested that if Mr. Lupton would

mind his own affairs it would be as well for the world
at large.

At the present crisis Dolly was very much excited.
When the dance was over, as a matter of course, he
offered the lady his arm, and as a matter of course she
accepted it. "You 'll take a turn; won't you?" he
said.

"It must be a very short turn," she said,—"as I am
expected to make myself busy."

"Oh, bother that."

"It bothers me; but it has to be done."

"You have set everything going now. They 'll begin dancing again without your telling them."

"I hope so."

"And I 've got something I want to say."

"Dear me;—what is it?"

They were now on a path close to the river-side, in
which there were many loungers. "Would you mind
coming up to the temple?" he said.

"What temple?"

"Oh, such a beautiful place! The Temple of the
Winds, I think they call it, or Venus;—or—or—Mrs.
Arthur de Bever."

"Was she a goddess?"

"It is something built to her memory. Such a view
of the river! I was here once before and they took me
up there. Everybody who comes here goes and sees
Mrs. Arthur de Bever. They ought to have told you."

"Let us go then," said Miss Boncassen. "Only it
must not be long."

"Five minutes will do it all." Then he walked rather
quickly up a flight of rural steps. "Lovely spot;
is n't it?"

"Yes, indeed."

"That's Maidenhead Bridge;—that's—somebody's place;—and now I've got something to say to you."

"You're not going to murder me now you've got me up here alone," said Miss Boncassen, laughing.

"Murder you!" said Dolly, throwing himself into an attitude that was intended to express devoted affection. "Oh no!"

"I am glad of that."

"Miss Boncassen!"

"Mr. Longstaff! If you sigh like that you'll burst yourself."

"I'll—what?"

"Burst yourself!" and she nodded her head at him. Then he slapped his hands together, and turned his head away from her towards the little temple. "I wonder whether she knows what love is," he said, as though he were addressing himself to Mrs. Arthur de Bever.

"No, she don't," said Miss Boncassen.

"But I do," he shouted, turning back towards her. "I do. If any man were ever absolutely, actually, really in love, I am the man."

"Are you indeed, Mr. Longstaff? Is n't it pleasant?"

"Pleasant;—pleasant? Oh, it could be so pleasant."

"But who is the lady? Perhaps you don't mean to tell me that."

"You mean to say you don't know?"

"Have n't the least idea in life."

"Let me tell you then that it could only be one person. It never was but one person. It never could have been but one person. It is you." Then he put his hand well on his heart.

"Me!" said Miss Boncassen, choosing to be un-grammatical in order that he might be more absurd.

"Of course it is you. Do you think that I should have brought you all the way up here to tell you that I was in love with anybody else?"

"I thought I was brought to see Mrs. de Somebody and the view."

"Not at all," said Dolly emphatically.

"Then you have deceived me."

"I will never deceive you. Only say that you will love me, and I will be as true to you as the North Pole."

"Is that true to me?"

"You know what I mean."

"But if I don't love you?"

"Yes, you do!"

"Do I?"

"I beg your pardon," said Dolly. "I did n't mean to say that. Of course a man should n't make sure of a thing."

"Not in this case, Mr. Longstaff; because, really I entertain no such feeling."

"But you can if you please. Just let me tell you who I am."

"That will do no good whatever, Mr. Longstaff."

"Let me tell you at any rate. I have a very good income of my own as it is."

"Money can have nothing to do with it."

"But I want you to know that I can afford it. You might perhaps have thought that I wanted your money."

"I will attribute nothing evil to you, Mr. Longstaff. Only it is quite out of the question that I should—re-spond as I suppose you wish me to; and therefore, pray, do not say anything further."

She went to the head of the little steps but he interrupted her. "You ought to hear me," he said.

"I have heard you."

"I can give you as good a position as any man without a title in England."

"Mr. Longstaff, I rather fancy that wherever I may be I can make a position for myself. At any rate I shall not marry with the view of getting one. If my husband were an English duke I should think myself nothing, unless I was something as Isabel Boncassen."

When she said this she did not bethink herself that Lord Silverbridge would in the course of nature become an English duke. But the allusion to an English duke told intensely on Dolly, who had suspected that he had a noble rival. "English dukes are n't so easily got," he said.

"Very likely not. I might have expressed my meaning better had I said an English prince."

"That 's quite out of the question," said Dolly. "They can't do it,—by Act of Parliament,—except in a hugger-mugger left-handed way that would n't suit you at all."

"Mr. Longstaff,—you must forgive me—if I say— that of all the gentlemen—I have ever met in this country or in any other—you are the—most obtuse." This she brought out in little disjointed sentences, not with any hesitation, but in a way to make every word she uttered more clear to an intelligence which she did not believe to be bright. But in this belief she did some injustice to Dolly. He was quite alive to the disgrace of being called obtuse, and quick enough to avenge himself at the moment.

"Am I?" said he. "How humble-minded you must

be when you think me a fool because I have fallen in love with such a one as yourself."

"I like you for that," she replied, laughing, "and withdraw the epithet as not being applicable. Now we are quits and can forget and forgive;—only let there be the forgetting."

"Never!" said Dolly, with his hand again on his heart.

"Then let it be a little dream of your youth,—that you once met a pretty American girl who was foolish enough to refuse all that you would have given her."

"So pretty! So awfully pretty!" Thereupon she curtsied. "I have seen all the handsome women going in England for the past ten years, and there has not been one who has made me think that it would be worth my while to get off my perch for her."

"And now you would desert your perch for me!"

"I have already."

"But you can get up again. Let it be all a dream. I know men like to have had such dreams. And in order that the dream may be pleasant the last word between us shall be kind. Such admiration from such a one as you is an honour,—and I will reckon it among my honours. But it can be no more than a dream." Then she gave him her hand. "It shall be so;—shall it not?" Then she paused. "It must be so, Mr. Longstaff."

"Must it?"

"That and no more. Now I wish to go down. Will you come with me? It will be better. Don't you think it is going to rain?"

Dolly looked up at the clouds. "I wish it would with all my heart."

"I know you are not so ill-natured.   It would spoil all."

"You have spoiled all."

"No, no.   I have spoiled nothing.   It will only be a little dream about 'that strange American girl, who really did make me feel queer for half an hour.'   Look at that.   A great big drop—and the cloud has come over us as black as Erebus.   Do hurry down."   He was leading the way.   "What shall we do for carriages to get us to the inn?"

"There's the summer-house."

"It will hold about half of us.   And think what it will be to be in there waiting till the rain shall be over! Everybody has been so good-humoured and now they will be so cross!"

The rain was falling in big heavy drops, slow and far between, but almost black with their size.   And the heaviness of the cloud which had gathered over them made everything black.

"Will you have my arm?" said Silverbridge, who saw Miss Boncassen scudding along, with Dolly Longstaff following as fast as he could.

"Oh dear, no.   I have got to mind my dress.   There; —I have gone right into a puddle.   Oh dear!"   So she ran on, and Silverbridge followed close behind her, leaving Dolly Longstaff in the distance.

It was not only Miss Boncassen who got her feet into a puddle and splashed her stockings.   Many did so who were not obliged by their position to maintain good-humour under their misfortunes.   The storm had come on with such unexpected quickness that there had been a general stampede to the summer-house.   As Isabel had said, there was comfortable room for not

more than half of them. In a few minutes people were
crushed who never ought to be crushed. A countess
for whom treble-piled sofas were hardly good enough
was seated on the corner of a table till some younger
and less gorgeous lady could be made to give way.
And the marchioness was declaring she was as wet
through as though she had been dragged in a river.
Mrs. Boncassen was so absolutely quelled as to have
retired into the kitchen attached to the summer-house.
Mr. Boncassen, with all his country's pluck and pride,
was proving to a knot of gentlemen round him on the
veranda, that such treachery in the weather was a
thing unknown in his happier country. Miss Boncassen had to do her best to console the splashed ladies.
"Oh Mrs. Jones, is it not a pity! What can I do for
you?"

"We must bear it, my dear. It often does rain, but
why on this special day should it come down out of
buckets?"

"I never was so wet in all my life," said Dolly
Longstaff, poking in his head.

"There's somebody smoking," said the countess
angrily. There was a crowd of men smoking out on
the veranda. "I never knew anything so nasty," the
countess continued, leaving it in doubt whether she
spoke of the rain, or the smoke, or the party generally.

Damp gauzes, splashed stockings, trampled muslins,
and features which have perhaps known something of
rouge and certainly encountered something of rain may
be made, but can only, by supreme high breeding, be
made compatible with good-humour. To be moist,
muddy, rumpled, and smeared, when by the very nature
of your position it is your duty to be clear-starched up

to the pellucidity of crystal, to be spotless as the lily, to be crisp as the ivy-leaf, and as clear in complexion as a rose,—is it not, oh gentle readers, felt to be a disgrace? It came to pass, therefore, that many were now very cross. Carriages were ordered under the idea that some improvement might be made at the inn which was nearly a mile distant. Very few, however, had their own carriages, and there was jockeying for the vehicles. In the midst of all this Silverbridge remained as near to Miss Boncassen as circumstances would permit. "You are not waiting for me," she said.

"Yes, I am. We might as well go up to town together."

"Leave me with father and mother. Like the captain of a ship, I must be the last to leave the wreck."

"But I 'll be the gallant sailor of the day who always at the risk of his life sticks to the skipper to the last moment."

"Not at all;—just because there will be no gallantry. But come and see us to-morrow and find out whether we have got through it alive."

CHAPTER VII.

THE LANGHAM HOTEL.

"What an abominable climate," Mrs. Boncassen had said when they were quite alone at Maidenhead.

"My dear, you did n't think you were to bring New York along with you when you came here," replied her husband.

"I wish I was going back to-morrow."

"That's a foolish thing to say. People here are very kind, and you are seeing a great deal more of the world than you would ever see at home. I am having a very good time. What do you say, Bell?"

"I wish I could have kept my stockings clean."

"But what about the young men?"

"Young men are pretty much the same everywhere, I guess. They never have their wits about them. They never mean what they say, because they don't understand the use of words. They are generally half impudent and half timid. When in love they do not at all understand what has befallen them. What they want they try to compass as a cow does when it stands stretching out its head towards a stack of hay which it cannot reach. Indeed there is no such thing as a young man, for a man is not really a man till he is middle-aged. But take them at their worst they are a deal too good for us, for they become men some day, whereas we must only be women to the end."

"My word, Bella!" exclaimed the mother.

"You have managed to be tolerably heavy upon

God's creatures, taking them in a lump," said the father. " Boys, girls, and cows! Something has gone wrong with you besides the rain."

" Nothing on earth, sir,—except the boredom."

" Some young man has been talking to you, Bella."

" One or two, mother; and I got to bethinking if any one of them should ask me to marry him, and if moved by some evil destiny I were to take him, whether I should murder him, or myself, or run away with one of the others."

" Could n't you bear with him till, according to your own theory, he would grow out of his folly? " said the father.

" Being a woman,—no. The present moment is always everything to me. When that horrid old harridan halloaed out that somebody was smoking, I thought I should have died. It was very bad just then."

" Awful! " said Mrs. Boncassen, shaking her head.

" I did n't seem to feel it much," said the father. " One does n't look to have everything just what one wants always. If I did I should go nowhere;—but my total of life would be less enjoyable. If ever you do get married, Bell, you should remember that."

" I mean to get married some day, so that I should n't be made love to any longer."

" I hope it will have that effect," said the father.

" Mr. Boncassen! " ejaculated the mother.

" What I say is true. I hope it will have that effect. It had with you, my dear."

" I don't know that people did n't think of me as much as of anybody else, even though I was married."

" Then, my dear, I never knew it."

Miss Boncassen, though she had behaved serenely

and with good temper during the process of Dolly's proposal, had not liked it. She had a very high opinion of herself, and was certainly entitled to have it by the undisguised admiration of all that came near her. She was not more indifferent to the admiration of young men than are other young ladies. But she was not proud of the admiration of Dolly Longstaff. She was here among strangers whose ways were unknown to her, whose rank and standing in the world were vague to her, and wonderful in their dimness. She knew that she was associating with men very different from those at home where young men were supposed to be under the necessity of earning their bread. At New York she would dance, as she had said, with bank clerks. She was not prepared to admit that a young London lord was better than a New York bank clerk. Judging the men on their own individual merits she might find the bank clerk to be the better of the two. But a certain sweetness of the aroma of rank was beginning to permeate her republican senses. The softness of a life in which no occupation was compulsory had its charms for her. Though she had complained of the insufficient intelligence of young men, she was alive to the delight of having nothings said to her pleasantly. All this had affected her so strongly that she had almost felt that a life among these English luxuries would be a pleasant life. Like most Americans who do not as yet know the country, she had come with an inward feeling that as an American and a republican she might probably be despised.

There is not uncommonly a savageness of self-assertion about Americans which arises from a too great anxiety to be admitted to fellowship with Britons. She had felt this, and conscious of reputation already made by herself in the social life of New York, she had half trusted that she would be well received in London, and had half convinced herself that she would be rejected. She had not been rejected. She must have become quite aware of that. She had dropped very quickly the idea that she would be scorned. Ignorant as she had been of English life, she perceived that she had at once become popular. And this had been so in spite of her mother's homeliness and her father's awkwardness. By herself and by her own gifts she had done it. She had found out concerning herself that she had that which would commend her to other society than that of the Fifth Avenue. Those lords of whom she had heard were as plenty with her as blackberries. Young Lord Silverbridge, of whom she was told that of all the young lords of the day he stood first in rank and wealth, was peculiarly her friend. Her brain was firmer than that of most girls, but even her brain was a little turned. She never told herself that it would be well for her to become the wife of such a one. In her more thoughtful moments she told herself that it would not be well. But still the allurement was strong upon her. Park Lane was sweeter than the Fifth Avenue. Lord Silverbridge was nicer than the bank clerk.

But Dolly Longstaff was not. She would certainly prefer the bank clerk to Dolly Longstaff. And yet Dolly Longstaff was the one among her English admirers who had come forward and spoken out. She did not desire that any one should come forward and speak out. But it was an annoyance to her that this special man should have done so.

The waiter at the Langham understood American

ways perfectly, and when a young man called between three and four o'clock, asking for Mrs. Boncassen, said that Miss Boncassen was at home. The young man took off his hat, brushed up his hair, and followed the waiter up to the sitting-room. The door was opened and the young man was announced. "Mr. Longstaff."

Miss Boncassen was rather disgusted. She had had enough of this English lover. Why should he have come after what had occurred yesterday? He ought to have felt that he was absolved from the necessity of making personal inquiries. "I am glad to see that you got home safe," she said, as she gave him her hand.

"And you too, I hope?"

"Well;—so, so; with my clothes a good deal damaged and my temper rather worse."

"I am so sorry."

"It should not rain on such days. Mother has gone to church."

"Oh;—indeed. I like going to church myself sometimes."

"Do you now?"

"I know what would make me like to go to church."

"And father is at the Athenæum. He goes there to do a little light reading in the library on Sunday afternoon."

"I shall never forget yesterday, Miss Boncassen."

"You would n't if your clothes had been spoilt as mine were."

"Money will repair that."

"Well; yes; but when I 've had a petticoat flounced particularly to order I don't like to see it ill-treated. There are emotions of the heart which money can't touch."

" Just so ;—emotions of the heart ! That's the very phrase."

She was determined if possible to prevent a repetition of the scene which had taken place up at Mrs. de Bever's temple. " All my emotions are about my dress."

" All? "

" Well ; yes ; all. I guess I don't care much for eating and drinking." In saying this she actually contrived to produce something of a nasal twang.

" Eating and drinking !" said Dolly. " Of course they are necessities ;—and so are clothes."

" But new things are such ducks ! "

" Trousers may be," said Dolly.

Then she took a prolonged gaze at him, wondering whether he was or was not such a fool as he looked.

" How funny you are," she said.

" A man does not generally feel funny after going through what I suffered yesterday, Miss Boncassen."

" Would you mind ringing the bell? "

" Must it be done quite at once? "

" Quite,—quite," she said. " I can do it myself for the matter of that." And she rang the bell somewhat violently. Dolly sank back again into his seat, remarking in his usual apathetic way that he had intended to obey her behest but had not understood that she was in so great a hurry. " I am always in a hurry," she said. " I like things to be done—sharp." And she hit the table a crack. " Please bring me some iced water," this of course was addressed to the waiter. " And a glass for Mr. Longstaff."

" None for me, thank you."

" Perhaps you 'd like soda and brandy."

" Oh dear, no ;—nothing of the kind. But I am so

much obliged to you all the same." As the water bottle was in fact standing in the room, and as the waiter had only to hand the glass, all this created but little obstacle. Still it had its effect, and Dolly, when the man had retired, felt that there was a difficulty in proceeding. "I have called to-day——" he began.

"That has been so kind of you. But mother has gone to church."

"I am very glad that she has gone to church, because I wish to——"

"Oh laws! There's a horse has tumbled down in the street. I heard it."

"He has got up again," said Dolly, looking leisurely out of the window. "But as I was saying——"

"I don't think that the water we Americans drink can be good. It makes the women become ugly so young."

"You will never become ugly."

She got up and curtsied to him, and then, still standing, made him a speech. "Mr. Longstaff, it would be absurd of me to pretend not to understand what you mean. But I won't have any more of it. Whether you are making fun of me, or whether you are in earnest, it is just the same."

"Making fun of you!"

"It does not signify. I don't care which it is. But I won't have it. There!"

"A gentleman should be allowed to express his feelings and to explain his position."

"You have expressed and explained more than enough, and I won't have any more. If you will sit down and talk about something else, or else go away, there shall be an end of it;—but if you go on, I will ring the bell again. What can a man gain by going on when a girl has spoken as I have done?" They were both at this time standing up, and he was now as angry as she was.

"I've paid you the greatest compliment a man can pay a woman," he began.

"Very well. If I remember rightly I thanked you for it yesterday. If you wish it, I will thank you again to-day. But it is a compliment which becomes very much the reverse if it be repeated too often. You are sharp enough to understand that I have done everything in my power to save us both from this trouble."

"What makes you so fierce, Miss Boncassen?"

"What makes you so foolish?"

"I suppose it must be something peculiar to American ladies."

"Just that;—something peculiar to American ladies. They don't like;—well; I don't want to say anything more that can be called fierce."

At this moment the door was again opened and Lord Silverbridge was announced. "Halloa, Dolly, are you here?"

"It seems that I am."

"And I am here too," said Miss Boncassen, smiling her prettiest.

"None the worse for yesterday's troubles, I hope?"

"A good deal the worse. I have been explaining all that to Mr. Longstaff, who has been quite sympathetic with me about my things."

"A terrible pity that shower," said Dolly.

"For you," said Silverbridge, "because, if I remember right, Miss Boncassen was walking with you;—but I was rather glad of it."

"Lord Silverbridge!"

"I regarded it as a direct interposition of Providence, because you would not dance with me."

"Any news to-day, Silverbridge?" asked Dolly.

"Nothing particular. They say that Coalheaver can't run for the Leger."

"What's the matter?" asked Dolly vigorously.

"Broke down at Ascot. But I dare say it's a lie."

"Sure to be a lie," said Dolly. "What do you think of Madame Scholzdam, Miss Boncassen?"

"I am not a good judge."

"Never heard anything equal to it yet in this world," said Dolly. "I wonder whether that's true about Coalheaver?"

"Tifto says so."

"Which at the present moment," asked Miss Boncassen, "is the greater favourite with the public, Madame Scholzdam or Coalheaver?"

"Coalheaver is a horse, Miss Boncassen."

"Oh,—a horse!"

"Perhaps I ought to say a colt."

"Oh,—a colt!"

"Do you suppose, Dolly, that Miss Boncassen does n't know all that?" asked Silverbridge.

"He supposes that my American ferocity has never been sufficiently softened for the reception of polite erudition."

"You two have been quarrelling, I fear."

"I never quarrel with a woman," said Dolly.

"Nor with a man in my presence, I hope," said Miss Boncassen.

"Somebody does seem to have got out of bed at the wrong side," said Silverbridge.

"I did," said Miss Boncassen. "I got out of bed at the wrong side. I am cross. I can't get over the spoiling of my flounces. I think you had better both go away and leave me. If I could walk about the room for half an hour and stamp my feet, I should get better." Silverbridge thought that as he had come last, he certainly ought to be left last. Miss Boncassen felt that, at any rate, Mr. Longstaff should go. Dolly felt that his manhood required him to remain. After what had taken place he was not going to leave the field vacant for another. Therefore he made no effort to move.

"That seems rather hard upon me," said Silverbridge. "You told me to come."

"I told you to come and ask after us all. You have come and asked after us, and have been informed that we are very bad. What more can I say? You accuse me of getting out of bed the wrong side, and I own that I did."

"I meant to say that Dolly Longstaff had done so."

"And I say it was Silverbridge," said Dolly.

"We aren't very agreeable together, are we? Upon my word I think you 'd better both go." Silverbridge immediately got up from his chair; upon which Dolly also moved.

"What the mischief is up?" asked Silverbridge, when they were under the porch together.

"The truth is, you never can tell what you are to do with those American girls."

"I suppose you have been making up to her."

"Nothing in earnest. She seemed to me to like admiration; so I told her I admired her."

"What did she say then?"

"Upon my word, you seem to be very great at cross-examining. Perhaps you had better go back and ask her."

"I will, next time I see her." Then he stepped into his cab, and in a loud voice ordered the man to drive him to the Zoo. But when he had gone a little way up Portland Place, he stopped the driver and desired he might be taken back again to the hotel. As he left the vehicle he looked round for Dolly, but Dolly had certainly gone. Then he told the waiter to take his card to Miss Boncassen, and explain that he had something to say which he had forgotten.

"So you have come back again," said Miss Boncassen, laughing.

"Of course I have. You did n't suppose I was going to let that fellow get the better of me. Why should I be turned out because he had made an ass of himself!"

"Who said he made an ass of himself?"

"But he had; had n't he?"

"No;—by no means," said she after a little pause.

"Tell me what he had been saying."

"Indeed I shall do nothing of the kind. If I told you all he said, then I should have to tell the next man all that you may say. Would that be fair?"

"I should not mind," said Silverbridge.

"I dare say not, because you have nothing particular to say. But the principle is the same. Lawyers and doctors and parsons talk of privileged communications. Why should not a young lady have her privileged communications?"

"But I have something particular to say."

"I hope not."

" Why should you hope not? "

" I hate having things said particularly. Nobody likes conversation so well as I do; but it should never be particular."

" I was going to tell you that I came back to London yesterday in the same carriage with old Lady Clanfiddle, and that she swore that no consideration on earth would ever induce her to go to Maidenhead again."

" That is n't particular."

" She went on to say;—you won't tell of me; will you? "

" It shall all be privileged."

" She went on to say that Americans could n't be expected to understand English manners."

" Perhaps they may be all the better for that."

" Then I spoke up. I swore I was awfully in love with you."

" You did n't."

" I did;—that you were, out and away, the finest girl I ever saw in my life. Of course you understand that her two daughters were there. And that as for manners,—unless the rain could be attributed to American manners,—I did not think anything had gone wrong."

" What about the smoking? "

" I told her they were all Englishmen, and that if she had been giving the party herself they would have smoked just as much. You must understand that she never does give any parties."

" How could you be so ill-natured? "

" There was ever so much more of it. And it ended in her telling me that I was a schoolboy. I found out the cause of it all. A great spout of rain had come upon her daughter's hat, and that had produced a most melancholy catastrophe."

"I would have given her mine willingly."

"An American hat;—to be worn by Lady Violet Clanfiddle!"

"It came from Paris last week, sir."

"But must have been contaminated by American contact."

"Now, Lord Silverbridge," said she, getting up, "if I had a stick I 'd whip you."

"It was such fun."

"And you come here and tell it all to me."

"Of course I do. It was a deal too good to keep it to myself. 'American manners!'" As he said this he almost succeeded in looking like Lady Clanfiddle.

At that moment Mr. Boncassen entered the room, and was immediately appealed to by his daughter. "Father, you must turn Lord Silverbridge out of the room."

"Dear me! If I must,—of course I must. But why?"

"He is saying everything horrid he can about Americans."

After this they settled down for a few minutes to general conversation, and then Lord Silverbridge again took his leave. When he was gone Isabel Boncassen almost regretted that the "something particular" which he had threatened to say had not been less comic in its nature.

CHAPTER VIII.

LORD POPPLECOURT.

WHEN the reader was told that Lord Popplecourt had found Lady Cantrip very agreeable it is to be hoped that the reader was disgusted. Lord Popplecourt would certainly not have given a second thought to Lady Cantrip unless he had been specially flattered. And why should such a man have been flattered by a woman who was in all respects his superior? The reader will understand. It had been settled by the wisdom of the elders that it would be a good thing that Lord Popplecourt should marry Lady Mary Palliser.

The mutual assent which leads to marriage should no doubt be spontaneous. Who does not feel that? Young love should speak from its first doubtful unconscious spark,—a spark which any breath of air may quench or cherish,—till it becomes a flame which nothing can satisfy but the union of the two lovers. No one should be told to love, or bidden to marry this man or that woman. The theory of this is plain to us all, and till we have sons or daughters whom we feel imperatively obliged to control, the theory is unassailable. But the duty is so imperative! The Duke had taught himself to believe that as his wife would have been thrown away on the world had she been allowed to marry Burgo Fitzgerald, so would his daughter be thrown away were she allowed to marry Mr. Tregear. Therefore the theory of spontaneous love must in this case be set aside. Therefore the spark,—would that it had been no more,—must be quenched. Therefore there could be no union of two lovers;—but simply a prudent and perhaps splendid marriage.

Lord Popplecourt was a man in possession of a large estate which was unencumbered. His rank in the peerage was not high; but his barony was of an old date,—and, if things went well with him, something higher in rank might be open to him. He had good looks of that sort which recommend themselves to pastors and masters, to elders and betters. He had regular features. He looked as though he were steady. He was not impatient nor rollicking. Silverbridge was also good-looking;—but his good looks were such as would give a pang to the hearts of anxious mothers of daughters. Tregear was the handsomest man of the three;—but then he looked as though he had no betters and did not care for his elders. Lord Popple-court, though a very young man, had once stammered through half-a-dozen words in the House of Lords and had been known to dine with the "Benevolent Funds." Lord Silverbridge had declared him to be a fool. No one thought him to be bright. But in the eyes of the Duke,—and of Lady Cantrip,—he had his good qualities.

But the work was very disagreeable. It was the more hard upon Lady Cantrip because she did not believe in it. If it could be done, it would be expedient. But she felt very strongly that it could not be done. No doubt that Lady Glencora had been turned from her evil destiny; but Lady Glencora had been younger than her daughter was now, and possessed of less character. Nor was Lady Cantrip blind to the difference between a poor man with a bad character, such as that Burgo had been, and a poor man with a good character, such as was Tregear. Nevertheless she undertook to aid the work, and condescended to pretend to be so interested in the portrait of some common ancestor as to persuade the young man to have it photographed, in order that the bringing down of the photograph might lead to something.

He took the photograph and Lady Cantrip said very much to him about his grandmother, who was the old lady in question. "She could," she said, "just remember the features of the dear old woman." She was not habitually a hypocrite and she hated herself for what she was doing, and yet her object was simply good,—to bring together two young people who might advantageously marry each other. The mere talking about the old woman would be of no service. She longed to bring out the offer plainly, and say, "There is Lady Mary Palliser. Don't you think she 'd make a good wife for you ? " But she could not, as yet, bring herself to be so indelicately plain. "You have n't seen the Duke since ? " she asked.

"He spoke to me only yesterday in the House. I like the Duke."

"If I may be allowed to say so, it would be for your advantage that he should like you ;—that is, if you mean to take a part in politics."

"I suppose I shall," said Popplecourt. "There is n't much else to do."

"You don't go to races." He shook his head. "I am glad of that," said Lady Cantrip. "Nothing is so bad as the turf. I fear Lord Silverbridge is devoting himself to the turf."

"I don't think it can be good for any man to have much to do with Major Tifto. I suppose Silverbridge knows what he 's about."

Here was an opportunity which might have been used. It would have been so easy for her to glide from the imperfections of the brother to the perfections of the sister. But she could not bring herself to do it quite at once. She approached the matter, however, as nearly as she could without making her grand proposition. She shook her head sadly in reference to Silverbridge, and then spoke of the Duke. "His father is so anxious about him."

"I dare say."

"I don't know any man who is more painfully anxious about his children. He feels the responsibility so much since his wife's death. There is Lady Mary."

"She 's all right, I should say."

"All right! oh yes. But when a girl is possessed of so many things,—rank, beauty, intelligence, large fortune,——"

"Will Lady Mary have much?"

"A large portion of her mother's money, I should say. When all these things are joined together a father of course feels most anxious as to their disposal."

"I suppose she is clever."

"Very clever," said Lady Cantrip.

"I think a girl may be too clever, you know," said Lord Popplecourt.

"Perhaps she may. But I know more who are too foolish. I am so much obliged to you for the photograph."

"Don't mention it."

"I really did not mean that you should send a man down."

On that occasion the two young people did not see each other. Lady Mary did not come down, and Lady Cantrip lacked the courage to send for her. As it was, might it not be possible that the young man should be induced to make himself agreeable to the young lady without any further explanation? But love-making between young people cannot well take place unless they be brought together. There was a difficulty in bringing them together at Richmond. The Duke had indeed spoken of meeting Lord Popplecourt at dinner there;—but this was to have followed the proposition which Lady Cantrip should make to him. She could not yet make the proposition, and therefore she hardly knew how to arrange the dinner. She was obliged at last to let the wished-for lover go away without arranging anything. When the Duke should have settled his autumn plans, then an attempt must be made to induce Lord Popplecourt to travel in the same direction.

That evening Lady Cantrip said a few words to Mary respecting the proposed suitor. "There is nothing I have such a horror of as gambling," she said.

"It is dreadful."

"I am very glad to think that Nidderdale does not do anything of that sort." It was perhaps on the cards that Nidderdale should do things of which she knew nothing. "I hope Silverbridge does not bet."

"I don't think he does."

"There's Lord Popplecourt,—quite a young man, —with everything at his own disposal, and a very large estate.   Think of the evil he might do if he were given that way."

"Does he gamble?"

"Not at all.   It must be such a comfort to his mother!"

"He looks to me as though he never would do anything," said Lady Mary.   Then the subject was dropped.

It was a week after this, towards the end of July, that the Duke wrote a line to Lady Cantrip, apologising for what he had done, but explaining that he had asked Lord Popplecourt to dine at The Horns on a certain Sunday.   He had, he said, been assured by Lord Cantrip that such an arrangement would be quite convenient.   It was clear from his letter that he was much in earnest.   Of course there was no reason why the dinner should not be eaten.   Only the speciality of the invitation to Lord Popplecourt must not be so glaring that he himself should be struck by the strangeness of it.   There must be a little party made up. Lord Nidderdale and his wife were therefore bidden to come down, and Silverbridge, who at first consented rather unwillingly,—and Lady Mabel Grex, as to whom the Duke made a special request that she might be asked.   This last invitation was sent express from Lady Mary, and included Miss Cass.   So the party was made up.   The careful reader will perceive that there were to be ten of them.

"Isn't it odd papa wanting to have Lady Mabel," Mary said to Lady Cantrip.

"Does he not know her, my dear?"

"He hardly ever spoke to her.   I'll tell you what; I expect Silverbridge is going to marry her."

"Why should n't he?"

"I don't know why he should n't. She is very beautiful, and very clever. But if so, papa must know all about it. It does seem so odd that papa of all people should turn match-maker, or even that he should think of it."

"So much is thrown upon him now," said Lady Cantrip.

"Poor papa!" Then she remembered herself, and spoke with a little start. "Of course I am not thinking of myself. Arranging a marriage is very different from preventing any one from marrying."

"Whatever he may think to be his duty he will be sure to do it," said the elder lady very solemnly.

Lady Mabel was surprised by the invitation, but she was not slow to accept it. "Papa will be here and will be so glad to meet you," Lady Mary had said. Why should the Duke of Omnium wish to meet her? "Silverbridge will be here too," Mary had gone on to say. "It is just a family party. Papa, you know, is not going anywhere; nor am I." By all this Lady Mabel's thoughts were much stirred, and her bosom somewhat moved. And Silverbridge also was moved by it. Of course he could not but remember that he had pledged himself to his father to ask Lady Mabel to be his wife. He had faltered since. She had been, he thought, unkind to him, or at any rate indifferent. He had surely said enough to her to make her know what he meant; and yet she had taken no trouble to meet him half way. And then Isabel Boncassen had intervened. Now he was asked to dinner in a most unusual manner!

Of all the guests invited Lord Popplecourt was perhaps the least disturbed. He was quite alive to the
honour of being noticed by the Duke of Omnium, and
alive also to the flattering courtesy shown to him by
Lady Cantrip. But justice would not be done him
unless it were acknowledged that he had as yet flattered
himself with no hopes in regard to Lady Mary Palliser.
He, when he prepared himself for his journey down to
Richmond, thought much more of the Duke than of
the Duke's daughter.

"Oh yes, I can drive you down if you like that kind
of thing," Silverbridge said to him on the Saturday
evening.

"And bring me back?"

"If you will come when I am coming. I hate
waiting for a fellow."

"Suppose we leave at half-past ten."

"I won't fix any time; but if we can't make it suit
there 'll be the governor's carriage."

"Will the Duke go down in his carriage?"

"I suppose so. It 's quicker and less trouble than
the railway." Then Lord Popplecourt reflected that
he would certainly come back with the Duke if he
could so manage it, and there floated before his eyes
visions of under-secretaryships, all of which might owe
their origin to this proposed drive up from Richmond.

At six o'clock on the Sunday evening Silverbridge
called for Lord Popplecourt. "Upon my word," said
he, "I did n't ever expect to see you in my cab."

"Why not me especially?"

"Because you 're not one of our lot."

"You 'd sooner have Tifto, I dare say."

"No, I would n't. Tifto is not at all a pleasant companion, though he understands horses. You 're going in for heavy politics I suppose."

"Not particularly heavy."

"If not, why on earth does my governor take you up? You won't mind my smoking, I dare say." After this there was no conversation between them.

CHAPTER IX.

"DON'T YOU THINK——— ?"

I<small>T</small> was pretty to see the Duke's reception of Lady
Mabel. "I knew your mother many years ago," he
said, "when I was young myself. Her mother and my
mother were first cousins and dear friends." He held
her hand as he spoke and looked at her as though he
meant to love her. Lady Mabel saw that it was so.
Could it be possible that the Duke had heard anything;—that he should wish to receive her? She had
told herself and had told Miss Cassewary that though
she had spared Silverbridge, yet she knew that she
would make him a good wife. If the Duke thought
so also, then surely she need not doubt.

"I knew we were cousins," she said, "and have been
so proud of the connection! Lord Silverbridge does
come and see us sometimes."

Soon after that Silverbridge and Popplecourt came
in. If the story of the old woman in the portrait may
be taken as evidence of a family connection between
Lady Cantrip and Lord Popplecourt, everybody there
was more or less connected with everybody else.
Nidderdale had been a first cousin of Lady Glencora
and he had married a daughter of Lady Cantrip.
They were manifestly a family party,—thanks to the
old woman in the picture.

It is a point of conscience among the—perhaps not
ten thousand, but say one thousand of bluest blood,—
that everybody should know who everybody is. Our

Duke, though he had not given his mind much to the pursuit, had nevertheless learned his lesson. It is a knowledge which the possession of the blue blood itself produces. There are countries with bluer blood than our own in which to be without such knowledge is a crime.

When the old lady in the portrait had been discussed, Popplecourt was close to Lady Mary. They two had no idea why such vicinity had been planned. The Duke knew of course, and Lady Cantrip. Lady Cantrip had whispered to her daughter that such a marriage would be suitable, and the daughter had hinted it to her husband. Lord Cantrip of course was not in the dark. Lady Mabel had expressed a hint on the matter to Miss Cass, who had not repudiated it. Even Silverbridge had suggested to himself that something of the kind might be in the wind, thinking that, if so, none of them knew much about his sister Mary. But Popplecourt himself was divinely innocent. His ideas of marriage had as yet gone no farther than a conviction that girls generally were things which would be pressed on him, and against which he must arm himself with some shield. Marriage would have to come no doubt; but not the less was it his duty to live as though it were a pit towards which he would be tempted by female allurements. But that a net should be spread over him here he was much too humble-minded to imagine.

" Very hot," he said to Lady Mary.

" We found it warm in church to-day."

" I dare say. I came down here with your brother in his hansom cab. What a very odd thing to have a hansom cab! "

" I should like one."

" Should you indeed ? "

" Particularly if I could drive it myself. Silverbridge does, at night, when he thinks people won't see him."

" Drive the cab in the streets! What does he do with his man? "

" Puts him inside. He was out once without the man and took up a fare,—an old woman, he said. And when she was going to pay him he touched his hat and said he never took money from ladies."

" Do you believe that? "

" Oh yes. I call that good fun, because it did no harm. He had his lark. The lady was taken where she wanted to go, and she saved her money."

" Suppose he had upset her," said Lord Popplecourt, looking as an old philosopher might have looked when he had found some clenching answer to another philosopher's argument.

" The real cabman might have upset her worse," said Lady Mary.

" Don't you feel it odd that we should meet here? " said Lord Silverbridge to his neighbour, Lady Mabel.

" Anything unexpected is odd," said Lady Mabel. It seemed to her to be very odd,—unless certain people had made up their minds as to the expediency of a certain event.

" That is what you call logic ;—is n't it? Anything unexpected is odd ! "

" Lord Silverbridge, I won't be laughed at. You have been at Oxford and ought to know what logic is."

" That at any rate is ill-natured," he replied, turning very red in the face.

" You don't think I meant it. Oh Lord Silverbridge,

say that you don't think I meant it. You cannot think
I would willingly wound you. Indeed, indeed, I was
not thinking." It had in truth been an accident. She
could not speak aloud because they were closely surrounded by others, but she looked up in his face to
see whether he were angry with her. " Say that you
do not think I meant it."

" I do not think you meant it."

" I would not say a word to hurt you,—oh, for more
than I can tell you."

" It is all bosh of course," he said, laughing ; " but I
do not like to hear the old place named. I have always made a fool of myself. Some men do it and
don't care about it. But I do it, and yet it makes me
miserable."

" If that be so you will soon give over making—what
you call a fool of yourself. For myself I like the idea
of wild oats. I look upon them like measles. Only
you should have a doctor ready when the disease shows
itself."

" What sort of a doctor ought I to have? "

" Ah ;—you must find out that yourself. That sort
of feeling which makes you feel miserable ;—that is a
doctor itself."

" Or a wife? "

" Or a wife,—if you can find a good one. There
are wives, you know, who aggravate the disease. If
I had a fast husband I should make him faster by being fast myself. There is nothing I envy so much as
the power of doing half-mad things."

" Women can do that too."

" But they go to the dogs. We are dreadfully re-
stricted. If you like champagne you can have a

bucketful. I am obliged to pretend that I only want a very little. You can bet thousands. I must confine myself to gloves. You can flirt with any woman you please. I must wait till somebody comes,—and put up with it if nobody does come."

"Plenty come,—no doubt."

"But I want to pick and choose. A man turns the girls over one after another as one does the papers when one is fitting up a room, or rolls them out as one rolls out the carpets. A very careful young man like Lord Popplecourt might reject a young woman because her hair did n't suit the colour of his furniture."

"I don't think that I shall choose my wife as I would paper and carpets."

The Duke, who sat between Lady Cantrip and her daughter, did his best to make himself agreeable. The conversation had been semi-political,—political to the usual feminine extent, and had consisted chiefly of sarcasms from Lady Cantrip against Sir Timothy Beeswax. "That England should put up with such a man," Lady Cantrip had said, "is to me shocking! There used to be a feeling in favour of gentlemen." To this the Duke had responded by asserting that Sir Timothy had displayed great aptitudes for parliamentary life, and knew the House of Commons better than most men. He said nothing against his foe, and very much in his foe's praise. But Lady Cantrip perceived that she had succeeded in pleasing him.

When the ladies were gone the politics became more serious. "That unfortunate quarrel is to go on the same as ever I suppose," said the Duke, addressing himself to the two young men who had seats in the House of Commons. They were both on the conservative side in politics. The three peers present were all liberals.

"Till next session, I think, sir," said Silverbridge.

"Sir Timothy, though he did lose his temper, has managed it well," said Lord Cantrip.

"Phineas Finn lost his temper worse than Sir Timothy," said Lord Nidderdale.

"But yet I think he had the feeling of the House with him," said the Duke. "I happened to be present in the gallery at the time."

"Yes," said Nidderdale, "because he ' owned up.' The fact is if you ' own up' in a genial sort of way the House will forgive anything. If I were to murder my grandmother, and when questioned about it were to acknowledge that I had done it." Then Lord Nidderdale stood up and made his speech as he might have made it in the House of Commons. " I regret to say, sir, that the old woman did get in my way when I was in a passion. Unfortunately I had a heavy stick in my hand and I did strike her over the head. Nobody can regret it so much as I do! Nobody can feel so acutely the position in which I am placed! I have sat in this House for many years, and many gentlemen know me well. I think, sir, that they will acknowledge that I am a man not deficient in filial piety or general humanity. Sir, I am sorry for what I did in a moment of heat. I have now spoken the truth, and I shall leave myself in the hands of the House. My belief is I should get such a round of applause as I certainly shall never achieve in any other way. It is not only that a popular man may do it,—like Phineas Finn,—but the most unpopular man in the House may make himself liked by owning freely that he has done something that he ought to be ashamed of." Nidderdale's unwonted eloquence was received in good part by the assembled legislators.

"Taking it altogether," said the Duke, "I know of no assembly in any country in which good-humour prevails so generally, in which the members behave to each other so well, in which rules are so universally followed, or in which the president is so thoroughly sustained by the feeling of the members."

"I hear men say that it is n't quite what it used to be," said Silverbridge.

"Nothing will ever be quite what it used to be."

"Changes for the worse, I mean. Men are doing all kinds of things, just because the rules of the House allow them."

"If they be within rule," said the Duke, "I don't know who is to blame them. In my time, if any man stretched a rule too far the House would not put up with it."

"That 's just it," said Nidderdale. "The House puts up with anything now. There is a great deal of good feeling no doubt, but there 's no earnestness about anything. I think you are more earnest than we; but then you are such horrid bores. And each earnest man is in earnest about something that nobody else cares for."

When they were again in the drawing-room, Lord Popplecourt was seated next to Lady Mary. "Where are you going this autumn?" he asked.

"I don't know in the least. Papa said something about going abroad."

"You won't be at Custins?" Custins was Lord Cantrip's country seat in Dorsetshire.

" I know nothing about myself as yet. But I don't think I shall go anywhere unless papa goes too."

" Lady Cantrip has asked me to be at Custins in the middle of October. They say it is about the best pheasant shooting in England."

" Do you shoot much? "

" A great deal. I shall be in Scotland on the twelfth. I and Reginald Dobbes have a place together. I shall get to my own partridges on the 1st of September. I always manage that. Popplecourt is in Suffolk, and I don't think any man in England can beat me for partridges."

" What do you do with all you slay ? "

" Leadenhall Market. I make it pay,—or very nearly. Then I shall run back to Scotland for the end of the stalking, and I can easily manage to be at Custins by the middle of October. I never touch my own pheasants till November."

" Why are you so abstemious? "

" The birds are heavier and it answers better. But if I thought you would be at Custins it would be much nicer." Lady Mary again told him that as yet she knew nothing of her father's autumn movements.

But at the same time the Duke was arranging his autumn movements, or at any rate those of his daughter. Lady Cantrip had told him that the desirable son-in-law had promised to go to Custins, and suggested that he and Mary should also be there. In his daughter's name he promised, but he would not bind himself. Would it not be better that he should be absent ? Now that the doing of this thing was brought nearer to him so that he could see and feel its details, he was disgusted by it. And yet it had answered so well with his wife!

" Is Lord Popplecourt intimate here? " Lady Mabel asked her friend, Lord Silverbridge.

" I don't know.   I am not."

" Lady Cantrip seems to think a great deal about him."

" I dare say.   I don't."

" Your father seems to like him."

" That's possible too.   They're going back to London together in the governor's carriage.   My father will talk high politics all the way, and Popplecourt will agree with everything."

" He isn't intended to—to——?   You know what I mean."

" I can't say that I do."

" To cut out poor Frank."

" It's quite possible."

" Poor Frank!"

" You had a great deal better say poor Popplecourt! —or poor governor, or poor Lady Cantrip."

" But a hundred countesses can't make your sister marry a man she does n't like."

" Just that.   They don't go the right way about it."

" What would you do? "

" Leave her alone.   Let her find out gradually that what she wants can't be done."

" And so linger on for years," said Lady Mabel reproachfully.

" I say nothing about that.   The man is my friend."

" And you ought to be proud of him."

" I never knew anybody yet that was proud of his friends.   I like him well enough, but I can quite understand that the governor should object."

" Yes, we all know that," said she sadly.

" What would your father say if you wanted to marry some one who had n't a shilling? "

" I should object myself,—without waiting for my father. But then,—neither have I a shilling. If I had money, do you think I would n't like to give it to the man I loved? "

" But this is a case of giving somebody else's money. They won't make her give it up by bringing such a young ass as that down here. If my father has per-sistency enough to let her cry her eyes out, he 'll succeed."

" And break her heart. Could you do that? "

" Certainly not. But then I 'm soft. I can't refuse."

" Can't you? "

" Not if the person who asks me is in my good books. You try me."

" What shall I ask for? "

" Anything."

" Give me that ring off your finger," she said. He at once took it off his hand. " Of course you know I am in joke. You don't imagine that I would take it from you." He still held it towards her. " Lord Sil-verbridge, I expect that with you I may say a foolish word without being brought to sorrow by it. I know that that ring belonged to your great-uncle,—and to fifty Pallisers before."

" What would it matter? "

" And it would be wholly useless to me, as I could not wear it."

" Of course it would be too big," said he, replacing the ring on his own finger. " But when I talk of any one being in my good books, I don't mean a thing like that. Don't you know there is nobody on earth I—"

there he paused and blushed, and she sat motionless, looking at him expecting, with her colour too somewhat raised,—" whom I like so well as I do you? " It was a lame conclusion. She felt it to be lame. But as regarded him, the lameness at the moment had come from a timidity which forbade him to say the word " love " even though he had meant to say it.

She recovered herself instantly. " I do believe it," she said. " I do think that we are real friends."

" Would you not take a ring from a—real friend? "

" Not that ring;—nor a ring at all after I had asked for it in joke. You understand it all. But to go back to what we were talking about,—if you can do anything for Frank, pray do. You know it will break her heart. A man of course bears it better, but he does not perhaps suffer the less. It is all his life to him. He can do nothing while this is going on. Are you not true enough to your friendship to exert yourself for him? " Silverbridge put his hand up and rubbed his head as though he were vexed. " Your aid would turn everything in his favour."

" You do not know my father."

" Is he so inexorable? "

" It is not that, Mabel. But he is so unhappy. I cannot add to his unhappiness by taking part against him."

In another part of the room Lady Cantrip was busy with Lord Popplecourt. She had talked about pheasants, and had talked about grouse, had talked about moving the address in the House of Lords in some coming session, and the great value of political alliances early in life, till the young peer began to think that Lady Cantrip was the nicest of women. Then after a short pause she changed the subject. "Don't you think Lady Mary very beautiful?"

"Uncommon," said his lordship.

"And her manners so perfect. She has all her mother's ease without any of that——— You know what I mean."

"Quite so," said his lordship.

"And then she has got so much in her."

"Has she though?"

"I don't know any girl of her age so thoroughly well educated. The Duke seems to take to you."

"Well, yes;—the Duke is very kind."

"Don't you think———?"

"Eh!"

"You have heard of her mother's fortune?"

"Tremendous!"

"She will have, I take it, quite a third of it. Whatever I say I 'm sure you will take in confidence; but she is a dear, dear girl; and I am anxious for her happiness almost as though she belonged to me."

Lord Popplecourt went back to town in the Duke's carriage, but was unable to say a word about politics. His mind was altogether filled with the wonderful words that had been spoken to him. Could it be that Lady Mary had fallen violently in love with him? He would not at once give himself up to the pleasing idea, having so thoroughly grounded himself in the belief that female nets were to be avoided. But when he got home he did think favourably of it. The daughter of a duke, —and such a duke! So lovely a girl, and with such gifts! And then a fortune which would make a material addition to his own large property!

CHAPTER X.

WE all know that very clever distich concerning the great fleas and the little fleas, which tells us that no animal is too humble to have its parasite. Even Major Tifto had his inferior friend. This was a certain Captain Green,—for the friend also affected military honours. He was a man somewhat older than Tifto, of whose antecedents no one was supposed to know anything. It was presumed of him that he lived by betting, and it was boasted by those who wished to defend his character that when he lost he paid his money like a gentleman. Tifto during the last year or two had been anxious to support Captain Green, and had always made use of this argument; "Where the d——he gets his money I don't know;—but when he loses, there it is."

Major Tifto had a little "box" of his own in the neighbourhood of Egham, at which he had a set of stables a little bigger than his house, and a set of kennels a little bigger than his stables. It was here he kept his horses and hounds, and himself too when business connected with his sporting life did not take him to town. It was now the middle of August and he had come to Tally-ho Lodge, there to look after his establishments, to make arrangements for cub-hunting, and to prepare for the autumn racing campaign. On this occasion Captain Green was enjoying his hospitality

and assisting him by sage counsels. Behind the little
box was a little garden,—a garden that was very little;
but, still, thus close to the parlour window, there was
room for a small table to be put on the grass-plat, and
for a couple of arm-chairs. Here the Major and the
Captain were seated about eight o'clock one evening,
with convivial good things within their reach. The
good things were gin and water and pipes. The two
gentlemen had not dressed strictly for dinner. They
had spent a great part of the day handling the hounds
and the horses, dressing wounds, curing sores, and min-
istering to canine ailments, and had been detained over
their work too long to think of their toilet. As it was,
they had an eye to business. The stables at one corner and the kennels at the other were close to the little
garden, and the doings of a man and a boy who were
still at work among the animals could be directed
from the arm-chairs on which the two sportsmen were
sitting.

It must be explained that ever since the Silverbridge
election there had been a growing feeling in Tifto's
mind that he had been ill-treated by his partner. The
feeling was strengthened by the admirable condition of
Prime Minister. Surely more consideration had been
due to a man who had produced such a state of things!

"I would n't quarrel with him, but I 'd make him
pay his way," said the prudent Captain.

"As for that, of course he does pay,—his share."

"Who does all the work?"

"That 's true."

"The fact is, Tifto, you don't make enough out of
it. When a small man like you has to deal with a big
man like that, he may take it out of him in one of two

ways. But he must be deuced clever if he can get it both ways."

"What are you driving at?" asked Tifto, who did not like being called a small man, feeling himself to be every inch a master of fox-hounds.

"Why, this!—Look at that d——d fellow fretting that 'orse with a switch. If you can't strap a 'orse without a stick in your hand, don't you strap him at all, you ——" Then there came a volley of abuse out of the Captain's mouth, in the middle of which the man threw down the rubber he was using and walked away.

"You come back," halloed Tifto, jumping up from his seat with his pipe in his mouth. Then there was a general quarrel between the man and his two masters, in which the man at last was victorious. And the horse was taken into the stable in an unfinished condition. "It's all very well to say 'get rid of him,' but where am I to get anybody better? It has come to such a pass that now if you speak to a fellow he walks out of the yard."

They then returned to the state of affairs, as it was between Tifto and Lord Silverbridge. "What I was saying is this," continued the Captain. "If you choose to put yourself up to live with a fellow like that on equal terms——"

"One gentleman with another, you mean?"

"Put it so. It don't quite hit it off, but put it so. Why, then, you get your wages when you take his arm and call him Silverbridge."

"I don't want wages from any man," said the indignant Major.

"That comes from not knowing what wages is. I do want wages. If I do a thing I like to be paid for it. You are paid for it after one fashion, I prefer the other."

" Do you mean he should give me—a salary ? "

" I 'd have it out of him someway. What 's the good of young chaps of that sort if they are n't made to pay? You 've got this young swell in tow. He 's going to be about the richest man in England ;—and what the deuce better are you for it? " Tifto sat meditating, thinking of the wisdom which was being spoken. The same ideas had occurred to him. The happy chance which had made him intimate with Lord Silverbridge had not yet enriched him. " What is the good of chaps of that sort if they are not made to pay? " The words were wise words. But yet how glorious he had been when he was elected at the Beargarden, and had entered the club as the special friend of the heir of the Duke of Omnium.

After a short pause, Captain Green pursued his discourse. " You said salary."

" I did mention the word."

" Salary and wages is one. A salary is a nice thing if it 's paid regular. I had a salary once myself for looking after a stud of 'orses at Newmarket, only the gentleman broke up and it never went very far."

" Was that Marley Bullock ? "

" Yes ; that was Marley Bullock. He's abroad somewhere now with nothing a year paid quarterly to live on. I think he does a little at cards. He 'd had a good bit of money once, but most of it was gone when he came my way."

" You did n't make by him? "

" I did n't lose nothing. I did n't have a lot of 'orses under me without getting something out of it."

"What am I to do?" asked Tifto. "I can sell him a horse now and again. But if I give him anything good there is n't much to come out of that."

"Very little, I should say. Don't he put his money on his 'orses?"

"Not very free. I think he's coming out freer now."

"What did he stand to win on the Derby?"

"A thousand or two, perhaps."

"There may be something got handsome out of that," said the Captain, not venturing to allow his voice to rise above a whisper. Major Tifto looked hard at him but said nothing. "Of course you must see your way."

"I don't quite understand."

"Race-'orses are expensive animals,—and races generally is expensive."

"That's true."

"When so much is dropped, somebody has to pick it up. That's what I've always said to myself. I'm as honest as another man."

"That's of course," said the Major civilly.

"But if I don't keep my mouth shut, somebody 'll have my teeth out of my head. Every one for himself and God for us all. I suppose there's a deal of money flying about. He'll put a lot of money on this 'orse of yours for the Leger if he's managed right. There's more to be got out of that than calling him Silverbridge and walking arm-in-arm. Business is business. I don't know whether I make myself understood."

The gentleman did not quite make himself understood; but Tifto endeavoured to read the riddle. He must in some way make money out of his friend Lord

Silverbridge.   Hitherto he had contented himself with
the brilliancy of the connection; but now his brilliant
friend had taken to snubbing him, and had on more
than one occasion made himself disagreeable.   It
seemed to him that Captain Green counselled him to
put up with that, but counselled him at the same time
to—pick up some of his friend's money.   He did n't
think that he could ask Lord Silverbridge for a salary,—
he who was a master of fox-hounds, and a member
of the Beargarden.   Then his friend had suggested
something about the young lord's bets.   He was en-
deavouring to unriddle all this with a brain that was
already somewhat muddled with alcohol, when Captain
Green got up from his chair, and, standing over the
Major, spoke his last words for that night as from an
oracle.   "Square is all very well, as long as others are
square to you;—but when they are n't, then I say
square be d——d!   Square! what comes of it?   Work
your heart out, and then it 's no good."

The Major thought about it much that night, and
was thinking about it still when he awoke on the next
morning.   He would like to make Lord Silverbridge
pay for his late insolence.   It would answer his purpose to make a little money,—as he told himself,—in
any honest way.   At the present moment he was in
want of money, and on looking into his affairs declared
to himself that he had certainly impoverished himself
by his devotion to Lord Silverbridge's interests.   At
breakfast on the following morning he endeavoured to
bring his friend back to the subject.   But the Captain
was cross, rather than oracular.   "Everybody," he said,
"ought to know his own business.   He was n't going to
meddle or make.   What he had said had been taken

amiss." This was hard upon Tifto, who had taken nothing amiss.

"Square be d——d!" There was a great deal in the lesson there enunciated which demanded consideration. Hitherto the Major had fought his battles with a certain adherence to squareness. If his angles had not all been perfect angles, still there had always been an attempt at geometrical accuracy. He might now and again have told a lie about a horse,—but who that deals in horses has not done that? He had been alive to the value of underhand information from racing-stables, but who won't use a tip if he can get it? He had lied about the expense of his hounds, in order to enhance the subscription of his members. Those were things which everybody did in his line. But Green had meant something beyond this.

As far as he could see out in the world at large, nobody was square. You had to keep your mouth shut, or your teeth would be stolen out of it. He did n't look into a paper without seeing that on all sides of him men had abandoned the idea of squareness. Chairmen, directors, members of Parliament, ambassadors,—all the world, as he told himself,—were trying to get on by their wits. He did n't see why he should be more square than anybody else. Why had n't Silverbridge taken him down to Scotland for the grouse?

CHAPTER XI.

GREX.

FAR away from all known places, in the northern limit of the Craven district, on the borders of Westmoreland but in Yorkshire, there stands a large, rambling, most picturesque old house called Grex. The people around call it the Castle, but it is not a castle. It is an old brick building supposed to have been erected in the days of James I. having oriel windows, twisted chimneys, long galleries, gable ends, a quadrangle of which the house surrounds three sides, terraces, sun-dials, and fishponds. But it is so sadly out of repair as to be altogether unfit for the residence of a gentleman and his family. It stands not in a park, for the land about it is divided into paddocks by low stone walls, but in the midst of lovely scenery, the ground rising all round it in low irregular hills or fells, and close to it, a quarter of a mile from the back of the house, there is a small dark lake,—not serenely lovely, as are some of the lakes in Westmoreland, but attractive by the darkness of its waters and the gloom of the woods around it.

This is the country seat of Earl Grex,—which, however, he had not visited for some years. Gradually the place had got into such a condition that his absence is not surprising. An owner of Grex, with large means at his disposal and with a taste for the picturesque to gratify,—one who could afford to pay for memories and who was willing to pay dearly for such luxuries, might no doubt restore Grex. But the Earl had neither the money nor the taste.

Lord Grex had latterly never gone near the place, nor was his son Lord Percival fond of looking upon the ruin of his property. But Lady Mabel loved it with a fond love. With all her lightness of spirit she was prone to memories, prone to melancholy, prone at times almost to seek the gratification of sorrow. Year after year when the London season was over she would come down to Grex and spend a week or two amidst its desolation. She was now going on to a seat in Scotland belonging to Mrs. Montacute Jones called Killancodlem; but she was now passing a desolate fortnight at Grex in company with Miss Casseway. The gardens were let,—and being let of course were not kept in further order than as profit might require. The man who rented them lived in the big house with his wife, and they on such occasions as this would cook and wait upon Lady Mabel.

Lady Mabel was at the home of her ancestors, and the faithful Miss Cass was with her. But at the moment and at the spot at which the reader shall see her Miss Cass was not with her. She was sitting on a rock about twelve feet above the lake looking upon the black water ; and on another rock a few feet from her was seated Frank Tregear. " No," she said, " you should not have come. Nothing can justify it. Of course as you are here I could not refuse to come out with you. To make a fuss about it would be the worst of all. But you should not have come."

" Why not? Whom does it hurt? It is a pleasure to me. If it be the reverse to you, I will go."

"Men are so unmanly. They take such mean advantages. You know it is a pleasure to me to see you."

"I had hoped so."

"But it is a pleasure I ought not to have,—at least not here."

"That is what I do not understand," said he. "In London, where the Earl could bark at me if he happened to find me, I could see the inconvenience. But here, where there is nobody but Miss Cass—— "

"There are a great many others. There are the rooks and stones and old women;—all of which have ears."

"But of what is there to be ashamed? There is nothing in the world to me so pleasant as the companionship of my friends."

"Then go after Silverbridge."

"I mean to do so;—but I am taking you by the way."

"It is all unmanly," she said, rising from her stone; "you know that it is so. Friends! Do you mean to say that it would make no difference whether you were here with me or with Miss Cass?"

"The greatest difference in the world."

"Because she is an old woman and I am a young one, and because in intercourse between young men and young women there is something dangerous to the woman and therefore pleasant to the man."

"I never heard anything more unjust. You cannot think I desire anything injurious to you."

"I do think so." She was still standing, and spoke now with great vehemence. "I do think so. You force me to throw aside the reticence I ought to keep. Would it help me in my prospects if your friend Lord Silverbridge knew that I was here?"

"How should he know?"

"But if he did? Do you suppose that I want to have visits paid to me of which I am afraid to speak? Would you dare to tell Lady Mary that you had been sitting alone with me on the rocks at Grex?"

"Certainly I would."

"Then it would be because you have not dared to tell her certain other things which have gone before. You have sworn to her no doubt that you love her better than all the world."

"I have."

"And you have taken the trouble to come here to tell me that,—to wound me to the core by saying so; to show me that, though I may still be sick, you have recovered,—that is, if you ever suffered! Go your way and let me go mine. I do not want you."

"Mabel!"

"I do not want you. I know you will not help me, but you need not destroy me."

"You know that you are wronging me."

"No! You understand it all though you look so calm. I hate your Lady Mary Palliser. There! But if by anything I could do I could secure her to you I would do it,—because you want it."

"She will be your sister-in-law,—probably."

"Never. It will never be so." .

"Why do you hate her?"

"There again! You are so little of a man that you can ask me why!" Then she turned away as though she intended to go down to the marge of the lake. But he rose up and stopped her. "Let us have this out, Mabel, before we go," he said. "Unmanly is a heavy word to hear from you, and you have used it a dozen times."

"It is because I have thought it a thousand times.
Go and get her if you can;—but why tell me about it?"

"You said you would help me."

"So I would, as I would help you to anything you
might want; but you can hardly think that after what
has passed I can wish to hear about her."

"It was you spoke of her."

"I told you you should not be here,—because of
her and because of me. And I tell you again, I hate
her. Do you think I can hear you speak of her as
though she were the only woman you had ever seen,
without feeling it? Did you ever swear that you loved
any one else?"

"Certainly, I have so sworn."

"Have you ever said that nothing could alter that
love?"

"Indeed I have."

"But it is altered. It has all gone. It has been
transferred to one who has more advantages of beauty,
youth, wealth, and position."

"Oh, Mabel, Mabel!"

"But it is so."

"When you say this do you not think of yourself?"

"Yes. But I have never been false to any one.
You are false to me."

"Have I not offered to face all the world with you?"

"You would not offer it now?"

"No," he said, after a pause,—"not now. Were I
to do so, I should be false. You bade me take my
love elsewhere, and I did so."

"With the greatest ease."

"We agreed that it should be so; and you have
done the same."

"That is false. Look me in the face and tell me whether you do not know it to be false?"

"And yet I am told that I am injuring you with Silverbridge."

"Oh,—so unmanly again! Of course I have to marry. Who does not know it? Do you want to see me begging my bread about the streets? You have bread; or if not, you might earn it. If you marry for money——"

"The accusation is altogether unjustifiable."

"Allow me to finish what I have to say. If you marry for money you will do that which is in itself bad, and which is also unnecessary. What other course would you recommend me to take? No one goes into the gutter while there is a clean path open. If there be no escape but through the gutter, one has to take it."

"You mean that my duty to you should have kept me from marrying all my life."

"Not that;—but a little while, Frank; just a little while. Your bloom is not fading; your charms are not running from you. Have you not a strength which I cannot have? Do you not feel that you are a tree, standing firm in the ground, while I am a bit of ivy that will be trodden in the dirt unless it can be made to cling to something? You should not liken yourself to me, Frank."

"If I could do you any good!"

"Good! What is the meaning of good? If you love, it is good to be loved again. It is good not to have your heart torn in pieces. You know that I love you." He was standing close to her, and put out his hand as though he would twine his arm round her waist. "Not for worlds," she said. "It belongs to that Palliser girl. And as I have taught myself to think that what there is left of me may perhaps belong to some other one, worthless as it is, I will keep it for him. I love you,—but there can be none of that softness of love between us." Then there was a pause, but as he did not speak she went on. "But remember, Frank,—our position is not equal. You have got over your little complaint. It probably did not go deep with you, and you have found a cure. Perhaps there is a satisfaction in finding that two young women love you."

"You are trying to be cruel to me."

"Why else should you be here? You know I love you,—with all my heart, with all my strength, and that I would give the world to cure myself. Knowing this you come and talk to me of your passion for this other girl."

"I had hoped we might both talk rationally as friends."

"Friends! Frank Tregear, I have been bold enough to tell you I love you; but you are not my friend, and cannot be my friend. If I have before asked you to help me in this mean catastrophe of mine, in my attack upon that poor boy, I withdraw my request. I think I will go back to the house now."

"I will walk back to Ledburgh if you wish it without going to the house again."

"No; I will have nothing that looks like being ashamed. You ought not to have come, but you need not run away." Then they walked back to the house together and found Miss Cassewary on the terrace. "We have been to the lake," said Mabel, "and have been talking of old days. I have but one ambition now in the world." Of course Miss Cassewary asked what the remaining ambition was. "To get money enough to purchase this place from the ruins of the Grex property. If I could own the house and the lake, and the paddocks about, and had enough income to keep one servant and bread for us to eat—of course including you, Miss Cass——"

"Thank 'ee, my dear; but I am not sure I should like it."

"Yes, you would. Frank would come and see us perhaps once a year. I don't suppose anybody else cares about the place, but to me it is the dearest spot in the world." So she went on in almost high spirits, though alluding to the general decadence of the Grex family, till Tregear took his leave.

"I wish he had not come," said Miss Cassewary when he was gone.

"Why should you wish that? There is not so much here to amuse me that you should begrudge me a stray visitor."

"I don't think that I grudge you anything in the way of pleasure, my dear; but still he should not have come. My lord, if he knew it, would be angry."

"Then let him be angry. Papa does not do so much for me that I am bound to think of him at every turn."

"But I am,—or rather I am bound to think of myself, if I take his bread."

"Bread!"

"Well;—I do take his bread, and I take it on the understanding that I will be to you what a mother might be,—or an aunt."

"Well,—and if so! Had I a mother living would

not Frank Tregear have come to visit her, and in visiting her would he not have seen me,—and should we not have walked out together?"

"Not after all that has come and gone."

"But you are not a mother nor yet an aunt, and you have to do just what I tell you. And don't I know that you trust me in all things? And am I not trustworthy?"

"I think you are trustworthy."

"I know what my duty is and I mean to do it. No one shall ever have to say of me that I have given way to self-indulgence. I could n't help his coming, you know."

That same night, after Miss Cassewary had gone to bed, when the moon was high in the heavens and the world around her was all asleep, Lady Mabel again wandered out to the lake, and again seated herself on the same rock, and there she sat thinking of her past life and trying to think of that before her. It is so much easier to think of the past than of the future,— to remember what has been than to resolve what shall be! She had reminded him of the offer which he had made and repeated to her more than once,—to share with her all his chances in life. There would have been almost no income for them. All the world would have been against her. She would have caused his ruin. Her light on the matter had been so clear that it had not taken her very long to decide that such a thing must not be thought of. She had at last been quite stern in her decision.

Now she was broken-hearted because she found that he had left her in very truth. Oh yes;—she would marry the boy, if she could so arrange. Since that meeting at Richmond he had sent her the ring reset. She was to meet him down in Scotland within a week or two from the present time. Mrs. Montacute Jones had managed that. He had all but offered to her a second time at Richmond. But all that would not serve to make her happy. She declared to herself that she did not wish to see Frank Tregear again; but still it was a misery to her that his heart should in truth be given to another woman.

CHAPTER XII.

CRUMMIE-TODDIE.

ALMOST at the last moment Silverbridge and his brother Gerald were induced to join Lord Popplecourt's shooting-party in Scotland. The party perhaps might more properly be called the party of Reginald Dobbes, who was a man knowing in such matters. It was he who made the party up. Popplecourt and Silverbridge were to share the expense between them, each bringing three guns. Silverbridge brought his brother and Frank Tregear,—having refused a most piteous petition on the subject from Major Tifto. With Popplecourt of course came Reginald Dobbes, who was, in truth, to manage everything, and Lord Nidderdale, whose wife had generously permitted him this recreation. The shooting was in the west of Perthshire, known as Crummie-Toddie, and comprised an enormous acreage of so-called forest and moor. Mr. Dobbes declared that nothing like it had as yet been produced in Scotland. Everything had been made to give way to deer and grouse. The thing had been managed so well that the tourist nuisance had been considerably abated. There was hardly a potato patch left in the district, nor a head of cattle to be seen. There were no inhabitants remaining, or so few that they could be absorbed in game-preserving or cognate duties. Reginald Dobbes, who was very great at grouse, and supposed to be

capable of outwitting a deer by venatical wiles more
perfectly than any other sportsman in Great Britain,
regarded Crummie-Toddie as the nearest thing there
was to a Paradise on earth. Could he have been allowed to pass one or two special laws for his own pro-
tection, there might still have been improvement. He
would like the right to have all intruders thrashed by
the gillies within an inch of their lives; and he would
have had a clause in his lease against the making of
any new roads, opening of footpaths, or building of
bridges. He had seen somewhere in print a plan for
running a railway from Callender to Fort Augustus
right through Crummie-Toddie! If this were done in
his time the beauty of the world would be over.
Reginald Dobbes was a man of about forty, strong,
active, well-made, about five feet ten in height, with
broad shoulders and greatly developed legs. He was
not a handsome man, having a protrusive nose, high
cheek-bones, and long upper lip; but there was a manliness about his face which redeemed it. Sport was
the business of his life, and he thoroughly despised all
who were not sportsmen. He fished and shot and
hunted during nine or ten months of the year, filling
up his time as best he might with coaching, polo, and
pigeon-shooting. He regarded it as a great duty to
keep his body in the firmest possible condition. All
his eating and all his drinking was done upon a system,
and he would consider himself to be guilty of weak self-
indulgence were he to allow himself to break through
sanitary rules. But it never occurred to him that his
whole life was one of self-indulgence. He could walk
his thirty miles with his gun on his shoulder as well
now as he could ten years ago; and being sure of this.

was thoroughly contented with himself. He had a
patrimony amounting to perhaps £1000 a year, which
he husbanded so as to enjoy all his amusements to
perfection. No one had ever heard of his sponging
on his friends. Of money he rarely spoke, sport being
in his estimation the only subject worthy of a man's
words. Such was Reginald Dobbes, who was now to
be the master of the shooting at Crummie-Toddie.

Crummie-Toddie was but twelve miles from Killancodlem, Mrs. Montacute Jones's highland seat; and it
was this vicinity which first induced Lord Silverbridge
to join the party. Mabel Grex was to be at Killancodlem, and, determined as he still was to ask her to
be his wife, he would make this his opportunity. Of
real opportunity there had been none at Richmond.
Since he had had his ring altered and had sent it to
her there had come but a word or two of answer.
"What am I to say? You unkindest of men! To
keep it or to send it back would make me equally
miserable. I shall keep it till you are married, and
then give it to your wife." This affair of the ring had
made him more intent than ever. After that he heard
that Isabel Boncassen would also be at Killancodlem,
having been induced to join Mrs. Montacute Jones's
swarm of visitors. Though he was dangerously devoid
of experience, still he felt that this was unfortunate.
He intended to marry Mabel Grex. And he could
assure himself that he thoroughly loved her. Nevertheless he liked making love to Isabel Boncassen. He
was quite willing to marry and settle down, and looked
forward with satisfaction to having Mabel Grex for his
wife. But it would be pleasant to have a six-months'
run of flirting and love-making before this settlement,

and he had certainly never seen any one with whom this would be so delightful as with Miss Boncassen. But that the two ladies should be at the same house was unfortunate.

He and Gerald reached Crummie-Toddie late on the evening of August 11th, and found Reginald Dobbes alone. That was on Wednesday. Popple-court and Nidderdale ought to have made their appearance on that morning, but had telegraphed to say that they would be detained two days on their route. Tregear, whom hitherto Dobbes had never seen, had left his arrival uncertain. This carelessness on such matters was very offensive to Mr. Dobbes, who loved discipline and exactitude. He ought to have received the two young men with open arms because they were punctual; but he had been somewhat angered by what he considered the extreme youth of Lord Gerald. Boys who could not shoot were, he thought, putting themselves forward before their time. And Silverbridge himself was by no means a first-rate shot. Such a one as Silverbridge had to be endured because from his position and wealth he could facilitate such arrangements as these. It was much to have to do with a man who would not complain if an extra fifty pounds were wanted. But he ought to have understood that he was bound in honour to bring down competent friends. Of Tregear's shooting Dobbes had been able to learn nothing. Lord Gerald was a lad from the universities; and Dobbes hated university lads. Popplecourt and Nidderdale were known to be efficient. They were men who could work hard and do their part of the required slaughter. Dobbes proudly knew that he could make up for some deficiency by his own prowess; but he could not struggle against three bad guns. What was the use of so perfecting Crummie-Toddie as to make it the best bit of ground for grouse and deer in Scotland, if the men who came there failed by their own incapacity to bring up the grand total of killed to a figure which would render Dobbes and Crummie-Toddie famous through the whole shooting world? He had been hard at work on other matters. Dogs had gone amiss,—or guns, and he had been made angry by the champagne which Popplecourt caused to be sent down. He knew what champagne meant. whiskey and water, and not much of it, was the liquor which Reginald Dobbes loved in the mountains.

"Don't you call this a very ugly country?" Silver-bridge asked as soon as he arrived. Now it is the case that the traveller who travels into Argyleshire, Perthshire, and Inverness, expects to find lovely scenery; and it was also true that the country through which they had passed for the last twenty miles had been not only bleak and barren, but uninteresting and ugly. It was all rough open moorland, never rising into mountains, and graced by no running streams, by no forest scenery, almost by no foliage. The lodge itself did indeed stand close upon a little river, and was reached by a bridge that crossed it; but there was nothing pretty either in the river or the bridge. It was a placid black little streamlet, which in that portion of its course was hurried by no steepness, had no broken rocks in its bed, no trees on its low banks, and played none of those gambols which make running water beautiful. The bridge was a simple low construction with a low parapet, carrying an ordinary roadway up to the hall door. The lodge itself was as ugly as a house could be, white, of two stories, with the door in the middle and windows on each side, with a slate roof, and without a tree near it.   It was in the middle of the shooting, and did not create a town around itself as do sumptuous mansions, to the great detriment of that seclusion which is favourable to game.   "Look at Killancodlem," Dobbes had been heard to say—"a very fine house for ladies to flirt in; but if you find a deer within six miles of it I will eat him first and shoot him afterwards."   There was a Spartan simplicity about Crummie-Toddie which pleased the Spartan mind of Reginald Dobbes.

"Ugly do you call it?"

"Infernally ugly," said Lord Gerald.

"What did you expect to find?   A big hotel, and a lot of cockneys.   If you come after grouse, you must come to what the grouse think pretty."

"Nevertheless, it is ugly," said Silverbridge, who did not choose to be "sat upon."   "I have been at shootings in Scotland before, and sometimes they are not ugly.   This I call beastly."   Whereupon Reginald Dobbes turned upon his heel and walked away.

"Can you shoot?" he said afterwards to Lord Gerald.

"I can fire off a gun, if you mean that," said Gerald.

"You never have shot much?"

"Not what you call very much.   I'm not so old as you are, you know.   Everything must have a beginning."   Mr. Dobbes wished "the beginning" might have taken place elsewhere; but there had been some truth in the remark.

"What on earth made you tell him crammers like that?" asked Silverbridge, as the brothers sat together afterwards smoking on the wall of the bridge.

"Because he made an ass of himself; asking me whether I could shoot."

On the next morning they started at seven. Dobbes had determined to be cross, because, as he thought, the young men would certainly keep him waiting; and was cross because by their punctuality they robbed him of any just cause for offence. During the morning on the moor they were hardly ever near enough each other for much conversation, and very little was said. According to arrangement made they returned to the house for lunch, it being their purpose not to go far from home till their numbers were complete. As they came over the bridge and put down their guns near the door, Mr. Dobbes spoke the first good-humoured word they had heard from his lips. "Why did you tell me such an infernal ——, I would say lie, only perhaps you might n't like it."

"I told you no lie," said Gerald.

"You 've only missed two birds all the morning, and you have shot forty-two. That 's uncommonly good sport."

"What have you done?"

"Only forty," and Mr. Dobbes seemed for the moment to be gratified by his own inferiority. "You are a deuced sight better than your brother."

"Gerald 's about the best shot I know," said Silverbridge.

"Why did n't he tell?"

"Because you were angry when we said the place was ugly."

"I see all about it," said Dobbes. "Nevertheless when a fellow comes to shoot he should n't complain because a place is n't pretty. What you want is a de

cent house as near as you can have it to your ground.
If there is anything in Scotland to beat Crummie-
Toddie I don't know where to find it. Shooting is
shooting, you know, and touring is touring."

Upon that he took very kindly to Lord Gerald, who,
even after the arrival of the other men, was second
only in skill to Dobbes himself. With Nidderdale,
who was an old companion, he got on very well.
Nidderdale ate and drank too much, and refused to be
driven beyond a certain amount of labour, but was in
other respects obedient and knew what he was about.
Popplecourt was disagreeable, but he was a fairly good
shot and understood what was expected of him.   Silverbridge was so good-humoured, that even his manifest faults,—shooting carelessly, lying in bed and wanting his dinner,—were, if not forgiven, at least endured.
But Tregear was an abomination. He could shoot
well enough and was active, and when he was at the
work seemed to like it ;—but he would stay away whole
days by himself, and when spoken to would answer in
a manner which seemed to Dobbes to be flat mutiny.
"We are not doing it for our bread," said Tregear.

" I don't know what you mean."

" There 's no duty in killing a certain number of
these animals." They had been driving deer on the
day before and were to continue the work on the day
in question.   " I 'm not paid fifteen shillings a week
for doing it."

" I suppose if you undertake to do a thing you mean
to do it.   Of course you 're not wanted. We can
make the double party without you."

" Then why the mischief should you growl at me ? "

" Because I think a man should do what he under-

takes to do. A man who gets tired after three days'
work of this kind would become tired if he were earning his bread."

"Who says I am tired? I came here to amuse myself."

"Amuse yourself!"

"And as long as it amuses me I shall shoot, and
when it does not I shall give it up."

This vexed the governor of Crummie-Toddie much.
He had learned to regard himself as the arbiter of the
fate of men while they were sojourning under the same
autumnal roof as himself. But a defalcation which
occurred immediately afterwards was worse. Silverbridge declared his intention of going over one morning to Killancodlem. Reginald Dobbes muttered a
curse between his teeth, which was visible by the anger
on his brow, to all the party. "I shall be back to-night,
you know," said Silverbridge.

"A lot of men and women who pretend to come
there for shooting," said Dobbes angrily, "but do all
the mischief they can."

"One must go and see one's friends, you know."

"Some girl!" said Dobbes.

But worse happened than the evil so lightly mentioned. Silverbridge did go over to Killancodlem;
and presently there came back a man with a cart, who
was to return with a certain not small proportion of
his luggage.

"It 's hardly honest, you know," said Reginald
Dobbes.

CHAPTER XIII.

KILLANCODLEM.

MR. DOBBES was probably right in his opinion that hotels, tourists, and congregations of men are detrimental to shooting. Crummie-Toddie was in all respects suited for sport. Killancodlem, though it had the name of a shooting-place, certainly was not so. Men going there took their guns. Gamekeepers were provided and gillies,—and, in a moderate quantity, game. On certain grand days a deer or two might be shot,—and would be very much talked about afterwards. But a glance at the place would suffice to show that Killancodlem was not intended for sport. It was a fine castellated mansion, with beautiful though narrow grounds, standing in the valley of the Archay river, with a mountain behind and the river in front. Between the gates and the river there was a public road on which a stage-coach ran, with loud-blown horns and the noise of many tourists. A mile beyond the Castle was the famous Killancodlem hotel which made up a hundred and twenty beds, and at which half as many more guests would sleep on occasions, under the tables. And there was the Killancodlem post-office half-way between the two. At Crummie-Toddie they had to send nine miles for their letters and newspapers. At Killancodlem there was lawn-tennis and a billiard-room and dancing every night. The costumes of the ladies were lovely, and those of the gentlemen, who were wonderful in knickerbockers, picturesque hats, and variegated stockings, hardly less so. And then there were carriages and saddle-horses, and paths had been made hither and thither through the rocks and hills for the sake of the scenery. Scenery! To hear Mr. Dobbes utter the single word was as good as a play Was it for such cockney purposes as those that Scot. land had been created, fit mother for grouse and deer ?

Silverbridge arrived just before lunch, and was soon made to understand that it was impossible that he should go back that day. Mrs. Jones was very great on that occasion. " You are afraid of Reginald Dobbes," she said severely.

" I think I am rather."

" Of course you are. How came it to pass that you of all men should submit yourself to such a tyrant? "

" Good shooting, you know," said Silverbridge.

" But you dare not call an hour your own,—or your soul. Mr. Dobbes and I are sworn enemies. We both like Scotland, and unfortunately we have fallen into the same neighbourhood. He looks upon me as the genius of sloth. I regard him as the incarnation of tyranny. He once said there should be no women in Scotland,—just an old one here and there, who would know how to cook grouse. I offered to go and cook his grouse! Any friend of mine," continued Mrs. Jones, " who comes down to Crummie-Toddie without staying a day or two with me,—will never be my friend any more. I do not hesitate to tell you, Lord Silver- bridge, that I call for your surrender, in order that I may show my power over Reginald Dobbes.   Are you a Dobbite?"

"Not thorough-going," said Silverbridge.

"Then be a Montacute-Jones-ite; or a Boncassen-ite, if, as is possible, you prefer a young woman to an old one."   At this moment Isabel Boncassen was standing close to them.

"Killancodlem against Crummie-Toddie forever," said Miss Boncassen, waving her handkerchief.   As a matter of course a messenger was sent back to Crummie-Toddie for the young lord's wearing apparel.

The whole of that afternoon he spent playing lawn-tennis with Miss Boncassen.   Lady Mabel was asked to join the party but she refused, having promised to take a walk to a distant waterfall where the Codlem falls into the Archay.   A gentleman in knickerbockers was to have gone with her, and two other young ladies; but when the time came she was weary, she said,—and she sat almost the entire afternoon looking at the game from a distance.   Silverbridge played well, but not so well as the pretty American.   With them were joined two others somewhat inferior, so that Silverbridge and Miss Boncassen were on different sides.   They played game after game, and Miss Boncassen's side always won.

Very little was said between Silverbridge and Miss Boncassen which did not refer to the game.   But Lady Mabel, looking on, told herself that they were making love to each other before her eyes.   And why should n't they?   She asked herself that question in perfect good faith.   Why should they not be lovers?   Was ever anything prettier than the girl in her country dress, active as a fawn and as graceful?   Or could anything be more handsome, more attractive to a girl, more good-humoured, or better bred in his playful emulation than Silverbridge?

> " ' When youth and pleasure meet,
> To chase the glowing hours with flying feet!' "

she said to herself over and over again.

But why had he sent her the ring? She would certainly give him back the ring and bid him bestow it at once upon Miss Boncassen. Inconstant boy! Then she would get up and wander away for a time and rebuke herself. What right had she even to think of inconstancy? Could she be so irrational, so unjust, as to be sick for his love, as to be angry with him because he seemed to prefer another? Was she not well aware that she herself did not love him;—but that she did love another man? She had made up her mind to marry him in order that she might be a duchess and because she could give herself to him without any of that horror which would be her fate in submitting to matrimony with one or another of the young men around her. There might be disappointment. If he escaped her there would be bitter disappointment. But seeing how it was, had she any further ground for hope? She certainly had no ground for anger!

It was thus, within her own bosom, she put questions to herself. And yet all this before her was simply a game of play in which the girl and the young man were as eager for victory as though they were children. They were thinking neither of love nor love-making. That the girl should be so lovely was no doubt a pleasure to him;—and perhaps to her also that he should be joyous to look at and sweet of voice.

But he, could he have been made to tell all the truth within him, would have still owned that it was his pur- pose to make Mabel his wife.

When the game was over and the propositions made for further matches and the like,—Miss Boncassen said that she would betake herself to her own room. " I never worked so hard in my life before," she said, " and I feel like a navvie. I could drink beer out of a jug and eat bread and cheese. I won't play with you any more, Lord Silverbridge, because I am begin- ning to think it is unladylike to exert myself."

" Are you not glad you came over ? " said Lady Mabel to him as he was going off the ground almost without seeing her.

" Pretty well," he said.

" Is not that better than stalking ? "

" Lawn-tennis ? "

" Yes ;—lawn-tennis,—with Miss Boncassen."

" She plays uncommonly well."

" And so do you."

" Ah, she has such an eye for distances."

" And you,—what have you an eye for ? Will you answer me a question ? "

" Well ;—yes ; I think so."

" Truly ? "

" Certainly ; if I do answer it."

" Do you not think her the most beautiful creature you ever saw in your life? " He pushed back his cap and looked at her without making any immediate an- swer. " I do. Now tell me what you think."

" I think that perhaps she is."

" I knew you would say so. You are so honest that you could not bring yourself to tell a fib,—even to me

about that. Come here and sit down for a moment."
Of course he sat down by her. " You know that Frank
came to see me at Grex ? "

" He never mentioned it."

" Dear me ;—how odd!"

" It was odd," said he in a voice which showed that
he was angry. She could hardly explain to herself
why she told him this at the present moment. It came
partly from jealousy, as though she had said to herself,
" Though he may neglect me, he shall know that there
is some one who does not ;"—and partly from an eager
half-angry feeling that she would have nothing con-
cealed. There were moments with her in which she
thought that she could arrange her future life in accordance with certain wise rules over which her heart
should have no influence. There were others, many
others, in which her feelings completely got the better
of her. And now she told herself that she would be
afraid of nothing. There should be no deceit, no
lies!

" He went to see you at Grex!" said Silverbridge.

" Why should he not have come to me at Grex? "

" Only it is so odd that he did not mention it. It
seems to me that he is always having secrets with you
of some kind."

" Poor Frank! There is no one else who would
come to see me at that tumble-down old place. But
I have another thing to say to you. You have behaved badly to me."

" Have I? "

" Yes, sir. After my folly about that ring you should
have known better than to send it to me. You must
take it back again."

"You shall do exactly what you said you would. You shall give it to my wife,—when I have one."

"That did very well for me to say in a note. I did not want to send my anger to you over a distance of two or three hundred miles by the postman. But now that we are together you must take it back."

"I will do no such thing," said he sturdily.

"You speak as though this were a matter in which you can have your own way."

"I mean to have mine about that."

"Any lady, then, must be forced to take any present that a gentleman may send her! Allow me to assure you that the usages of society do not run in that direction. Here is the ring. I knew that you would come over to see—well, to see some one here, and I have kept it ready in my pocket."

"I came over to see you."

"Lord Silverbridge! But we know that in certain employments all things are fair." He looked at her not knowing what were the employments to which she alluded. "At any rate you will oblige me by—by —by not being troublesome, and putting this little trinket into your pocket."

"Never! Nothing on earth shall make me do it."

At Killancodlem they did not dine till half-past eight. Twilight was now stealing on these two, who were still out in the garden, all the others having gone in to dress. She looked round to see that no other eyes were watching them as she still held the ring. "It is there," she said, putting it on the bench between them. Then she prepared to rise from the seat so that she might leave it with him.

But he was too quick for her, and was away at a

distance before she had collected her dress. And from a distance he spoke again, "If you choose that it shall be lost, so be it."

"You had better take it," said she, following him slowly. But he would not turn back;—nor would she. They met again in the hall for a moment. "I should be sorry it should be lost," said he, "because it belonged to my great-uncle. And I had hoped that I might live to see it very often."

"You can fetch it," she said, as she went to her room. He, however, would not fetch it. She had accepted it, and he would not take it back again, let the fate of the gem be what it might.

But to the feminine and more cautious mind the very value of the trinket made its position out there on the bench, within the grasp of any dishonest gardener, a burden to her. She could not reconcile it to her conscience that it should be so left. The diamond was a large one, and she had heard it spoken of as a stone of great value,—so much so, that Silverbridge had been blamed for wearing it ordinarily. She had asked for it in joke, regarding it as a thing which could not be given away. She could not go down herself and take it up again; but neither could she allow it to remain. As she went to her room she met Mrs. Jones already coming from hers. "You will keep us all waiting," said the hostess.

"Oh no;—nobody ever dressed so quickly. But, Mrs. Jones, will you do me a favour?"

"Certainly."

"And will you let me explain something?"

"Anything you like,—from a hopeless engagement down to a broken garter."

"I am suffering neither from one or the other. But there is a most valuable ring lying out in the garden. Will you send for it?" Then of course the story had to be told. "You will, I hope, understand how I came to ask for it foolishly. It was because it was the one thing which I was sure he would not give away."

"Why not take it?"

"Can't you understand? I would n't for the world. But you will be good enough,—won't you,—to see that there is nothing else in it?"

"Nothing of love?"

"Nothing in the least. He and I are excellent friends. We are cousins, and intimate, and all that. I thought I might have had my joke, and now I am punished for it. As for love, don't you see he is over head and ears in love with Miss Boncassen?"

This was very imprudent on the part of Lady Mabel, who, had she been capable of clinging fast to her policy, would not now in a moment of strong feeling have done so much to raise obstacles in her own way. "But you will send for it, won't you, and have it put on his dressing-table to-night?" When he went to bed Lord Silverbridge found it on his table.

But before that time came he had twice danced with Miss Boncassen, Lady Mabel having refused to dance with him. "No," she said, "I am angry with you. You ought to have felt that it did not become you as a gentleman to subject me to inconvenience by throwing upon me the charge of that diamond. You may be foolish enough to be indifferent about its value, but as you have mixed me up with it I cannot afford to have it lost."

"It is yours."

"No, sir; it is not mine, nor will it ever be mine. But I wish you to understand that you have offended me."

This made him so unhappy for the time that he almost told the story to Miss Boncassen. "If I were to give you a ring," he said, "would not you accept it?"

"What a question!"

"What I mean is, don't you think all those conventional rules about men and women are absurd?"

"As a progressive American of course I am bound to think all conventional rules are an abomination."

"If you had a brother and I gave him a stick he'd take it."

"Not across his back, I hope."

"Or if I gave your father a book?"

"He'd take books to any extent, I should say."

"And why not you a ring?"

"Who said I wouldn't? But after all this you must n't try me."

"I was not thinking of it."

"I'm so glad of that! Well;—if you'll promise that you'll never offer me one, I'll promise that I'll take it when it comes. But what does all this mean?"

"It is not worth talking about."

"You have offered somebody a ring, and somebody has n't taken it. May I guess?"

"I had rather you did not."

"I could, you know."

"Never mind about that. Now come and have a turn. I am bound not to give you a ring; but you are bound to accept anything else I may offer."

"No, Lord Silverbridge;—not at all. Nevertheless we 'll have a turn."

That night before he went up to his room he had
told Isabel Boncassen that he loved her.   And when
he spoke he was telling her the truth.   It had seemed
to him that Mabel had become hard to him, and had
over and over again rejected the approaches to tenderness which he had attempted to make in his intercourse with her.   Even though she were to accept him,
what would that be worth to him if she did not love
him?   So many things had been added together!
Why had Tregear gone to Grex, and having gone there
why had he kept his journey a secret?   Tregear he
knew was engaged to his sister;—but for all that, there
was a closer intimacy between Mabel and Tregear than
between Mabel and himself.   And surely she might
have taken his ring!

And then Isabel Boncassen was so perfect!   Since
he had first met her he had heard her loveliness talked
of on all sides.   It seemed to be admitted everywhere
that so beautiful a creature had never before been seen
in London.   There is even a certain dignity attached
to that which is praised by all lips.   Miss Boncassen
as an American girl, had she been judged to be beautiful only by his own eyes,—might perhaps have seemed
to him to be beneath his serious notice.   In such a
case he might have felt himself unable to justify so ex-
traordinary a choice.   But there was an acclamation
of assent as to this girl!   Then came the dancing,—
the one dance after another; the pressure of the hand,
the entreaty that she would not, just on this occasion,
dance with any other man, the attendance on her when
she took her glass of wine, the whispered encouragement of Mrs. Montacute Jones, the half-resisting and
yet half-yielding conduct of the girl.   "I shall not

dance at all again," she said when he asked her to stand up for another. "Think of all that lawn-tennis this morning."

"But you will play to-morrow?"

"I thought you were going."

"Of course I shall stay now," he said, and as he said it he put his hand on her hand, which was on his arm. She drew it away at once. "I love you so dearly," he whispered to her; "so dearly."

"Lord Silverbridge!"

"I do. I do. Can you say that you will love me in return?"

"I cannot," she said slowly. "I have never dreamed of such a thing. I hardly know now whether you are in earnest."

"Indeed, indeed I am."

"Then I will say good night, and think about it. Everybody is going. We will have our game to-morrow at any rate."

When he went to his room he found the ring on his dressing-table.

CHAPTER XIV.

ON the next morning Miss Boncassen did not appear at breakfast. Word came that she had been so fatigued by the lawn-tennis as not to be able to leave her bed. " I have been to her." said Mrs. Montacute Jones, whispering to Lord Silverbridge, as though he were particularly interested. " There 's nothing really the matter. She will be down to lunch."

" I was afraid she might be ill," said Silverbridge, who was now hardly anxious to hide his admiration.

" Oh no ;—nothing of that sort ; but she will not be able to play again to-day. It was your fault. You should not have made her dance last night." After that Mrs. Jones said a word about it all to Lady Mabel. " I hope the Duke will not be angry with me."

" Why should he be angry with you ? "

" I don't suppose he will approve of it, and perhaps he 'll say I brought them together on purpose."

Soon afterwards Mabel asked Silverbridge to walk with her to the waterfall. She had worked herself into such a state of mind that she hardly knew what to do, what to wish, or how to act. At one moment she would tell herself that it was better in every respect that she should cease to think of being Duchess of Omnium. It was not fit that she should think of it. She herself cared but little for the young man, and he,

136

—she would tell herself,—now appeared to care as
little for her. And yet to be Duchess of Omnium!
But was it not clear that he was absolutely in love
with this other girl? She had played her cards so
badly that the game was now beyond her powers.
Then other thoughts would come. Was it beyond her
powers? Had he not told her in London that he loved
her ? Had he not given her the ring which she well
knew he valued? Ah;—if she could but have been
aware of all that had passed between Silverbridge and
the Duke, how different would have been her feelings!
And then would it not be so much better for him that
he should marry her, one of his own class, than this
American girl, of whom nobody knew anything. And
then,—to be the daughter of the Duke of Omnium, to
be the future Duchess, to escape from all the cares
which her father's vices and follies had brought upon
her, to have come to an end of all her troubles!
Would it not be sweet ?

She had made her mind up to nothing when she
asked him to walk up to the waterfall. There was
present to her only the glimmer of an idea that she
ought to caution him not to play with the American
girl's feelings. She knew herself to be aware that when
the time for her own action came her feminine feelings
would get the better of her purpose. She could not
craftily bring him to the necessity of bestowing himself
upon her. Had that been within the compass of her
powers, opportunities had not been lacking to her. On
such occasions she had always "spared him." And
should the opportunity come again, again she would
spare him. But she might perhaps do some good,—
not to herself, that was now out of the question,—but

to him by showing him how wrong he was in trifling
with this girl's feelings.

And so they started for their walk. He of course
would have avoided it had it been possible. When
men in such matters have two strings to their bow,
much inconvenience is felt when the two become en-
tangled. Silverbridge no doubt had come over to
Killancodlem for the sake of making love to Mabel
Grex, and instead of doing so he had made love to
Isabel Boncassen. And during the watches of the
night, and as he had dressed himself in the morning,
and while Mrs. Jones had been whispering to him her
little bulletin as to the state of the young lady's health,
he had not repented himself of the change. Mabel
had been, he thought, so little gracious to him that he
would have given up that notion earlier, but for his indiscreet declaration to his father. On the other hand,
making love to Isabel Boncassen seemed to him to
possess some divine afflatus of joy which made it of all
imaginable occupations the sweetest and most charming. She had admitted of no embrace. Indeed he
had attempted none, unless that touch of the hand
might be so called, from which she had immediately
withdrawn. Her conduct had been such that he had
felt it to be incumbent on him, at the very moment, to
justify the touch by a declaration of love. Then she
had told him that she would not promise to love him
in return. And yet it had been so sweet, so heavenly
sweet!

During the morning he had almost forgotten Mabel.
When Mrs. Jones told him that Isabel would keep her
room, he longed to ask for leave to go and make some
inquiry at the door. She would not play lawn-tennis

with him.   Well ;—he did not now care much for that.
After what he had said to her she must at any rate
give him some answer.   She had been so gracious to
him that his hopes ran very high.   It never occurred
to him to fancy that she might be gracious to him because he was heir to the Dukedom of Omnium.   She
herself was so infinitely superior to all wealth, to all
rank, to all sublunary arrangements, conventions, and
considerations, that there was no room for confidence
of that nature.   But he was confident because her smile
had been sweet, and her eyes bright,—and because he
was conscious, though unconsciously conscious, of
something of the sympathy of love.

But he had to go to the waterfall with Mabel.
Lady Mabel was always dressed perfectly,—having
great gifts of her own in that direction.   There was a
freshness about her which made her morning costume
more charming than that of the evening, and never did
she look so well as when arrayed for a walk.   On this
occasion she had certainly done her best.   But he,
poor blind idiot, saw nothing of this.   The white gauzy
fabric which had covered Isabel's satin petticoat on
the previous evening still filled his eyes.   Those perfect boots, the little glimpses of party-coloured stockings above them, the looped-up skirt, the jacket fitting
but never binding that lovely body and waist, the jaunty
hat with its small fresh feathers, all were nothing to him.

Nor was the bright honest face beneath the hat anything to him now ;—for it was an honest face, though
misfortunes which had come had somewhat marred the
honesty of the heart.

At first the conversation was about indifferent things,
—Killancodlem and Mrs. Jones, Crummie-Toddie and

Reginald Dobbes. They had gone along the high-road as far as the post-office, and had turned up through the wood and reached a seat whence there was a beautiful view down upon the Archay before a word was said affecting either Miss Boncassen or the ring. "You got the ring safe," she said.

"Oh yes."

"How could you be so foolish as to risk it?"

"I did not regard it as mine. You had accepted it, —I thought."

"But if I had, and then repented of my fault in doing so, should you not have been willing to help me in setting myself right with myself? Of course, after what had passed, it was a trouble to me when it came. What was I to do? For a day or two I thought I would take it, not as liking to take it, but as getting rid of the trouble in that way. Then I remembered its value, its history, the fact that all who knew you would want to know what had become of it,—and I felt that it should be given back. There is only one person to whom you must give it."

"Who is that?" he said quickly.

"Your wife;—or to her who is to become your wife. No other woman can be justified in accepting such a present."

"There has been a great deal more said about it than it's worth," said he, not anxious at the present moment to discuss any matrimonial projects with her. "Shall we go on to the Fall?" Then she got up and led the way till they came to the little bridge from which they could see the Falls of the Codlem below them. "I call that very pretty," he said.

"I thought you would like it."

"I never saw anything of that kind more jolly. Do you care for scenery, Mabel?"

"Very much. I know no pleasure equal to it. You have never seen Grex?"

"Is it like this?"

"Not in the least. It is wilder than this, and there are not so many trees; but to my eyes it is very beautiful. I wish you had seen it."

"Perhaps I may some day."

"That is not likely now," she said. "The house is in ruins. If I had just money enough to keep it for myself, I think I could live alone there and be happy."

"You;—alone! Of course you mean to marry?"

"Mean to marry! Do persons marry because they mean it? With nineteen men out of twenty the idea of marrying them would convey the idea of hating them. You can mean to marry. No doubt you do mean it."

"I suppose I shall,—some day. How very well the house looks from here." It was incumbent upon him at the present moment to turn the conversation.

But when she had a project in her head it was not so easy to turn her away. "Yes, indeed," she said, "very well. But as I was saying,—you can mean to marry."

"Anybody can mean it."

"But you can carry out a purpose. What are you thinking of doing now?"

"Upon my honour, Mabel, that is unfair."

"Are we not friends?"

"I think so."

"Dear friends?"

"I hope so."

"Then may I not tell you what I think? If you do not mean to marry that American young lady you should not raise false hopes."

"False—hopes!" He had hopes, but he had never thought that Isabel could have any.

"False hopes;—certainly. Do you not know that every one was looking at you last night?"

"Certainly not."

"And that that old woman is going about talking of it as her doing, pretending to be afraid of your father, whereas nothing would please her better than to humble a family so high as yours."

"Humble!" exclaimed Lord Silverbridge.

"Do you think your father would like it? Would you think that another man would be doing well for himself by marrying Miss Boncassen?"

"I do," said he energetically.

"Then you must be very much in love with her."

"I say nothing about that."

"If you are so much in love with her that you mean to face the displeasure of all your friends——"

"I do not say what I mean. I could talk more freely to you than to any one else, but I won't talk about that even to you. As regards Miss Boncassen, I think that any man might marry her without discredit. I won't have it said that she can be inferior to me,— or to anybody."

There was a steady manliness in this which took Lady Mabel by surprise. She was convinced that he intended to offer his hand to the girl, and now was act-

uated chiefly by a feeling that his doing so would be
an outrage to all English propriety. If a word might
have an effect it would be her duty to speak that word.
" I think you are wrong there, Lord Silverbridge."

" I am sure I am right."

" What have you yourself felt about your sister and
Mr. Tregear ? "

" It is altogether different ;—altogether. Frank's
wife will be simply his wife. Mine, should I outlive
my father, will be Duchess of Omnium."

" But your father ? I have heard you speak with
bitter regret of this affair of Lady Mary's, because it
vexes him. Would your marriage with an American
lady vex him less ? "

" Why should it vex him at all ? Is she vulgar, or
ill to look at, or stupid ? "

" Think of her mother."

" I am not going to marry her mother. Nor for the
matter of that am I going to marry her. You are
taking all that for granted in a most unfair way."

" How can I help it after what I saw yesterday ? "

" I will not talk any more about it. We had better
go down or we shall get no lunch." Lady Mabel, as
she followed him, tried to make herself believe that all
her sorrow came from regret that so fine a scion of the
British nobility should throw himself away upon an
American adventuress.

The guests were still at lunch when they entered the
dining-room, and Isabel was seated close to Mrs. Jones.
Silverbridge at once went up to her,—and place was
made for him as though he had almost a right to be
next to her. Miss Boncassen herself bore her honours
well, seeming to regard the little change at table as

though it was of no moment. "I became so eager about that game," she said, "that I went on too long."

"I hope you are now none the worse."

"At six o'clock this morning I thought I should never use my legs again."

"Were you awake at six?" said Silverbridge, with pitying voice.

"That was it. I could not sleep. Now I begin to hope that sooner or later I shall unstiffen."

During every moment, at every word that he uttered, he was thinking of the declaration of love which he had made to her. But it seemed to him as though the matter had not dwelt on her mind. When they drew their chairs away from the table he thought that not a moment was to be lost before some further explanation of their feelings for each other should be made. Was not the matter which had been so far discussed of vital importance for both of them? And, glorious as she was above all other women, the offer which he had made must have some weight with her. He did not think that he proposed to give more than she deserved, but still, that which he was so willing to give was not a little. Or was it possible that she had not understood his meaning? If so, he would not willingly lose a moment before he made it plain to her. But she seemed content to hang about with the other women, and when she sauntered about the grounds seated herself on a garden-chair with Lady Mabel, and discussed with great eloquence the general beauty of Scotch scenery. An hour went on in this way. Could it be that she knew that he had offered to make her his wife? During this time he went and returned more

than once,—but still she was there, on the same gar-
den-seat, talking to those who came in her way.

Then on a sudden she got up and put her hand
on his arm. " Come and take a turn with me," she
said.

" Lord Silverbridge, do you remember anything of
last night? "

" Remember! "

" I thought for a while this morning that I would let
it all pass as though it had been mere trifling."

" It would have wanted two to let it pass in that
way," he said, almost indignantly.

On hearing this she looked up at him, and there
came over her face that brilliant smile, which to him
was perhaps the most potent of her spells. " What do
you mean by—wanting two? "

" I must have a voice in that as well as you."

" And what is your voice? "

" My voice is this. I told you last night that I loved
you. This morning I ask you to be my wife."

" It is a very clear voice," she said,—almost in a
whisper; but in a tone so serious that it startled him.

" It ought to be clear," he said doggedly.

" Do you think I don't know that? Do you think
that if I liked you well last night I don't like you
better now? "

" But do you—like me? "

" That is just the thing that I am going to say nothing about."

" Isabel! "

" Just the one thing that I will not allude to. Now
you must listen to me."

" Certainly."

"I know a great deal about you. We Americans are an inquiring people, and I have found out pretty much everything." His mind misgave him as he felt that she had ascertained his former purpose respecting Mabel. "You," she said, "among young men in England are about the foremost, and therefore,—as I think,—about the foremost in the world. And you have all personal gifts;—youth and spirits—— Well, I will not go on and name the others. You are, no doubt, supposed to be entitled to the best and sweetest of God's feminine creatures."

"You are she."

"Whether you be entitled to me or not I cannot yet say. Now I will tell you something of myself. My father's father came to New York as a labourer from Holland, and worked upon the quays in that city. Then he built houses, and became rich, and was almost a miser;—with the good sense, however, to educate his only son. What my father is you see. To me he is sterling gold, but he is not like your people. My dear mother is not at all like your ladies. She is not a lady in your sense,—though with her unselfish devotion to others she is something infinitely better. For myself I am,—well, meaning to speak honestly, I will call myself pretty and smart. I think I know how to be true."

"I am sure you do."

"But what right have you to suppose I shall know how to be a duchess?"

"I am sure you will."

"Now listen to me. Go to your friends and ask them. Ask that Lady Mabel;—ask your father;—ask that Lady Cantrip. And above all, ask yourself. And allow me to require you to take three months to do this. Do not come to see me for three months."

" And then? "

" What may happen then I cannot tell, for I want three months also to think of it myself. Till then good-bye." She gave him her hand and left it in his for a few seconds. He tried to draw her to him ; but she resisted him, still smiling. Then she left him.

CHAPTER XV.

ISCHEL.

It was a custom with Mrs. Finn almost every autumn to go off to Vienna, where she possessed considerable property, and there to inspect the circumstances of her estate. Sometimes her husband would accompany her, and he did so in this year of which we are now speaking. One morning in September they were together at an hotel at Ischel, whither they had come from Vienna, when as they went through the hall into the courtyard, they came, in the very doorway, upon the Duke of Omnium and his daughter. The Duke and Lady Mary had just arrived, having passed through the mountains from the salt-mine district, and were about to take up their residence in the hotel for a few days. They had travelled very slowly, for Lady Mary had been ill, and the Duke had expressed his determination to see a doctor at Ischel.

There is no greater mistake than in supposing that only the young blush. But the blushes of middle life are luckily not seen through the tan which has come from the sun and the gas and the work and the wiles of the world. Both the Duke and Phineas blushed; and though their blushes were hidden, that peculiar glance of the eye which always accompanies a blush was visible enough from one to the other. The elder lady kept her countenance admirably, and the younger one had no occasion for blushing. She at once ran forward and kissed her friend. The Duke stood with his hat off waiting to give his hand to the lady, and then took that of his late colleague. "How odd that we should meet here," he said, turning to Mrs. Finn.

"Odd enough to us that your Grace should be here," she said, "because we had heard nothing of your intended coming."

"It is so nice to find you," said Lady Mary. "We are this moment come. Don't say that you are this moment going."

"At this moment we are only going as far as Halstadt."

"And are coming back to dinner? Of course they will dine with us. Will they not, papa?" The Duke said that he hoped they would. To declare that you are engaged at an hotel, unless there be some real engagement, is amost an impossibility. There was no escape, and before they were allowed to get into their carriage they had promised they would dine with the Duke and his daughter.

"I don't know that it is especially a bore," Mrs. Finn said to her husband in the carriage. "You may be quite sure that of whatever trouble there may be in it, he has much more than his share."

"His share should be the whole," said her husband. "No one else has done anything wrong."

When the Duke's apology had reached her, so that there was no longer any ground for absolute hostility, then she had told the whole story to her husband. He at first was very indignant. What right had the Duke to expect that any ordinary friend should act duenna over his daughter in accordance with his caprices? This was said and much more of the kind. But any

humour towards quarrelling which Phineas Finn might
have felt for a day or two was quieted by his wife's
prudence. "A man," she said, "can do no more than
apologise. After that there is no room for reproach."

At dinner the conversation turned at first on British
politics, in which Mrs. Finn was quite able to take her
part. Phineas was decidedly of opinion that Sir Timothy Beeswax and Lord Drummond could not live
another session. And on this subject a good deal was
said. Later in the evening the Duke found himself
sitting with Mrs. Finn in the broad veranda over the
hotel garden, while Lady Mary was playing to Phineas
within. "How do you think she is looking?" asked
the father.

"Of course I see that she has been ill. She tells me
that she was far from well at Saltzburg."

"Yes ;—indeed for three or four days she frightened
me much. She suffered terribly from headaches."

"Nervous headaches?"

"So they said there. I feel quite angry with myself
because I did not bring a doctor with us. The trouble
and ceremony of such an accompaniment is no doubt
disagreeable."

"And I suppose seemed when you started to be unnecessary?"

"Quite unnecessary."

"Does she complain again now?"

"She did to-day—a little."

The next morning Lady Mary could not leave her
bed ; and the Duke in his sorrow was obliged to apply
to Mrs. Finn. After what had passed on the previous
day Mrs. Finn of course called, and was shown at once
up to her young friend's room. There she found the

girl in great pain, lying with her two thin hands up to her head, and hardly able to utter more than a word. Shortly after that Mrs. Finn was alone with the Duke, and then there took place a conversation between them which the lady thought to be very remarkable.

"Had I better send for a doctor from England?" he asked. In answer to this Mrs. Finn expressed her opinion that such a measure was hardly necessary, that the gentleman from the town who had been called in seemed to know what he was about, and that the illness, lamentable as it was, did not seem to be in any way dangerous. "One cannot tell what it comes from," said the Duke dubiously.

"Young people, I fancy, are often subject to such maladies."

"It must come from something wrong."

"That may be said of all sickness."

"And therefore one tries to find out the cause. She says that she is unhappy." These last words he spoke slowly and in a low voice. To this Mrs. Finn could make no reply. She did not doubt but that the girl was unhappy, and she knew well why; but the source of Lady Mary's misery was one to which she could not very well allude. "You know all the misery about that young man."

"That is a trouble that requires time to cure it," she said,—not meaning to imply that time would cure it by enabling the girl to forget her lover; but because in truth she had not known what else to say.

"If time will cure it."

"Time, they say, cures all sorrows."

"But what should I do to help time? There is no sacrifice I would not make,—no sacrifice! Of myself,

I mean. I would devote myself to her,—leaving everything else on one side. We purpose being back in England in October; but I would remain here if I thought it better for her comfort."

"I cannot tell, Duke."

"Neither can I. But you are a woman and might know better than I do. It is so hard that a man should be left with a charge of which from its very nature he cannot understand the duties." Then he paused, but she could find no words which would suit at the moment. It was almost incredible to her that after what had passed he should speak to her at all as to the condition of his daughter. "I cannot, you know," he said very seriously, "encourage a hope that she should be allowed to marry that man."

"I do not know."

"You yourself, Mrs. Finn, felt that when she told you about it at Matching."

"I felt that you would disapprove of it."

"Disapprove of it! How could it be otherwise? Of course you felt that. There are ranks in life in which the first comer that suits a maiden's eye may be accepted as a fitting lover. I will not say but that they who are born to such a life may be the happier. They are, I am sure, free from troubles to which they are incident whom fate has called to a different sphere. But duty is—duty;—and whatever pang it may cost, duty should be performed."

"Certainly."

"Certainly;—certainly; certainly," he said, re-echoing her word.

"But then, Duke, one has to be so sure what duty requires. In many matters this is easy enough, and

the only difficulty comes from temptation. There are
cases in which it is so hard to know."

" Is this one of them? "

" I think so."

" Then the maiden should—in any class of life—be
allowed to take the man—that just suits her eye? " As
he said this his mind was intent on his Glencora and
on Burgo Fitzgerald.

" I have not said so. A man may be bad, vicious,
a spendthrift,—eaten up by bad habits." Then he
frowned, thinking that she also had her mind intent on
his Glencora and on that Burgo Fitzgerald, and being
most unwilling to have the difference between Burgo
and Frank Tregear pointed out to him. " Nor have I
said," she continued, " that even were none of these
faults apparent in the character of a suitor, the lady
should in all cases be advised to accept a young man
because he has made himself agreeable to her. There
may be discrepancies."

" There are," said he, still with a low voice, but with
infinite energy,—" insurmountable discrepancies."

" I only said that this was a case in which it might
be difficult for you to see your duty plainly."

" Why should it be ? "

" You would not have her—break her heart? "
Then he was silent for a while, turning over in his mind
the proposition which now seemed to have been made
to him. If the question came to that,—should she be
allowed to break her heart and die, or should he save
her from that fate by sanctioning her marriage with
Tregear? If the choice could be put to him plainly
by some supernal power what then would he choose?
If duty required him to prevent this marriage, his duty

could not be altered by the fact that his girl would avenge herself upon him by dying! If such a marriage were in itself wrong, that wrong could not be made right by the fear of such a catastrophe. Was it not often the case that duty required that some one should die? And yet as he thought of it,—thought that the some one whom his mind had suggested was the one female creature now left belonging to him,—he put his hand up to his brow and trembled with agony. If he knew, if in truth he believed that such would be the result of firmness on his part,—then he would be infirm, then he must yield. Sooner than that, he must welcome this Tregear to his house. But why should he think that she would die? This woman had now asked him whether he would be willing to break his girl's heart. It was a frightful question; but he could see that it had come naturally in the sequence of the conversation which he had forced upon her. Did girls break their hearts in such emergencies? Was it not all romance? "Men have died and worms have eaten them,—but not for love." He remembered it all and carried on the argument in his mind, though the pause was but for a minute. There might be suffering no doubt. The higher the duties the keener the pangs! But would it become him to be deterred from doing right because she for a time might find that she had made the world bitter to herself? And were there not feminine wiles, —tricks by which women learn to have their way in opposition to the judgment of their lords and masters? He did not think that his Mary was wilfully guilty of any scheme. The suffering he knew was true suffering. But not the less did it become him to be on his guard against attacks of this nature.

"No," he said at last; "I would not have her break her heart,—if I understand what such words mean. They are generally, I think, used fantastically."

"You would not wish to see her overwhelmed by sorrow."

"Wish it! What a question to ask a father!"

"I must be more plain in my language, Duke. Though such a marriage be distasteful to you it might perhaps be preferable to see her sorrowing always."

"Why should it? I have to sorrow always. We are told that man is born to sorrow as surely as the sparks fly upwards."

"Then I can say nothing further."

"You think I am cruel."

"If I am to say what I really think I shall offend you."

"No;—not unless you mean offence."

"I shall never do that to you, Duke. When you talk as you do now you hardly know yourself. You think you could see her suffering and not be moved by it. But were it to be continued long you would give way. Though we know that there is an infinity of grief in this life, still we struggle to save those we love from grieving. If she be steadfast enough to cling to her affection for this man, then at last you will have to yield." He looked at her frowning but did not say a word. "Then it will perhaps be a comfort for you to know that the man himself is trustworthy and honest."

There was a terrible rebuke in this; but still, as he had called it down upon himself, he would not resent it, even in his heart. "Thank you," he said, rising from his chair. "Perhaps you will see her again this afternoon." Of course she assented, and as the interview had taken place in his rooms she took her leave.

This which Mrs. Finn had said to him was all to the same effect as that which had come from Lady Cantrip; only it was said with a higher spirit. Both the women saw the matter in the same light. There must be a fight between him and his girl; but she, if she could hold out for a certain time, would be the conqueror. He might take her away and try what absence would do, or he might have recourse to that specific which had answered so well in reference to his own wife; but if she continued to sorrow during absence, and if she would have nothing to do with the other lover,—then he must at last give way! He had declared that he was willing to sacrifice himself,—meaning thereby that if a lengthened visit to the cities of China, or a prolonged sojourn in the Western States of America would wean her from her love, he would go to China or to the Western States. At present his self-banishment had been carried no farther than Vienna. During their travels hitherto Tregear's name had not once been mentioned. The Duke had come away from home resolved not to mention it,—and she was minded to keep it in reserve till some seeming catastrophe should justify a declaration of her purpose. But from first to last she had been sad, and latterly she had been ill. When asked as to her complaint she would simply say that she was not happy. To go on with this through the Chinese cities could hardly be good for either of them. She would not wake herself to any enthusiasm in regard to scenery, costume, pictures, or even discomforts. Wherever she was taken it was all barren to her.

As their plans stood at present they were to return to England so as to enable her to be at Custins by the middle of October. Had he taught himself to hope that any good could be done by prolonged travelling he would readily have thrown over Custins and Lord Popplecourt. He could not bring himself to trust much to the Popplecourt scheme. But the same contrivance had answered on that former occasion. When he spoke to her about their plans, she expressed herself quite ready to go back to England. When he suggested those Chinese cities, her face became very long, and she was immediately attacked by paroxysms of headaches.

"I think I should take her to some place on the sea-shore in England," said Mrs. Finn.

"Custins is close to the sea," he replied. "It is Lord Cantrip's place in Dorsetshire. It was partly settled that she was to go there."

"I suppose she likes Lady Cantrip."

"Why should she not?"

"She has not said a word to me to the contrary. I only fear she would feel that she was being sent there, —as to a convent."

"What ought I to do then?"

"How can I venture to answer that? What she would like best, I think, would be to return to Match-ing with you, and to settle down in a quiet way for the winter." The Duke shook his head. That would be worse than travelling. She would still have headaches and still tell him that she was unhappy. "Of course I do not know what your plans are, and pray believe me that I should not obtrude my advice if you did not ask me."

"I know it," he said. "I know how good you are

and how reasonable. I know how much you have to forgive."

"Oh no."

"And if I have not said so as I should have done it has not been from want of feeling. I do believe you did what you thought best when Mary told you that story at Matching."

"Why should your Grace go back to that?"

"Only that I may acknowledge my indebtedness to you, and say to you somewhat fuller than I could do in my letter that I am sorry for the pain which I gave you."

"All that is over now,—and shall be forgotten."

Then he spoke of his immediate plans. He would at once go back to England by slow stages,—by very slow stages,—staying a day or two at Saltzburg, at Ratisbon, at Nuremberg, at Frankfort, and so on. In this way he would reach England about the 10th of October, and Mary would then be ready to go to Custins by the time appointed.

In a day or two Lady Mary was better. "It is terrible while it lasts," she said, speaking to Mrs. Finn of her headache, "but when it has gone then I am quite well. Only "—she added after a pause—" only I never can be happy again while papa thinks as he does now." Then there was a party made up before they separated for an excursion to the Hintersee and the Obersee. On this occasion Lady Mary seemed to enjoy herself, as she liked the companionship of Mrs. Finn. Against Lady Cantrip she never said a word. But Lady Cantrip was always a duenna to her, whereas Mrs. Finn was a friend. While the Duke and Phineas were discussing politics together, thoroughly enjoying the weakness of Lord Drummond and the iniquity of Sir Timothy, which they did with augmented vehemence from their ponies' backs, the two women in lower voices talked over their own affairs. "I dare say you will be happy at Custins," said Mrs. Finn.

"No; I shall not. There will be people there whom I don't know, and I don't want to know. Have you heard anything about him, Mrs. Finn?"

Mrs. Finn turned round and looked at her,—for a moment almost angrily. Then her heart relented. "Do you mean—Mr. Tregear?"

"Yes, Mr. Tregear."

"I think I heard that he was shooting with Lord Silverbridge."

"I am glad of that," said Mary.

"It will be pleasant for both of them."

"I am very glad they should be together. While I know that, I feel that we are not altogether separated. I will never give it up, Mrs. Finn,—never; never. It is no use taking me to China." In that Mrs. Finn quite agreed with her.

CHAPTER XVI.

AGAIN AT KILLANCODLEM.

SILVERBRIDGE remained at Crummie-Toddie under the dominion of Reginald Dobbes till the second week of September. Popplecourt, Nidderdale, and Gerald Palliser were there also, very obedient, and upon the whole efficient. Tregear was intractable, occasional, and untrustworthy. He was the cause of much trouble to Mr. Dobbes. He would entertain a most heterodox and injurious idea that as he had come to Crummie-Toddie for amusement, he was not bound to do anything that did not amuse him. He would not understand that in sport as in other matters there should be an ambition, driving a man on to excel always and be ahead of others. In spite of this Mr. Dobbes had cause for much triumph. It was going to be the greatest thing ever done by six guns in Scotland. As for Gerald, whom he had regarded as a boy, and who had offended him by saying that Crummie-Toddie was ugly,—he was ready to go round the world for him. He had indoctrinated Gerald with all his ideas of a sportsman,—even to a contempt for champagne and a conviction that tobacco should be moderated. The three lords, too, had proved themselves efficient, and the thing was going to be a success. But just when a day was of vital importance, when it was essential that there should be a strong party for a drive, Silverbridge found

it absolutely necessary that he should go over to Killancodlem.

"She has gone," said Nidderdale.

"Who the —— is she?" asked Silverbridge, almost
angrily.

"Everybody knows who she is," said Popplecourt.

"It will be a good thing when some she has got
hold of you, my boy, so as to keep you in your proper
place."

"If you cannot withstand that sort of attraction you
ought not to go in for shooting at all," said Dobbes.

"I should n't wonder at his going," continued Nidderdale, "if we did n't all know that the American is
no longer there. She has gone to—Bath, I think they
say."

"I suppose it 's Mrs. Jones herself," said Popplecourt.

"My dear boys," said Silverbridge, "you may be
quite sure that when I say that I am going to Killancodlem I mean to go to Killancodlem, and that no
chaff about young ladies,—which I think very disgust-
ing,—will stop me. I shall be sorry if Dobbes's roll
of the killed should be lessened by a single hand, seeing that his ambition sets that way. Considering the
amount of slaughter we have perpetrated, I really think
that we need not be overanxious." After this nothing
further was said. Tregear, who knew that Mabel Grex
was still at Killancodlem, had not spoken.

In truth, Mabel had sent for Lord Silverbridge, and
this had been her letter:

"Dear Lord Silverbridge,—Mrs. Montacute Jones
is cut to the heart because you have not been over to

see her again, and she says that it is lamentable to think that such a man as Reginald Dobbes should have so much power over you. 'Only twelve miles,' she says, 'and he knows that we are here!' I told her that you knew Miss Boncassen was gone.

"But though Miss Boncassen has left us we are a very pleasant party, and surely you must be tired of such a place as Crummie-Toddie. If only for the sake of getting a good dinner once in a way do come over again. I shall be here yet for ten days. As they will not let me go back to Grex I don't know where I could be more happy. I have been asked to go to Custins, and suppose I shall turn up there some time in the autumn.

"And now shall I tell you what I expect? I do expect that you will come over to—see me. 'I did see her the other day,' you will say, 'and she did not make herself pleasant.' I know that. How was I to make myself pleasant when I found myself so completely snuffed out by your American beauty? Now she is away, and Richard will be himself. Do come, because in truth I want to see you.

"Yours always sincerely,
"MABEL GREX."

On receiving this he at once made up his mind to go to Killancodlem, but he could not make up his mind why it was that she had asked him. He was sure of two things: sure in the first place that she had intended to let him know that she did not care about him; and then sure that she was aware of his intention in regard to Miss Boncassen. Everybody at Killancodlem had seen it,—to his disgust; but still that it was so had been manifest. And he had consoled himself, feeling that it would matter nothing should he be accepted, She had made an attempt to talk him out of his purpose. Could it be that she thought it possible a second attempt might be successful? If so, she did not know him.

She had in truth thought not only that this, but that something further than this might be possible. Of course the prize loomed larger before her eyes as the prospects of obtaining it became less. She could not doubt that he had intended to offer her his hand when he had spoken to her of his love in London. Then she had stopped him;—had "spared him," as she had told her friend. Certainly she had then been swayed by some feeling that it would be ungenerous in her to seize greedily the first opportunity he had given her. But he had again made an effort. He surely would not have sent her the ring had he not intended her to regard him as her lover. When she received the ring her heart had beat very high. Then she had sent that little note, saying that she would keep it till she could give it to his wife. When she wrote that she had intended the ring should be her own. And other things pressed upon her mind. Why had she been asked to the dinner at Richmond? Why was she invited to Custins? Little hints had reached her of the Duke's good-will towards her. If on that side the marriage were approved, why should she destroy her own hopes?

Then she had seen him with Miss Boncassen, and in her pique had forced the ring back upon him. During that long game on the lawn her feelings had been very bitter. Of course the girl was the lovelier of the two. All the world was raving of her beauty. And there was no doubt as to the charm of her wit and manner. And then she had no touch of that blasé used-up way of life of which Lady Mabel was conscious herself. It was natural that it should be so. And was she, Mabel Grex, the girl to stand in his way and to force herself upon him, if he loved another? Certainly not,—though there might be a triple ducal coronet to be had.

But were there not other considerations? Could it be well that the heir of the House of Omnium should marry an American girl, as to whose humble birth whispers were already afloat? As his friend, would it not be right that she should tell him what the world would say? As his friend, therefore, she had given him her counsel.

When he was gone the whole thing weighed heavily upon her mind. Why should she lose the prize if it might still be her own? To be Duchess of Omnium! She had read of many of the other sex and of one or two of her own who by settled resolution had achieved greatness in opposition to all obstacles. Was this thing beyond her reach? To hunt him, and catch him, and marry him to his own injury,—that would be impossible to her. She was sure of herself there. But how infinitely better would this be for him! Would she not have all his family with her,—and all the world of England? In how short a time would he not repent his marriage with Miss Boncassen? Whereas, were she his wife, she would so stir herself for his joys, for his good, for his honour, that there should be no possibility of repentance. And he certainly had loved her. Why else had he followed her, and spoken such words to her? Of course he had loved her! But then there had come this blaze of beauty and had carried off,— not his heart, but his imagination. Because he had yielded to such fascination was she to desert him, and also to desert herself? From day to day she thought of it, and then she wrote that letter. She hardly knew what she would do, what she might say; but she would trust to the opportunity to do and say something.

" If you have no room for me," he said to Mrs. Jones, " you must scold Lady Mab. She has told me that you told her to invite me."

" Of course I did. Do you think I would not sleep in the stables, and give you up my own bed if there were no other? It is so good of you to come!"

" So good of you, Mrs. Jones, to ask me."

" So very kind to come when all the attraction has gone!" Then he blushed and stammered, and was just able to say that his only object in life was to pour out his adoration at the feet of Mrs. Montacute Jones herself.

There was a certain Lady Fawn,—a pretty mincing married woman of about twenty-five, with a husband much older, who liked mild flirtations with mild young men. " I am afraid we 've lost your great attraction," she whispered to him.

" Certainly not as long as Lady Fawn is here," he said, seating himself close to her on a garden-bench, and seizing suddenly hold of her hand. She gave a little scream and a jerk, and so relieved herself from him. " You see," said he, " people do make such mistakes about a man's feelings!"

" Lord Silverbridge!"

" It 's quite true, but I 'll tell you all about it another time," and so he left her. All these little troubles, his experience in the House, the necessity of snubbing Tifto, the choice of a wife, and his battles with Reginald Dobbes, were giving him by degrees age and flavour.

Lady Mabel had fluttered about him on his first coming, and had been very gracious, doing the part of an old friend. "There is to be a big shooting to-morrow," she said, in presence of Mrs. Jones.

"If it is to come to that," he said, "I might as well go back to Dobbydom."

"You may shoot if you like," said Lady Mabel.

"I have n't even brought a gun with me."

"Then we 'll have a walk,—a whole lot of us," she said.

In the evening, about an hour before dinner, Silverbridge and Lady Mabel were seated together on the bank of a little stream which ran on the other side of the road, but on a spot not more than a furlong from the hall-door. She had brought him there, but she had done so without any definite scheme. She had made no plan of campaign for the evening, having felt relieved when she found herself able to postpone the project of her attack till the morrow. Of course there must be an attack, but how it should be made she had never had the courage to tell herself. The great women of the world, the Semiramises, the Pocahontases, the Ida Ppeffers, and the Charlotte Cordays, had never been wanting to themselves when the moment for action came. Now she was pleased to have this opportunity added to her; this pleasant minute in which some soft preparatory word might be spoken; but the great effort should be made on the morrow.

"Is not this nicer than shooting with Mr. Dobbes?" she asked.

"A great deal nicer. Of course I am bound to say so."

"But in truth. I want to find out what you really like. Men are so different. You need not pay me any compliment; you know that well enough."

"I like you better than Dobbes,—if you mean that."

"Even so much is something."

"But I am fond of shooting."

"Only a man may have enough of it."

"Too much, if he is subject to Dobbes, as Dobbes likes them to be. Gerald likes it."

"Did you think it odd," she said after a pause, "that I should ask you to come over again?"

"Was it odd?" he replied.

"That is as you may take it. There is certainly no other man in the world to whom I would have done it."

"Not to Tregear?"

"Yes," she said; "yes,—to Tregear, could I have been as sure of a welcome for him as I am for you. Frank is in all respects the same as a brother to me. That would not have seemed odd;—I mean to my-self."

"And has this been—odd,—to yourself?"

"Yes. Not that anybody else has felt it so. Only I,—and perhaps you. You felt it so?"

"Not especially. I thought you were a very good fellow. I have always thought that;—except when you made me take back the ring."

"Does that still fret you?"

"No man likes to take back a thing. It makes him seem to have been awkward and stupid in giving it."

"It was the value——"

"You should have left me to judge of that."

" If I have offended you I will beg your pardon.
Give me anything else, anything but that, and I will
take it."

" But why not that? " said he.

" Now that you have fitted it for a lady's finger it
should go to your wife.   No one else should have it."
Upon this he brought the ring once more out of his
pocket, and again offered it to her.   " No; anything
but that.   That your wife must have."   Then he put
the ring back again.   " It would have been nicer for
you had Miss Boncassen been here."   In saying this
she followed no plan.   It came rather from pique.   It
was almost as though she had asked him whether Miss
Boncassen was to have the ring.

" What makes you say that? "

" But it would."

" Yes, it would," he replied stoutly, turning round
as he lay upon the ground and facing her.

" Has it come to that? "

" Come to what?   You ask me a question and I
answer you truly."

" You cannot be happy without her? "

" I did not say so.   You ask me whether I should
like to have her here,—and I say yes.   What would
you think of me if I said no? "

" My being here is not enough? "   This should not
have been said, of course, but the little speech came
from the exquisite pain of the moment.   She had
meant to have said hardly anything.   She had intended
to be happy with him, just touching lightly on things
which might lead to that attack which must be made
on the morrow.   But words will often lead whither the
speaker has not intended.   So it was now, and in the

soreness of her heart she spoke. "My being here is not enough?"

"It would be enough," he said, jumping on his feet, "if you understood all, and would be kind to me."

"I will at any rate be kind to you," she replied, as she sat upon the bank looking at the running water.

"I have asked Miss Boncassen to be my wife."

"And she has accepted?"

"No; not as yet. She is to take three months to think of it. Of course I love her best of all. If you will sympathise with me in that, then I will be as happy with you as the day is long."

"No," said she, "I cannot. I will not."

"Very well."

"There should be no such marriage. If you have told me in confidence——"

"Of course I have told you in confidence."

"It will go no farther; but there can be no sympathy between us. It—it—it is not,—is not——" Then she burst into tears.

"Mabel!"

"No, sir, no; no! What did you mean? But never mind. I have no questions to ask, not a word to say. Why should I? Only this,—that such a marriage will disgrace your family. To me it is no more than to anybody else. But it will disgrace your family."

How she got back to the house she hardly knew; nor did he. That evening they did not again speak to each other, and on the following morning there was no walk to the mountains. Before dinner he drove himself back to Crummie-Toddie, and when he was taking his leave she shook hands with him with her usual pleasant smile.

CHAPTER XVII.

WHAT HAPPENED AT DONCASTER.

THE Leger this year was to be run on the 14th September, and while Lord Silverbridge was amusing himself with the deer at Crummie-Toddie, and at Killancodlem with the more easily pursued young ladies, the indefatigable Major was hard at work in the stables. This came a little hard on him. There was the cub-hunting to be looked after, which made his presence at Runnymede necessary, and then that "pig-headed fellow, Silverbridge," would not have the horses trained anywhere but at Newmarket. How was he to be in two places at once? Yet he was in two places almost at once, cub-hunting in the morning at Egham and Bagshot, and sitting on the same evening at the stable-door at Newmarket, with his eyes fixed upon Prime Minister.

Gradually had he and Captain Green come to understand each other, and though they did at last understand each other, Tifto would talk as though there were no such correct intelligence ;—when for instance he would abuse Lord Silverbridge for being pig-headed. On such occasions the Captain's remark would generally be short. "That be blowed!" he would say, implying that that state of things between the two partners, in which such complaints might be natural, had now been brought to an end. But on one occasion, about a week before the race, he spoke out a little

170

plainer. "What 's the use of your going on with all
that before me?   It 's settled what you 've got to do."

"I don't know that anything is settled," said the
Major.

"Ain't it?   I thought it was.   If it are n't you 'll
find yourself in the wrong box.   You 've as straight a
tip as a man need wish for, but if you back out you 'll
come to grief.   Your money 's all on the other way
already."

On the Friday before the race Silverbridge dined
with Tifto at the Beargarden.   On the next morning
they went down to Newmarket to see the horse get a
gallop, and came back the same evening.   During all
this time Tifto was more than ordinarily pleasant to
his patron.   The horse and the certainty of the horse's
success were the only subjects mooted.   "It is n't what
I say," repeated Tifto, "but look at the betting.   You
can't get five to four against him.   They tell me that
if you want to do anything on the Sunday the pull will
be the other way."

"I stand to lose over £20,000 already," said Silverbridge, almost frightened by the amount.

"But how much are you on to win?" said Tifto.   "I
suppose you could sell your bets for £5,000 down."

"I wish I knew how to do it," said Silverbridge.
But this was an arrangement, which, if made just now,
would not suit the Major's views.

They went to Newmarket, and there they met Captain Green.   "Tifto," said the young lord, "I won't
have that fellow with us when the horse is galloping."

"There is n't an honester man, or a man who
understands a horse's paces better in all England,"
said Tifto.

"I won't have him standing alongside of me on the
Heath," said his lordship.

"I don't know how I 'm to help it."

"If he 's there I 'll send the horse in;—that 's all."
Then Tifto found it best to say a few words to Captain
Green. But the Captain also said a few words to himself. "D—— young fool; he don't know what he 's
dropping into." Which assertion, if you lay aside the
unnecessary expletive, was true to the letter. Lord
Silverbridge was a young fool, and did not at all know
into what a mess he was being dropped by the united
experience, perspicuity, and energy of the man whose
company on the Heath he had declined.

The horse was quite a "picture to look at." Mr.
Pook, the trainer, assured his lordship that for health
and condition he had never seen anything better.
"Stout all over," said Mr. Pook, "and not an ounce
of what you may call flesh. And bright! just feel his
coat, my lord! That 's 'ealth,—that is; not dressing,
nor yet macassar!"

And then there were various evidences produced of
his pace,—how he had beaten that horse, giving him
two pounds; how he had been beaten by that, but
only on a mile course; the Leger distance was just the
thing for Prime Minister; how by a lucky chance that
marvellous quick rat of a thing that had won the Derby had not been entered for the autumn race; how
Coalheaver was known to have bad feet. "He 's a
stout 'orse, no doubt,—is the 'Eaver," said Mr. Pook,
"and that 's why the betting men have stuck to him.
But he 'll be nowhere on Wednesday. They 're beginning to see it now, my lord. I wish they was n't so
sharp-sighted."

In the course of the day, however, they met a gentleman who was of a different opinion. He said loudly that he looked on the Heaver as the best three-year-old in England. Of course as matters stood he was n't going to back the Heaver at even money;—but he 'd take twenty-five to thirty in hundreds between the two. All this ended in the bet being accepted and duly booked by Lord Silverbridge. And in this way Lord Silverbridge added two thousand four hundred pounds to his responsibilities.

But there was worse than this coming. On the Sunday afternoon he went down to Doncaster, of course in company with the Major. He was alive to the necessity of ridding himself of the Major; but it had been acknowledged that that duty could not be performed till after this race had been run. As he sat opposite to his friend on their journey to Doncaster, he thought of this in the train. It should be done immediately on their return to London after the race. But the horse, his Prime Minister, was by this time so dear to him that he intended if possible to keep possession of the animal.

When they reached Doncaster the racing men were all occupied with Prime Minister. The horse and Mr. Pook had arrived that day from Newmarket, viâ Cambridge and Peterborough. Tifto, Silverbridge, and Mr. Pook visited him together three times that afternoon and evening;—and the Captain also visited the horse, though not in company with Lord Silverbridge. To do Mr. Pook justice, no one could be more careful. When the Captain came round with the Major Mr. Pook was there. But Captain Green did not enter the box,—had no wish to do so, was of opinion that on such occasions no one whose business did not carry him there should go near a horse. His only object seemed to be to compliment Mr. Pook as to his care, skill, and good fortune.

It was on the Tuesday evening that the chief mischief was done. There was a club at which many of the racing men dined, and there Lord Silverbridge spent his evening. He was the hero of the hour, and everybody flattered him. It must be acknowledged that his head was turned. They dined at eight, and much wine was drunk. No one was tipsy, but many were elated; and much confidence in their favourite animals was imparted to men who had been sufficiently cautious before dinner. Then cigars and soda and brandy became common, and our young friend was not more abstemious than others. Large sums were named, and at last in three successive bets Lord Silverbridge backed his horse for more than £40,000. As he was making the second bet Mr. Lupton came across to him and begged him to hold his hand. "It will be a nasty sum for you to lose, and winning it will be nothing to you," he said. Silverbridge took it good-humouredly, but said that he knew what he was about. "These men will pay," whispered Lupton; "but you can't be quite sure what they 're at." The young man's brow was covered with perspiration. He was smoking quick and had already smoked more than was good for him. "All right," he said. "I 'll mind what I 'm about." Mr. Lupton could do no more, and retired. Before the night was over bets had been booked to the amount stated, and the Duke's son, who had promised that he would never plunge, stood to lose about £70,000 upon the race.

While this was going on Tifto sat not far from his patron, but completely silent. During the day and early in the evening a few sparks of the glory which scintillated from the favourite horse flew in his direction. But he was on this occasion unlike himself, and though the horse was to be run in his name had very little to say in the matter. Not a boast came out of his mouth during dinner or after dinner. He was so moody that his partner, who was generally anxious to keep him quiet, more than once endeavoured to encourage him. But he was unable to rouse himself. It was still within his power to run straight;—to be on the square, if not with Captain Green, at any rate with Lord Silverbridge. But to do so he must make a clean breast with his lordship and confess the intended sin. As he heard all that was being done, his conscience troubled him sorely. With pitch of this sort he had never soiled himself before. He was to have £3,000 from Green, and then there would be the bets he himself had laid against the horse,—by Green's assistance! It would be the making of him. Of what use had been all his "square" work to him? And then Silverbridge had behaved so badly to him! But still, as he sat there during the evening, he would have given a hand to have been free from the attempt. He had had no conception before that he could become subject to such misery from such a cause. He would make it straight with Silverbridge this very night, —but that Silverbridge was ever lighting fresh cigars and ever having his glass refilled. It was clear to him that on this night Silverbridge could not be made to understand anything about it. And the deed in which he himself was to be the chief actor was to be done

very early in the following morning.   At last he slunk
away to bed.

On the following morning, the morning of the day
on which the race was to be run, the Major tapped at
his patron's door about seven o'clock.   Of course there
was no answer though the knock was repeated.   When
young men overnight drink as much brandy and water
as Silverbridge had done, and smoke as many cigars,
they are apt not to hear knocks at their door made at
seven o'clock.   Nor was his lordship's servant up,—so
that Tifto had no means of getting at him except by
personal invasion of the sanctity of his bedroom.   But
there was no time, not a minute, to be lost.   Now,
within this minute that was pressing on him, Tifto
must choose his course.   He opened the door and was
standing at the young man's head.

"What the d—— does this mean?" said his lordship
angrily, as soon as his visitor had succeeded in waking
him.   Tifto muttered something about the horse which
Silverbridge failed to understand.   The young man's
condition was by no means pleasant.   His mouth was
furred by the fumes of tobacco.   His head was aching.
He was heavy with sleep, and this intrusion seemed to
him to be a final indignity offered to him by the man
whom he now hated.   "What business have you to
come in here?" he said, leaning on his elbow.   "I
don't care a straw for the horse.   If you have anything
to say send my servant.   Get out!"

"Oh;—very well," said Tifto;—and Tifto got out.

It was about an hour afterwards that Tifto returned,
and on this occasion a groom from the stables, and the
young lord's own servant, and two or three other men
were with him.   Tifto had been made to understand

that the news now to be communicated must be communicated by himself, whether his lordship were angry
or not.   Indeed, after what had been done his lordship's anger was not of much moment.   In his present
visit he was only carrying out the pleasant little plan
which had been arranged for him by Captain Green.
" What the mischief is up ? " said Silverbridge, rising in
his bed.

Then Tifto told his story, sullenly, doggedly, but still
in a perspicuous manner, and with words which admitted of no doubt.   But before he told the story he
had excluded all but himself and the groom.   He and
the groom had taken the horse out of the stable, it being the animal's nature to eat his corn better after slight
exercise, and while doing so a nail had been picked up.

" Is it much? " asked Silverbridge, jumping still
higher in his bed.   Then he was told that it was very
much,—that the iron had driven itself into the horse's
frog, and that there was actually no possibility that the
horse should run on that day.

" He can't walk, my lord," said the groom, in that
authoritative voice which grooms use when they desire
to have their own way, and to make their masters understand that they at any rate are not to have theirs.

" Where is Pook? " asked Silverbridge.   But Mr.
Pook was also still in bed.

It was soon known to Lord Silverbridge as a fact
that in very truth the horse could not run.   Then, sick
with headache, with a stomach suffering unutterable
things, he had, as he dressed himself, to think of his
£70,000.   Of course the money would be forthcoming.   But how would his father look at him?   How
would it be between him and his father now?   After

such a misfortune how would he be able to break that other matter to the Duke, and say that he had changed his mind about his marriage,—that he was going to abandon Lady Mabel Grex and give his hand and a future duchess's coronet to an American girl whose grandfather had been a porter?

A nail in his foot! Well! He had heard of such things before. He knew that such accidents had happened. What an ass must he have been to risk such a sum on the well-being and safety of an animal who might any day pick up a nail in his foot! Then he thought of the caution which Lupton had given him. What good would the money have done him had he won it? What more could he have than he now enjoyed? But to lose such a sum of money! With all his advantages of wealth he felt himself to be as forlorn and wretched as though he had nothing left in the world before him.

CHAPTER XVIII.

HOW IT WAS DONE.

THE story was soon about the town, and was the
one matter for discussion in all racing quarters. About
the town! It was about England, about all Europe.
It had travelled to America and the Indies, to Australia
and the Chinese cities before two hours were over.
Before the race was run the accident was discussed and
something like the truth surmised in Cairo, Calcutta,
Melbourne, and San Francisco. But at Doncaster it
was so all-pervading a matter that down to the trades-
men's daughters and the boys at the free-school the
town was divided into two parties, one party believing
it to have been a "plant," and the other holding that
the cause had been natural. It is hardly necessary to
say that the ring, as a rule, belonged to the former
party. The ring always suspects. It did not behove
even those who would win by the transaction to stand
up for its honesty.

The intention had been to take the horse round a
portion of the outside of the course near to which his
stable stood. A boy rode him, and the groom and
Tifto went with him. At a certain spot on their return
Tifto had exclaimed that the horse was going lame in
his off fore-foot. As to this exclamation the boy and
the two men were agreed. The boy was then made to
dismount and run for Mr. Pook; and as he started
Tifto commenced to examine the horse's foot. The

boy saw him raise the off fore-leg. He himself had not found the horse lame under him, but had been so hustled and hurried out of the saddle by Tifto and the groom that he had not thought on that matter till he was questioned. So far the story told by Tifto and the groom was corroborated by the boy,—except as to the horse's actual lameness. So far the story was believed by all men,—except in regard to the actual lameness. And so far it was true. Then, according to Tifto and the groom, the other foot was looked at, but nothing was seen. This other foot, the near fore-foot, was examined by the groom, who declared himself to be so flurried by the lameness of such a horse at such a time that he hardly knew what he saw or what he did not see. At any rate then in his confusion he found no cause of lameness, but the horse was led into the stable as lame as a tree. Here Tifto found the nail inserted into the very cleft of the frog of the near fore-foot, and so inserted that he could not extract it till the farrier came. That the farrier had extracted the nail from the part of the foot indicated was certainly a fact.

Then there was the nail. Only those who were most peculiarly privileged were allowed to see the nail. But it was buzzed about the racing quarters that the head of the nail,—an old rusty, straight, and well-pointed nail,—bore on it the mark of a recent hammer. In answer to this it was alleged that the blacksmith in extracting the nail with his pincers had of course operated on its head, had removed certain particles of rust, and might easily have given it the appearance of having been struck. But in answer to this the farrier, who was a sharp fellow, and quite beyond suspicion in the matter, declared that he had very particularly looked at the nail before he extracted it,—had looked at it with the feeling on his mind that something base might too probably have been done,—and that he was ready to swear that the clear mark on the head of the nail was there before he touched it. And then not in the stable, but lying under the little dung-heap away from the stable-door, there was found a small piece of broken iron bar, about a foot long, which might have answered for a hammer,—a rusty bit of iron; and amidst the rust of this was found such traces as might have been left had it been used in striking such a nail. There were some who declared that neither on the nail nor on the iron could they see anything. And among these was the Major. But Mr. Lupton brought a strong magnifying-glass to bear, and the world of examiners was satisfied that the marks were there.

It seemed, however, to be agreed that nothing could be done. Silverbridge would not lend himself at all to those who suspected mischief. He was miserable enough, but in this great trouble he would not separate himself from Tifto. "I don't believe a word of all that," he said to Mr. Lupton.

"It ought to be investigated, at any rate," said Lupton.

"Mr. Pook may do as he likes, but I will have nothing to do with it."

Then Tifto came to him swaggering. Tifto had to go through a considerable amount of acting, for which he was not very well adapted. The Captain would have done it better. He would have endeavoured to put himself altogether into the same boat with his partner, and would have imagined neither suspicion or enmity on his partner's part till suspicion or enmity had been shown. But Tifto, who had not expected that the matter would be allowed to pass over without some inquiry, began by assuming that Silverbridge would think evil of him. Tifto, who at this moment would have given all that he had in the world not to have done the deed, who now hated the instigator of the deed, and felt something almost akin to love for Silverbridge, found himself to be forced by circumstances to defend himself by swaggering. "I don't understand all this that 's going on, my lord," he said.

"Neither do I," replied Silverbridge.

"Any horse is subject to an accident. I am, I suppose, as great a sufferer as you are, and a deuced sight less able to bear it."

"Who has said anything to the contrary? As for bearing it, we must take it as it comes,—both of us. You may as well know now as later that I have done with racing—forever."

"What do you tell me that for? You can do as you like and I can do as I like about that. If I had had my way about the horse this never would have happened. Taking a horse out at that time in the morning,—before a race!"

"Why, you went with him yourself!"

"Yes;—by Pook's orders. You allowed Pook to do just as he pleased. I should like to know what money Pook has got on it, and which way he laid it." This disgusted Silverbridge so much that he turned away and would have no more to say to Tifto.

Before one o'clock, at which hour it was stated nominally that the races would commence, general opinion had formed itself,—and general opinion had nearly hit the truth. General opinion declared that the nail had been driven in wilfully,—that it had been done by Tifto himself, and that Tifto had been instigated by Captain Green. Captain Green perhaps overacted his part a little. His intimacy with the Major was well known, and yet, in all this turmoil, he kept himself apart as though he had no interest in the matter. "I have got my little money on, and what little I have I lose," he said in answer to inquiries. But every one knew that he could not but have a great interest in a race as to which the half-owner of the favourite was a peculiarly intimate friend of his own. Had he come down to the stables and been seen about the place with Tifto it might have been better. As it was, though he was very quiet, his name was soon mixed up in the matter. There was one man who asserted it as a fact known to himself that Green and Villiers,—one Gilbert Villiers,—were in partnership together. It was very well known that Gilbert Villiers would win £2,500 from Lord Silverbridge.

Then minute investigation was made into the betting of certain individuals. Of course there would be great plunder, and where would the plunder go? Who would get the money which poor Silverbridge would lose? It was said that one at least of the large bets made on that Tuesday evening could be traced to the same Villiers, though not actually made by him. More would be learned when the settling day should come. But there was quite enough already to show that there were many men determined to get to the bottom of it all if possible.

There came upon Silverbridge in his trouble a keen sense of his position and a feeling of the dignity which

he ought to support. He clung during great part of
the morning to Mr. Lupton. Mr. Lupton was much
his senior, and they had never been intimate; but now
there was comfort in his society. "I am afraid you
are hit heavily," said Mr. Lupton.

"Something over £70,000!"

"Looking at what will be your property it is of course
nothing. But if——"

"If what?"

"If you go to the Jews for it then it will become a
great deal."

"I shall certainly not do that."

"Then you may regard it as a trifle," said Lupton.

"No, I can't. It is not a trifle. I must tell my
father. He'll find the money."

"There is no doubt about that."

"He will. But I feel at present that I would rather
change places with the poorest gentleman I know than
have to tell him. I have done with races, Lupton."

"If so, this will have been a happy day for you. A
man in your position can hardly make money by it,
but he may lose so much! If a man really likes the
amusement,—as I do,—and risks no more than what
he has in his pocket, that may be very well."

"At any rate, I have done with it."

Nevertheless he went to see the race run, and everybody seemed to be touched with pity for him. He
carried himself well, saying as little as he could of his
own horse, and taking, or affecting to take, great interest in the race. After the race he managed to see
all those to whom he had lost heavy stakes,—having
to own to himself as he did so that not one of them
was a gentleman to whom he should like to give his

hand. To them he explained that his father was abroad,—that probably his liabilities could not be settled till after his father's return. He, however, would consult his father's agent, and would then appear on settling day. They were all full of the blandest courtesies. There was not one of them who had any doubt as to getting his money,—unless the whole thing might be disputed on the score of Tifto's villainy. Even then payment could not be disputed unless it was proved that he who demanded the money had been one of the actual conspirators. After having seen his creditors he went up alone to London.

When in London he went to Carlton Terrace and spent the night in absolute solitude. It had been his plan to join Gerald for some partridge-shooting at Matching, and then to go yachting till such time as he should be enabled to renew his suit to Miss Boncassen. Early in November he would again ask her to be his wife. These had been his plans. But now it seemed that everything was changed. Partridge-shooting and yachting must be out of the question till this terrible load was taken off his shoulders. Soon after his arrival at the house two telegrams followed him from Doncaster. One was from Gerald. "What is all this about Prime Minister? Is it a sell? I am so unhappy." The other was from Lady Mabel,—for among other luxuries Mrs. Montacute Jones had her own telegraph-wire at Killancodlem. "Can this be true? We are all so miserable. I do so hope it is not much." From which he learned that his misfortune was already known to all his friends.

And now what was he to do? He eat his supper, and then without hesitating for a moment,—feeling that if he did hesitate the task would not be done on that night,—he sat down and wrote the following letter:

"Carlton Terrace, Sept. 14, 18—.

"My dear Mr. Morton,—I have just come up from Doncaster. You have probably heard what has been Prime Minister's fate. I don't know whether any horse has ever been such a favourite for the Leger. Early in the morning he was taken out and picked up a nail. The consequence was he could not run.

"Now I must come to the bad part of my story. I have lost £70,000! It is no use beating about the bush. The sum is something over that. What am I to do? If I tell you that I shall give up racing altogether I dare say you will not believe me. It is a sort of thing a man always says when he wants money; but I feel now I cannot help saying it.

"But what shall I do? Perhaps, if it be not too much trouble, you will come up to town and see me. You can send me a word by the wires.

"You may be sure of this, I shall make no attempt to raise the money elsewhere, unless I find that my father will not help me. You will understand that of course it must be paid. You will understand also what I must feel about telling my father, but I shall do so at once. I only wait till I can hear from you.

"Yours faithfully,
"SILVERBRIDGE."

During the next day two despatches reached Lord Silverbridge, both of them coming as he sat down to his solitary dinner. The first consisted of a short but very civil note.

"Messrs. Comfort & Criball present their compliments to the Earl of Silverbridge.

"Messrs. C. & C. beg to offer their apologies for interfering, but desire to inform his lordship that should cash be wanting to any amount in consequence of the late races, they will be happy to accommodate his lordship on most reasonable terms at a moment's notice, upon his lordship's single bond.

"Lord Silverbridge may be sure of absolute secrecy.

"Crasham Court, Crutched Friars, Sept. 15, 18—."

The other despatch was a telegram from Mr. Morton, saying that he would be in Carlton Gardens by noon on the following day.

CHAPTER XIX.

"THERE SHALL NOT BE ANOTHER WORD ABOUT IT."

EARLY in October the Duke was at Matching with his daughter, and Phineas Finn and his wife were both with them. On the day after they parted at Ischel the first news respecting Prime Minister had reached him, —namely, that his son's horse had lost the race. This would not have annoyed him at all, but that the papers which he read contained some vague charge of swindling against somebody, and hinted that Lord Silverbridge had been a victim. Even this would not have troubled him,—might in some sort have comforted him, —were it not made evident to him that his son had been closely associated with swindlers in these transactions. If it were a mere question of money, that might be settled without difficulty. Even though the sum lost might have grown out of what he might have expected into some few thousands, still he would bear it without a word, if only he could separate his boy from bad companions. Then came Mr. Morton's letter telling the whole.

At the meeting which took place between Silverbridge and his father's agent at Carlton Terrace it was settled that Mr. Morton should write the letter. Silverbridge tried and found that he could not do it. He did not know how to humiliate himself sufficiently, and yet could not keep himself from making attempts to prove that according to all recognised chances his bets had been good bets.

Mr. Morton was better able to accomplish the task. He knew the Duke's mind. A very large discretion had been left in Mr. Morton's hands in regard to moneys which might be needed on behalf of that dangerous heir ;—so large that he had been able to tell Lord Silverbridge that if the money was in truth lost according to jockey-club rules, it should all be forthcoming on the settling day,—certainly without assistance from Messrs. Comfort & Criball. The Duke had been nervously afraid of such men of business as Comfort & Criball, and from the earliest days of his son's semi-manhood had been on his guard against them. Let any sacrifice be made so that his son might be kept clear from Comforts and Criballs. To Mr. Morton he had been very explicit. His own pecuniary resources were so great that they could bear some ravaging without serious detriment. It was for his son's character and standing in the world, for his future respectability and dignity, that his fears were so keen, and not for his own money. By one so excitable, so fond of pleasure as Lord Silverbridge, some ravaging would probably be made. Let it be met by ready money. Such had been the Duke's instructions to his own trusted man of business, and, acting on these instructions, Mr. Morton was able to tell the heir that the money should be forthcoming.

Mr. Morton, after detailing the extent and the nature of the loss, and the steps which he had decided upon taking, went on to explain the circumstances as best he could. He had made some inquiry, and felt no doubt that a gigantic swindle had been perpetrated by Major

Tifto and others.   The swindle had been successful.
Mr. Morton had consulted certain gentlemen of high
character versed in affairs of the turf.   He mentioned
Mr. Lupton among others,—and had been assured that
though the swindle was undoubted, the money had
better be paid.   It was thought to be impossible to
connect the men who had made the bets with the per-
petrators of the fraud;—and if Lord Silverbridge were
to abstain from paying his bets because his own partner
had ruined the animal which belonged to them jointly,
the feeling would be against him rather than in his
favour.   In fact, the jockey club could not sustain
him in such refusal.   Therefore the money would be
paid.   Mr. Morton, with some expressions of doubt,
trusted that he might be thought to have exercised a
wise discretion.   Then he went on to express his own
opinion in regard to the lasting effect which the matter
would have upon the young man.   "I think," said he,
"that his lordship is heartily sickened of racing, and
that he will never return to it."

The Duke was of course very wretched when these
tidings first reached him.   Though he was a rich man,
and of all men the least careful of his riches, still
he felt that £70,000 was a large sum of money to
throw away among a nest of swindlers.   And then it
was excessively grievous to him that his son should
have been mixed up with such men.   Wishing to
screen his son, even from his own anger, he was careful to remember that the promise made that Tifto
should be dismissed was not to take effect till after this
race had been run.   There had been no deceit in that.
But then Silverbridge had promised that he would not
"plunge."   There are, however, promises which from

their very nature may be broken without falsehood. Plunging is a doubtful word, and the path down to it, like all doubtful paths, is slippery and easy! If that assurance with which Mr. Morton ended his letter could only be made true, he could bring himself to forgive even this offence. The boy must be made to settle himself in life. The Duke resolved that his only revenge should be to press on that marriage with Mabel Grex.

At Coblenz, on their way home, the Duke and his daughter were caught up by Mr. and Mrs. Finn, and the matter of the young man's losses was discussed. Phineas had heard all about it, and was loud in denunciations against Tifto, Captain Green, Gilbert Villiers, and others whose names had reached him. The money, he thought, should never have been paid. The Duke, however, declared that the money would not cause a moment's regret, if only the whole thing could be got rid of at that cost. It had reached Finn's ears that Tifto was already at loggerheads with his associates. There was some hope that the whole thing might be brought to light by this means. For all that the Duke cared nothing. If only Silverbridge and Tifto could for the future be kept apart, as far as he and his were concerned, good would have been done rather than harm. While they were in this way together on the Rhine it was decided that very soon after their return to England Phineas and Mrs. Finn should go down to Matching.

When the Duke arrived in London his sons were not there. Gerald had gone back to Oxford, and Silverbridge had merely left an address. Then his sister wrote him a very short letter. "Papa will be so glad if you will come to Matching. Do come." Of course he came, and presented himself some few days after the Duke's arrival.

But he dreaded this meeting with his father, which, however, let it be postponed for ever so long, must come at last. In reference to this he made a great resolution,—that he would go instantly as soon as he might be sent for. When the summons came he started; but, though he was by courtesy an earl, and by fact was not only a man but a member of Parliament, though he was half engaged to marry one young lady and ought to have been engaged to marry another, though he had come to an age at which Pitt was a great minister and Pope a great poet, still his heart was in his boots, as a school-boy's might be, when he was driven up to the house at Matching.

In two minutes, before he had washed the dust from his face and hands, he was with his father. "I am glad to see you, Silverbridge," said the Duke, putting out his hand.

"I hope I see you well, sir."

"Fairly well. Thank you. Travelling I think agrees with me. I miss, not my comforts, but a certain knowledge of how things are going on, which comes to us I think through our skins when we are at home. A feeling of absence pervades me. Otherwise I like it. And you;—what have you been doing?"

"Shooting a little," said Silverbridge, in a moon-calf tone.

"Shooting a great deal, if what I see in the newspapers be true about Mr. Reginald Dobbes and his party. I presume it is a religion to offer up hecatombs to the autumnal gods—who must surely take a keener delight in blood and slaughter than those bloodthirsty gods of old."

" You should talk to Gerald about that, sir."

" Has Gerald been so great at his sacrifices? How will that suit with Plato? What does Mr. Simcox say? "

" Of course they were all to have a holiday just at that time. But Gerald is reading. I fancy that Gerald is clever."

" And he is a great Nimrod ? "

" As to hunting."

" Nimrod, I fancy, got his game in any way that he could compass it. I do not doubt but that he trapped foxes."

" With a rifle at deer, say for four hundred yards, I would back Gerald against any man of his age in England or Scotland."

" As for backing, Silverbridge, do not you think that we had better have done with that? " This was said hardly in a tone of reproach, with something even of banter in it; and as the question was asked the Duke was smiling. But in a moment all that sense of joyousness which the young man had felt in singing his brother's praises was expelled. His face fell, and he stood before his father almost like a culprit. "We might as well have it out about this racing," continued the Duke. " Something has to be said about it. You have lost an enormous sum of money." The Duke's tone in saying this became terribly severe. Such at least was its sound in his son's ears. He did not mean to be severe.

But when he did speak of that which displeased him his voice naturally assumed that tone of indignation with which in days of yore he had been wont to de-

nounce the public extravagance of his opponents in the
House of Commons.   The father paused, but the son
could not speak at the moment.   "And worse than
that," continued the Duke; "you have lost it in as bad
company as you could have found had you picked all
England through."

"Mr. Lupton and Sir Henry Playfair, and Lord
Stirling were in the room when the bets were made."

"Were the gentlemen you named concerned with
Major Tifto?"

"No, sir."

"Who can tell with whom he may be in a room?
Though rooms of that kind are, I think, best avoided."
Then the Duke paused again, but Silverbridge was now
sobbing so that he could hardly speak.   "I am sorry
that you should be so grieved," continued the father,
"but such delights cannot, I think, lead to much real
joy."

"It is for you, sir," said the son, rubbing his eyes
with the hand which supported his head.

"My grief in the matter might soon be cured."

"How shall I cure it?   I will do anything to cure it."

"Let Major Tifto and the horses go."

"They are gone," said Silverbridge, energetically
jumping from his chair as he spoke.   "I will never
own a horse again, or a part of a horse.   I will have
nothing more to do with races.   You will believe me?"

"I will believe anything that you tell me."

"I won't say I will not go to another race, because——"

"No; no.   I would not have you hamper yourself.
Nor shall you bind yourself by any further promises.
You have done with racing."

"Indeed, indeed I have, sir."

Then the father came up to the son and put his arms round the young man's shoulders and embraced him. "Of course it made me unhappy."

"I knew it would."

"But if you are cured of this evil, the money is nothing. What is it all for but for you and your brother and sister? It was a large sum, but that shall not grieve me. The thing itself is so dangerous that if with that much of loss we can escape, I will think that we have made not a bad market. Who owns the horse now?"

"The horses shall be sold."

"For anything they may fetch so that we may get clear of this dirt. And the Major?"

"I know nothing of him. I have not seen him since that day."

"Has he claims on you?"

"Not a shilling. It is all the other way."

"Let it go, then. Be quit of him, however it may be. Send a messenger, so that he may understand that you have abandoned racing altogether. Mr. Morton might perhaps see him."

That his father should forgive so readily and yet himself suffer so deeply, affected the son's feelings so strongly that for a time he could hardly repress his sobs. "And now there shall not be a word more said about it," said the Duke suddenly.

Silverbridge in his confusion could make no answer.

"There shall not be another word said about it," said the Duke again. "And now, what do you mean to do with yourself immediately?"

"I 'll stay here, sir, as long as you do. Finn and Warburton and I have still a few coverts to shoot."

"That's a good reason for staying anywhere."

"I meant that I would remain while you remained, sir."

"That at any rate is a good reason, as far as I am concerned. But we go to Custins next week."

"There's a deal of shooting to be done at Gatherum," said the heir.

"You speak of it as if it were the business of your life,—on which your bread depended."

"One can't expect game to be kept up if nobody goes to shoot it."

"Can't one? I did n't know. I should have thought that the less was shot the more there would be to shoot; but I am ignorant in such matters." Silverbridge then broke forth into a long explanation as to coverts, game-keepers, poachers, breeding, and the expectations of the neighbourhood at large, in the middle of which he was interrupted by the Duke. "I am afraid, my dear boy, that I am too old to learn. But as it is so mani-festly a duty, go and perform it like a man. Who will go with you?"

"I will ask Mr. Finn to be one."

"He will be very hard upon you in the way of politics."

"I can answer him better than I can you, sir. Mr. Lupton said he would come for a day or two. He'll stand to me."

After that his father stopped him as he was about to leave the room. "One more word, Silverbridge. Do you remember what you were saying when you walked down to the House with me from your club that night?" Silverbridge remembered very well what he had said. He had undertaken to ask Mabel Grex to be his wife, and had received his father's ready approval to the proposition. . But at this moment he was unwilling to refer to that matter. "I have thought about it very much since that," said the Duke. "I may say that I have been thinking of it every day. If there were anything to tell me, you would let me know;—would you not?"

"Yes, sir."

"Then there is nothing to be told? I hope you have not changed your mind."

Silverbridge paused a moment, trusting that he might be able to escape the making of any answer;—but the Duke evidently intended to have an answer. "It appeared to me, sir, that it did not seem to suit her," said the hardly driven young man. He could not now say that Mabel had shown a disposition to reject his offer, because as they had been sitting by the brook-side at Killancodlem, even he, with all his self-diffidence, had been forced to see what were her wishes. Her confusion and too evident despair when she heard of the offer to the American girl had plainly told her tale. He could not now plead to his father that Mabel Grex would refuse his offer. But his self-defence when first he found that he had lost himself in love for the American had been based on that idea. He had done his best to make Mabel understand him. If he had not actually offered to her, he had done the next thing to it. And he had run after her till he was ashamed of such running. She had given him no encouragement;—and therefore he had been justified. No doubt he must have been mistaken; that he now perceived; but still he felt himself to be justified. It was impossible that he should explain all this to his father. One thing he certainly could not say,—just at present. After his folly in regard to those heavy debts he could not at once risk his father's renewed anger by proposing to him an American daughter-in-law. That must stand over, at any rate till the girl had accepted him positively. "I am afraid it won't come off, sir," he said at last.

"Then I am to presume that you have changed your mind?"

"I told you when we were speaking of it that I was not confident."

"She has not——"

"I can't explain it all, sir,—but I fear it won't come off."

Then the Duke, who had been sitting, got up from his chair, and with his back to the fire made a final little speech. "We decided just now, Silverbridge, that nothing more should be said about that unpleasant racing business, and nothing more shall be said by me. But you must not be surprised if I am anxious to see you settled in life. No young man could be more bound by duty to marry early than you are. In the first place you have to repair the injury done by my inaptitude for society. You have explained to me that it is your duty to have the Barsetshire coverts properly shot, and I have acceded to your views. Surely it must be equally your duty to see your Barsetshire neighbours. And you are a young man every feature of whose character would be improved by matrimony. As far as means are concerned you are almost as free to make arrangements as though you were already the head of the family."

"No, sir."

" I could never bring myself to dictate to a son in regard to his choice of a wife. But I will own that when you told me that you had chosen I was much gratified. Try and think again, when you are pausing amidst your sacrifices at Gatherum, whether that be possible. If it be not, still I would wish you to bear in mind what is my idea as to your duty." Silver-bridge said that he would bear this in mind, and then escaped from the room.

CHAPTER XX.

LADY MARY'S DREAM.

When the Duke and his daughter reached Custins they found a large party assembled, and were somewhat surprised at the crowd. Lord and Lady Nidderdale were there, which might have been expected, as they were part of the family. With Lord Popplecourt had come his recent friend Adolphus Longstaff. That too might have been natural. Mr. and Miss Boncassen were there also, who at this moment were quite strangers to the Duke; and Mr. Lupton. The Duke also found Lady Chiltern, whose father-in-law had more than once sat in the same Cabinet with himself, and Mr. Monk, who was generally spoken of as the head of the coming liberal Government, and the Ladies Adelaide and Flora Fitz-Howard, the still unmarried but not very juvenile daughters of the Duke of St. Bungay. These with a few others made a large party, and rather confused the Duke, who had hardly reflected that discreet and profitable love-making was more likely to go on among numbers, than if the two young people were thrown together with no other companions.

Lord Popplecourt had been made to understand what was expected of him, and after some hesitation had submitted himself to the conspiracy. There would not be less at any rate than £200,000;—and the connection would be made with one of the highest families in Great Britain. Though Lady Cantrip had

said very few words, those words had been expressive ; and the young bachelor peer had given in his
adhesion. Some vague, half-defined tale had been told
him,—not about Tregear, as Tregear's name had not
been mentioned,—but respecting some dream of a
young man who had flitted across the girl's path during her mother's lifetime. " All girls have such dreams,"
Lady Cantrip had suggested. Whereupon Lord Popplecourt said that he supposed it was so. " But a softer,
purer, more unsullied flower never waited on its stalk
till the proper fingers should come to pluck it," said
Lady Cantrip, rising to unaccustomed poetry on behalf
of her friend the Duke. Lord Popplecourt accepted the
poetry and was ready to do his best to pluck the flower.

Soon after the Duke's arrival Lord Popplecourt
found himself in one of the drawing-rooms with Lady
Cantrip and his proposed father-in-law. A hint had
been given him that he might as well be home early
from shooting, so as to be in the way. As the hour in
which he was to make himself specially agreeable, both
to the father and to the daughter, had drawn nigh, he
became somewhat nervous, and now, at this moment,
was not altogether comfortable. Though he had been
concerned in no such matter before, he had an idea
that love was a soft kind of thing which ought to steal
on one unawares and come and go without trouble.
In his case it came upon him with a rough demand
for immediate hard work. He had not previously
thought that he was to be subjected to such labours,
and at this moment almost resented the interference
with his ease. He was already a little angry with Lady
Cantrip, but at the same time felt himself to be so
much in subjection to her that he could not rebel.

The Duke himself when he saw the young man was hardly more comfortable. He had brought his daughter to Custins, feeling that it was his duty to be with her; but he would have preferred to leave the whole operation to the care of Lady Cantrip. He hardly liked to look at the fish whom he wished to catch for his daughter. Whenever this aspect of affairs presented itself to him, he would endeavour to console himself by remembering the past success of a similar transaction. He thought of his own first interview with his wife. "You have heard," he had said, "what our friends wish." She had pouted her lips, and when gently pressed had at last muttered, with her shoulder turned to him, that she supposed it was to be so. Very much more coercion had been used to her then than either himself or Lady Cantrip had dared to apply to his daughter. He did not think that his girl in her present condition of mind would signify to Lord Popplecourt that "she supposed it was to be so." Now that the time for the transaction was present he felt almost sure it would never be transacted. But still he must go on with it. Were he now to abandon his scheme, would it not be tantamount to abandoning everything? So he wreathed his face in smiles,—or made some attempt at it,—as he greeted the young man.

"I hope you and Lady Mary had a pleasant journey abroad," said Lord Popplecourt. Lord Popplecourt, being aware that he had been chosen as a son-in-law, felt himself called upon to be familiar as well as pleasant. "I often thought of you and Lady Mary, and wondered what you were about."

"We were visiting lakes and mountains, churches

and picture-galleries, cities and salt-mines," said the Duke.

"Does Lady Mary like that sort of thing?"

"I think she was pleased with what she saw."

"She has been abroad a great deal before, I believe. It depends so much on whom you meet when abroad."

This was unfortunate, because it recalled Tregear to the Duke's mind. "We saw very few people whom we knew," he said.

"I've been shooting in Scotland with Silverbridge, and Gerald, and Reginald Dobbes, and Nidderdale,— and that fellow Tregear, who is so thick with Silverbridge."

"Indeed!"

"I'm told that Lord Gerald is going to be the great shot of his day," said Lady Cantrip.

"It is a distinction," said the Duke bitterly.

"He did not beat me by so much," continued Popplecourt. "I think Tregear did the best with his rifle. One morning he potted three. Dobbes was disgusted. He hated Tregear."

"Isn't it stupid,—half-a-dozen men getting together in that way?" asked Lady Cantrip.

"Nidderdale is always jolly."

"I am glad to hear that," said the mother-in-law.

"And Gerald is a regular brick." The Duke bowed. "Silverbridge used always to be going off to Killancodlem, where there were a lot of ladies. He is very sweet, you know, on this American girl whom you have here." Again the Duke winced. "Dobbes is awfully good as to making out the shooting, but then he is a tyrant. Nevertheless I agree with him, if you mean to do a thing you should do it."

"Certainly," said the Duke.   "But you should make
up your mind first whether the thing is worth doing."

"Just so," said Popplecourt.   "And as grouse and
deer together are about the best things out, most of us
made up our minds that it was worth doing.   But that
fellow Tregear would argue it out.   He said a gentleman ought n't to play billiards as well as a marker."

"I think he was right," said the Duke.

"Do you know Mr. Tregear, Duke?"

"I have met him—with my son."

"Do you like him?"

"I have seen very little of him."

"I cannot say I do.   He thinks so much of himself.
Of course he is very intimate with Silverbridge, and
that is all that any one knows of him."   The Duke
bowed almost haughtily, though why he bowed he
could hardly have explained to himself.   Lady Cantrip
bit her lips in disgust.   "He 's just the fellow," continued Popplecourt, "to think that some princess has
fallen in love with him."   Then the Duke left the room.

"You had better not talk to him about Mr. Tregear,"
said Lady Cantrip.

"Why not?"

"I don't know whether he approves of the intimacy
between him and Lord Silverbridge."

"I should think not;—a man without any position
or a shilling in the world."

"The Duke is peculiar.   If a subject is distasteful
to him he does not like it to be mentioned.   You had
better not mention Mr. Tregear."   Lady Cantrip as
she said this blushed inwardly at her own hypocrisy.

It was of course contrived at dinner that Lord Popplecourt should take out Lady Mary.   It is impossible

to discover how such things get wind, but there was already an idea prevalent at Custins that Lord Popplecourt had matrimonial views, and that these views were looked upon favourably. "You may be quite sure of it, Mr. Lupton," Lady Adelaide Fitz-Howard had said. "I'll make a bet they're married before this time next year."

"It will be a terrible case of Beauty and the Beast," said Lupton.

Lady Chiltern had whispered a suspicion of the same kind, and had expressed a hope that the lover would be worthy of the girl. And Dolly Longstaff had chaffed his friend Popplecourt on the subject, Popplecourt having laid himself open by indiscreet allusions to Dolly's love for Miss Boncassen. "Everybody can't have it as easily arranged for him as you,—a duke's daughter and a pot of money without so much as the trouble of asking for it!"

"What do you know about the Duke's daughter?"

"That's what it is to be a lord and not to have a father." Popplecourt tried to show that he was disgusted; but he felt himself all the more strongly bound to go on with his project.

It was therefore a matter of course that these should-be lovers would be sent out of the room together. "You'll give your arm to Mary," Lady Cantrip said, dropping the ceremonial prefix. Lady Mary of course went out as she was bidden. Though everybody else knew it, no idea of what was intended had yet come across her mind.

The should-be lover immediately reverted to the Austrian tour, expressing a hope that his neighbour had enjoyed herself. "There's nothing I like so much my-

self," said he, remembering some of the Duke's words,
" as mountains, cities, salt-mines, and all that kind of
thing.   There 's such a lot of interest about it."

" Did you ever see a salt-mine ? "

" Well,—not exactly a salt-mine; but I have coal-
mines on my property in Staffordshire.   I 'm very fond
of coal.   I hope you like coal."

" I like salt a great deal better,—to look at."

" But which do you think pays best ?   I don't mind
telling you,—though it 's a kind of thing I never talk
about to strangers,—the royalties from the Blogownie
and Toodlem mines go up regularly £2,000 every
year."

" I thought we were talking about what was pretty
to look at."

" So we were.   I 'm as fond of pretty things as anybody.   Do you know Reginald Dobbes? "

" No, I don't.   Is he pretty? "

" He used to be so angry with Silverbridge, because
Silverbridge would say Crummie-Toddie was ugly."

" Was Crummie-Toddie ugly? "

" Just a plain house on a moor."

" That sounds ugly."

" I suppose your family like pretty things."

" I hope so."

" I do, I know."   Lord Popplecourt endeavoured to
look as though he intended her to understand that she
was the pretty thing which he most particularly liked.
She partly conceived his meaning, and was disgusted
accordingly.   On the other side of her sat Mr. Boncassen, to whom she had been introduced in the drawing-room,—and who had said a few words to her about
some Norwegian poet.   She turned round to him, and

asked him some question about the Skald, and so, getting into conversation with him, managed to turn her shoulder to her suitor. On the other side of him sat Lady Rosina De Courcy, to whom, as being an old woman and an old maid, he felt very little inclined to be courteous. She said a word, asking him whether he did not think the weather was treacherous. He answered her very curtly, and sat bolt upright, looking forward on the table, and taking his dinner as it came to him. He had been put there in order that Lady Mary Palliser might talk to him, and he regarded interference on the part of that old American as being ungentlemanlike. But the old American disregarded him, and went on with his quotations from the Scandinavian bard. But Mr. Boncassen sat next to Lady Cantrip, and when at last he was called upon to give his ear to the Countess, Lady Mary was again vacant for Popplecourt's attentions. "Are you very fond of poetry?" he asked.

"Very fond."

"So am I. Which do you like best, Tennyson or Shakespeare?"

"They are very unlike."

"Yes;—they are unlike. Or Moore's Melodies. I'm very fond of 'When in death I shall calm recline.' I think this equal to anything. Reginald Dobbes would have it that poetry is all bosh."

"Then I think that Mr. Reginald Dobbes must be all bosh himself."

"There was a man there named Tregear who had brought some books." Then there was a pause. Lady Mary had not a word to say. "Dobbes used to declare that he was always pretending to read poetry."

"Mr. Tregear never pretends anything."

"Do you know him?" asked the rival.

"He is my brother's most particular friend."

"Ah; yes. I dare say Silverbridge has talked to you about him. I think he's a stuck-up sort of fellow." To this there was not a word of reply. "Where did your brother pick him up?"

"They were at Oxford together."

"I must say I think he gives himself airs;—because, you know, he's nobody."

"I don't know anything of the kind," said Lady Mary, becoming very red. "And as he is my brother's most particular friend,—his very friend of friends,—I think you had better not abuse him to me."

"I don't think the Duke is very fond of him."

"I don't care who is fond of him. I am very fond of Silverbridge and I won't hear his friend ill-spoken of. I dare say he had some books with him. He is not at all the sort of man to go to a place and satisfy himself with doing nothing but killing animals."

"Do you know him, Lady Mary?"

"I have seen him, and of course I have heard a great deal of him from Silverbridge. I would rather not talk any more about him."

"You seem to be very fond of Mr. Tregear," he said angrily.

"It is no business of yours, Lord Popplecourt, whether I am fond of anybody or not. I have told you that Mr. Tregear is my brother's friend, and that ought to be enough."

Lord Popplecourt was a young man possessed of a certain amount of ingenuity. It was said of him that he knew on which side his bread was buttered, and that if you wished to take him in you must get up early. After dinner and during the night he pondered a good deal on what he had heard. Lady Cantrip had told him that there had been a—dream. What was he to believe about that dream? Had he not better avoid the error of putting too fine a point upon it, and tell himself at once that a dream in this instance meant a—lover! Lady Mary had already been troubled by a lover! He was disposed to believe that young ladies often do have objectionable lovers, and that things get themselves right afterwards. Young ladies can be made to understand the beauty of coal-mines almost as readily as young gentlemen. There would be the £200,000; and there was the girl, beautiful, well-born, and thoroughly well-mannered. But what if this Tregear and the dream were one and the same? If so, had he not received plenty of evidence that the dream had not yet passed away? A remnant of affection for the dream would not have been a fatal barrier, had not the girl been so fierce with him in defence of her dream. He remembered, too, what the Duke had said about Tregear, and Lady Cantrip's advice to him to be silent in respect to this man. And then do girls generally defend their brothers' friends as she had defended Tregear? He thought not. Putting all these things together, on the following morning he had come to an uncomfortable belief that Tregear was the dream.

Soon after that he found himself near to Dolly Longstaff as they were shooting. "You know that fellow Tregear, don't you?"

"Oh Lord, yes. He is Silverbridge's pal."

"Did you ever hear anything about him?"

"What sort of thing?"

"Was he ever—ever in love with any one?"

"I fancy he used to be awfully spooney on Mab Grex. I remember hearing that they were to have been married, only that neither of them had sixpence."

"Oh—Lady Mabel Grex! That's a horse of another colour."

"And which is the horse of your colour?"

"I have n't got a horse," said Lord Popplecourt, going away to his own corner.

CHAPTER XXI.

MISS BONCASSEN'S IDEA OF HEAVEN.

IT was generally known that Dolly Longstaff had been heavily smitten by the charms of Miss Boncassen; but the world hardly gave him credit for the earnestness of his affection. Dolly had never been known to be in earnest in anything;—but now he was in very truth in love. He had agreed to be Popplecourt's companion at Custins because he had heard that Miss Boncassen would be there. He had thought over the matter with more consideration than he had ever before given to any subject. He had gone so far as to see his own man of business, with a view of ascertaining what settlements he could make and what income he might be able to spend. He had told himself over and over again that he was not the "sort of fellow" that ought to marry; but it was all of no avail. He confessed to himself that he was completely "bowled over,"—"knocked off his pins!"

"Is a fellow to have no chance?" he said to Miss Boncassen at Custins.

"If I understand what a fellow means, I am afraid not."

"No man alive was ever more in earnest than I am."

"Well, Mr. Longstaff; I do not suppose that you have been trying to take me in all this time."

"I hope you do not think ill of me."

"I may think well of a great many gentlemen without wishing to marry them."

"But does love go for nothing?" said Dolly, putting his hand upon his heart. "Perhaps there are so many that love you."

"Not above half-a-dozen or so."

"You can make a joke of it, when I—— But I don't think, Miss Boncassen, you at all realise what I feel. As to settlements and all that, your father could do what he likes with me."

"My father has nothing to do with it, and I don't know what settlements mean. We never think anything of settlements in our country. If two young people love each other they go and get married."

"Let us do the same here."

"But the two young people don't love each other. Look here, Mr. Longstaff; it's my opinion that a young woman ought not to be pestered."

"Pestered!"

"You force me to speak in that way. I've given you an answer ever so many times. I will not be made to do it over and over again."

"It's that d——d fellow, Silverbridge," he exclaimed, almost angrily. On hearing this Miss Boncassen left the room without speaking another word, and Dolly Longstaff found himself alone. He saw what he had done as soon as she was gone. After that he could hardly venture to persevere again,—here at Custins. He weighed it over in his mind for a long time, almost coming to a resolution in favour of hard drink. He had never felt anything like this before. He was so uncomfortable that he couldn't eat his luncheon, though in accordance with his usual habit he had breakfasted off soda and brandy and a morsel of devilled toast.   He did not know himself in his changed character.   "I wonder whether she understands that I have £4,000 a year of my own, and shall have £12,000 more when my governor goes!   She was so head-strong that it was impossible to explain anything to her."

"I'm off to London," he said to Popplecourt that afternoon.

"Nonsense! you said you'd stay for ten days."

"All the same, I'm going at once.   I've sent to Bridport for a trap, and I shall sleep to-night at Dorchester."

"What's the meaning of it all?"

"I've had some words with somebody.   Don't mind asking any more."

"Not with the Duke?"

"The Duke!   No;—I have n't spoken to him."

"Or Lord Cantrip?"

"I wish you would n't ask questions."

"If you've quarreled with anybody you ought to consult a friend."

"It's nothing of that kind."

"Then it's a lady.   It's the American girl!"

"Don't I tell you, I don't want to talk about it? I'm going.   I've told Lady Cantrip that my mother was n't well and wants to see me.   You'll stop your time out, I suppose?"

"I don't know."

"You've got it all square, no doubt.   I wish I'd a handle to my name.   I never cared for it before."

"I'm sorry you're so down in the mouth.   Why don't you try again?   The thing is to stick to 'em like wax. If ten times of asking won't do, go in twenty times."

Dolly shook his head despondently. "What can you do when a girl walks out of the room and slams the door in your face? She'll get it hot and heavy before she has done. I know what she's after. She might as well cry for the moon." And so Dolly got into the trap and went to Bridport and slept that night at the hotel at Dorchester.

Lord Popplecourt, though he could give such excellent advice to his friend, had been able as yet to do very little in his own case. He had been a week at Custins, and had said not a word to denote his passion. Day after day he had prepared himself for the encounter, but the lady had never given him the opportunity. When he sat next to her at dinner she would be very silent. If he stayed at home on a morning she was not visible. During the short evenings he could never get her attention. And he made no progress with the Duke. The Duke had been very courteous to him at Richmond, but here he was monosyllabic and almost sullen.

Once or twice Lord Popplecourt had a little conversation with Lady Cantrip. "Dear girl," said her ladyship. "She is so little given to seeking admiration."

"I dare say."

"Girls are so different, Lord Popplecourt. With some of them it seems that a gentleman need have no trouble in explaining what it is that he wishes."

"I don't think Lady Mary is like that at all."

"Not in the least. Any one who addresses her must be prepared to explain himself fully. Nor ought he to hope to get much encouragement at first. I do not think that Lady Mary will bestow her heart till she is sure she can give it with safety." There was an amount of falsehood in this which was proof at any rate of very strong friendship on the part of Lady Cantrip.

After a few days Lady Mary became more intimate with the American and his daughter than with any others of the party. Perhaps she liked to talk about the Scandinavian poets, of whom Mr. Boncassen was so fond. Perhaps she felt sure that her transatlantic friend would not make love to her. Perhaps it was that she yielded to the various allurements of Miss Boncassen. Miss Boncassen saw the Duke of Omnium for the first time at Custins, and there had the first opportunity of asking herself how such a man as that would receive from his son and heir such an announcement as Lord Silverbridge would have to make him should she at the end of three months accept his offer. She was quite aware that Lord Silverbridge need not repeat the offer unless he were so pleased. But she thought that he would come again. He had so spoken that she was sure of his love; and had so spoken as to obtain hers. Yes;—she was sure that she loved him. She had never seen anything like him before; —so glorious in his beauty, so gentle in his manhood, so powerful and yet so little imperious, so great in condition, and yet so little confident in his own greatness, so bolstered up with external advantages, and so little apt to trust to anything but his own heart and his own voice. In asking for her love he had put forward no claim but his own love. She was glad he was what he was. She counted at their full value all his natural advantages. To be an English duchess! Oh—yes;

her ambition understood it all! But she loved him, because in the expression of his love no hint had fallen from him of the greatness of the benefits which he could confer upon her. Yes, she would like to be a duchess; but not to be a duchess would she become the wife of a man who should begin his courtship by assuming a superiority.

Now the chances of society had brought her into the company of his nearest friends. She was in the house with his father and with his sister. Now and again the Duke spoke a few words to her, and always did so with a peculiar courtesy. But she was sure that the Duke had heard nothing of his son's courtship. And she was equally sure that the matter had not reached Lady Mary's ears. She perceived that the Duke and her father would often converse together. Mr. Boncassen would discuss republicanism generally, and the Duke would explain that theory of monarchy as it prevails in England, which but very few Americans have ever been made to understand. All this Miss Boncassen watched with pleasure. She was still of opinion that it would not become her to force her way into a family which would endeavour to repudiate her. She would not become this young man's wife if all connected with the young man were resolved to reject the contact. But if she could conquer them,—then,— then she thought that she could put her little hand into that young man's grasp with a happy heart.

It was in this frame of mind that she laid herself out not unsuccessfully to win the esteem of Lady Mary Palliser. "I do not know whether you approve it," Lady Cantrip said to the Duke; "but Mary has become very intimate with our new American friend."

At this time Lady Cantrip had become very nervous, —so as almost to wish that Lady Mary's difficulties might be unravelled elsewhere than at Custins.

"They seem to be sensible people," said the Duke. "I don't know when I have met a man with higher ideas on politics than Mr. Boncassen."

"His daughter is popular with everybody."

"A nice ladylike girl," said the Duke, "and appears to have been well educated."

It was now near the end of October, and the weather was peculiarly fine. Perhaps in our climate, October would of all months be the most delightful if something of its charms were not detracted from by the feeling that with it will depart the last relics of the delights of summer. The leaves are still there with their gorgeous colouring, but they are going. The last rose still lingers on the bush, but it is the last. The woodland walks are still pleasant to the feet, but caution is heard on every side as to the coming winter.

The park at Custins, which was spacious, had many woodland walks attached to it, from which, through vistas of the timber, distant glimpses of the sea were caught. Within half a mile of the house the woods were reached, and within a mile the open sea was in sight,—and yet the wanderers might walk for miles without going over the same ground. Here, without other companions, Lady Mary and Miss Boncassen found themselves one afternoon, and here the latter told her story to her lover's sister. "I so long to tell you something," she said.

"Is it a secret?" asked Lady Mary.

"Well; yes; it is,—if you will keep it so. I would rather you should keep it a secret. But I will tell you."

Then she stood still, looking into the other's face. "I wonder how you will take it?"

"What can it be?"

"Your brother has asked me to be his wife."

"Silverbridge!"

"Yes;—Lord Silverbridge. You are astonished."

Lady Mary was very much astonished,—so much astonished that words escaped from her, which she regretted afterwards. "I thought there was some one else."

"Who else?"

"Lady Mabel Grex. But I know nothing."

"I think not," said Miss Boncassen slowly. "I have seen them together and I think not. There might be somebody, though I think not her. But why do I say that? Why do I malign him, and make so little of myself. There is no one else, Lady Mary. Is he not true?"

"I think he is true."

"I am sure he is true. And he has asked me to be his wife."

"What did you say?"

"Well;—what do you think? What is it probable that such a girl as I would say when such a man as your brother asks her to be his wife? Is he not such a man as a girl would love?"

"Oh yes."

"Is he not handsome as a god?" Mary stared at her with all her eyes. "And sweeter than any god those pagan races knew? And is he not good-tempered, and loving;—and has he not that perfection of manly dash without which I do not think I could give my heart to any man?"

"Then you have accepted him?"

"And his rank and his wealth! The highest position in all the world in my eyes."

"I do not think you should take him for that."

"Does it not all help? Can you put yourself in my place? Why should I refuse him? No, not for that. I would not take him for that. But if I love him,—because he is all that my imagination tells me that a man ought to be;—if to be his wife seems to me to be the greatest bliss that could happen to a woman; if I feel that I could die to serve him, that I could live to worship him, that his touch would be sweet to me, his voice music, his strength the only support in the world on which I would care to lean,—what then?"

"Is it so?"

"Yes, it is so. It is after that fashion that I love him. He is my hero;—and not the less so because there is none higher than he among the nobles of the greatest land under the sun. Would you have me for a sister?" Lady Mary could not answer all at once. She had to think of her father;—and then she thought of her own lover. Why should not Silverbridge be as well entitled to his choice as she considered herself to be? And yet how would it be with her father? Silverbridge would in process of time be the head of the family. Would it be proper that he should marry an American?

"You would not like me for a sister?"

"I was thinking of my father. For myself I like you."

"Shall I tell you what I said to him?"

"If you will."

"I told him that he must ask his friends;—that I

would not be his wife to be rejected by them all. Nor will I. Though it be heaven I will not creep there through a hole. If I cannot go in with my head upright, I will not go even there." Then she turned round as though she were prepared in her emotion to walk back to the house alone. But Lady Mary ran after her, and having caught her put her arm round her waist and kissed her.

"I at any rate will love you," said Lady Mary.

"I will do as I have said," continued Miss Boncassen. "I will do as I have said. Though I love your brother down to the ground he shall not marry me without his father's consent." Then they returned arm-in-arm close together; but very little more was said between them.

When Lady Mary entered the house she was told that Lady Cantrip wished to see her in her own room.

CHAPTER XXII.

THE PARTY AT CUSTINS IS BROKEN UP.

THE message was given to Lady Mary after so
solemn a fashion that she was sure some important
communication was to be made to her. Her mind at
that moment had been filled with her new friend's story.
She felt that she required some time to meditate before
she could determine what she herself would wish; but
when she was going to her own room, in order that
she might think it over, she was summoned to Lady
Cantrip. " My dear," said the Countess, " I wish you
to do something to oblige me."

" Of course I will."

" Lord Popplecourt wants to speak to you."

" Who? "

" Lord Popplecourt."

" What can Lord Popplecourt have to say to me ? "

" Can you not guess ? Lord Popplecourt is a young
nobleman, standing very high in the world, possessed
of ample means, just in that position in which it be-
hoves such a man to look about for a wife." Lady
Mary pressed her lips together, and clenched her two
hands. " Can you not imagine what such a gentleman
may have to say? " Then there was a pause, but she
made no immediate answer. " I am to tell you, my
dear, that your father would approve of it."

" Approve of what ? "

"He approves of Lord Popplecourt as a suitor for your hand."

"How can he?"

"Why not, Mary? Of course he has made it his business to ascertain all particulars as to Lord Popplecourt's character and property."

"Papa knows that I love somebody else."

"My dear Mary, that is all vanity."

"I don't think that papa can want to see me married to a man when he knows that with all my heart and soul—— "

"Oh Mary!"

"When he knows," continued Mary, who would not be put down, "that I love another man with all my heart. What will Lord Popplecourt say if I tell him that? If he says anything to me, I shall tell him. Lord Popplecourt! He cares for nothing but his coal-mines. Of course, if you bid me see him I will; but it can do no good. I despise him, and if he troubles me I shall hate him. As for marrying him,—I would sooner die this minute."

After this Lady Cantrip did not insist on the interview. She expressed her regret that things should be as they were,—explained in sweetly innocent phrases that in a certain rank of life young ladies could not always marry the gentlemen to whom their fancies might attach them, but must, not unfrequently, postpone their youthful inclinations to the will of their elders,—or in less delicate language, that though they might love in one direction they must marry in another; and then expressed a hope that her dear Mary would think over these things and try to please her father. "Why does he not try to please me?" said Mary.

Then Lady Cantrip was obliged to see Lord Popple-court, a necessity which was a great nuisance to her. "Yes;—she understands what you mean.   But she is not prepared for it yet.   You must wait awhile."

"I don't see why I am to wait."

"She is very young,—and so are you, indeed.   There is plenty of time."

"There is somebody else, I suppose."

"I told you," said Lady Cantrip, in her softest voice, "that there has been a dream across her path."

"It's that Tregear!"

"I am not prepared to mention names," said Lady Cantrip, astonished that he should know so much. "But indeed you must wait."

"I don't see it, Lady Cantrip."

"What can I say more ?   If you think that such a girl as Lady Mary Palliser, the daughter of the Duke of Omnium, possessed of fortune, beauty, and every good gift, is to come like a bird to your call, you will find yourself mistaken.   All that her friends can do for you will be done.   The rest must remain with yourself." During that evening Lord Popplecourt endeavoured to make himself pleasant to one of the Fitz-Howard young ladies, and on the next morning he took his leave of Custins.

"I will never interfere again in reference to any-body else's child as long as I live," Lady Cantrip said to her husband that night.

Lady Mary was very much tempted to open her heart to Miss Boncassen.   It would be delightful to her to have a friend ; but were she to engage Miss Boncassen's sympathies on her behalf, she must of course sympathise with Miss Boncassen in return.   And

what if, after all, Silverbridge were not devoted to the
American beauty! What if it should turn out that he
were going to marry Lady Mabel Grex. "I wish you
would call me Isabel," her friend said to her. "It is
so odd,—since I have left New York I have never
heard my name from any lips except father's and
mother's."

"Has not Silverbridge ever called you by your
christian name?"

"I think not. I am sure he never has." But he
had, though it had passed by her at the moment without attention. "It all came from him so suddenly.
And yet I expected it. But it was too sudden for
christian names and pretty talk. I do not even know
what his name is."

"Plantagenet;—but we always call him Silverbridge."

"Plantagenet is very much prettier. I shall always
call him Plantagenet. But I recall that. You will not
remember that against me?"

"I will remember nothing that you do not wish."

"I mean that if,—if all the grandeurs of all the Pallisers could consent to put up with poor me, if heaven
were opened to me with a straight gate, so that I could
walk out of our republic into your aristocracy with my
head erect, with the stars and stripes waving proudly
round me till I had been accepted into the shelter of
the Omnium griffins,—then I would call him——"

"There's one Palliser would welcome you."

"Would you, dear? Then I will love you so dearly.
May I call you Mary?"

"Of course you may."

"Mary is the prettiest name under the sun. But

Plantagenet is so grand!   Which of the kings did you branch off from? "

" I know nothing about it.   From none of them, I should think.   There is some story about a Sir Guy, who was a king's friend.   I never trouble myself about it.   I hate aristocracy."

" Do you, dear ? "

" Yes," said Mary, full of her own grievances.   " It is an abominable bondage, and I do not see that it does any good at all."

" I think it is so glorious," said the American. " There is no such mischievous nonsense in all the world as equality.   That is what father says.   What men ought to want is liberty."

" It is terrible to be tied up in a small circle," said the Duke's daughter.

" What do you mean, Lady Mary? "

" I thought you were to call me Mary.   What I mean is this.   Suppose that Silverbridge loves you better than all the world."

" I hope he does.   I think he does."

" And suppose he cannot marry you, because of his —aristocracy ? "

" But he can."

" I thought you were saying yourself—— "

" Saying what ?   That he could not marry me! No, indeed!   But that under certain circumstances I would not marry him.   You don't suppose that I think he would be disgraced?   If so I would go away at once, and he should never again see my face or hear my voice.   I think myself good enough for the best man God ever made.   But if others think differently, and those others are so closely concerned with him and

would be so closely concerned with me, as to trouble
our joint lives,—then will I neither subject him to such
sorrow nor will I encounter it myself."

" It all comes from what you call aristocracy."

" No, dear;—but from the prejudices of an aristocracy. To tell the truth, Mary, the more difficult a
place is to get into, the more the right of going in is
valued. If everybody could be a duchess and a Palliser, I should not perhaps think so much about it."

" I thought it was because you loved him."

" So I do. I love him entirely. I have said not a
word of that to him;—but I do, if I know at all what
love is. But if you love a star, the pride you have in
your star will enhance your love. Though you know
that you must die of your love, still you must love
your star."

And yet Mary could not tell her tale in return. She
could not show the reverse picture;—that she being a
star was anxious to dispose of herself after the fashion
of poor human rushlights. It was not that she was
ashamed of her love, but that she could not bring herself to yield altogether in reference to the great descent
which Silverbridge would have to make.

On the day after this,—the last day of the Duke's
sojourn at Custins, the last also of the Boncassens'
visit,—it came to pass that the Duke and Mr. Boncassen, with Lady Mary and Isabel, were all walking in
the woods together. And it so happened when they
were at a little distance from the house, each of the
girls was walking with the other girl's father. Isabel
had calculated what she would say to the Duke should
a time for speaking come to her. She could not tell

him of his son's love.   She could not ask his permission.
She could not explain to him all her feelings, or tell
him what she thought of her proper way of getting into
heaven.   That must come afterwards if it should ever
come at all.   But there was something that she could
tell.   "We are so different from you," she said, speaking of her own country.

"And yet so like," said the Duke, smiling;—"your
language, your laws, your habits!"

"But still there is such a difference!   I do not think
there is a man in the whole Union more respected than
father."

"I dare say not."

"Many people think that if he would only allow
himself to be put in nomination, he might be the next
president."

"The choice, I am sure, would do your country
honour."

"And yet his father was a poor labourer who earned
his bread among the shipping at New York.   That
kind of thing would be impossible here."

"My dear young lady, there you wrong us."

"Do I?"

"Certainly!   A Prime Minister with us might as
easily come from the same class."

"Here you think so much of rank.   You are—a
duke."

"But a Prime Minister can make a duke, and if a
man can raise himself by his own intellect to that position, no one will think of his father or his grandfather.
The sons of merchants have with us been Prime Min-
isters more than once, and no Englishmen ever were

more honoured among their countrymen. Our peerage is being continually recruited from the ranks of the people, and hence it gets its strength."

" Is it so? "

" There is no greater mistake than to suppose that inferiority of birth is a barrier to success in this country." She listened to this and to much more on the same subject with attentive ears,—not shaken in her ideas as to the English aristocracy in general, but thinking that she was perhaps learning something of his own individual opinions. If he were more liberal than others, on that liberality might perhaps be based her own happiness and fortune.

He in all this was quite unconscious of the working of her mind. Nor in discussing such matters generally did he ever mingle his own private feelings, his own pride of race and name, his own ideas of what was due to his ancient rank with the political creed by which his conduct in public life was governed. The peer who sat next to him in the House of Lords, whose grandmother had been a washerwoman and whose father an innkeeper, was to him every whit as good a peer as himself. And he would as soon sit in counsel with Mr. Monk, whose father had risen from a mechanic to be a merchant, as with any nobleman who could count ancestors against himself. But there was an inner feeling in his bosom as to his own family, his own name, his own children, and his own personal self, which was kept altogether apart from his grand political theories. It was a subject on which he never spoke ; but the feeling had come to him as a part of his birthright. And he conceived that it would pass through him to his children after the same fashion. It was this which made the idea of a marriage between his daughter and Tregear intolerable to him, and which would operate as strongly in regard to any marriage which his son might comtemplate. Lord Grex was not a man with whom he would wish to form any intimacy. He was, we may say, a wretched unprincipled old man, bad all round; and such the Duke knew him to be. But the blue blood and the rank were there; and as the girl was good herself he would have been quite contented that his son should marry the daughter of Lord Grex. That one and the same man should have been in one part of himself so unlike the other part,—that he should have one set of opinions so contrary to another set,—poor Isabel Boncassen did not understand.

CHAPTER XXIII.

THE MAJOR'S FATE.

THE affair of Prime Minister and the nail was not allowed to fade away into obscurity. Through September and October it was made matter for pungent inquiry. The Jockey Club was alive. Mr. Pook was very instant,—with many Pookites anxious to free themselves from suspicion. Sporting men declared that the honour of the turf required that every detail of the case should be laid open. But by the end of October, though every detail had been surmised, nothing had in truth been discovered. Nobody doubted but that Tifto had driven the nail into the horse's foot, and that Green and Gilbert Villiers had shared the bulk of the plunder. They had gone off on their travels together, and the fact that each of them had been in possession of about £20,000 was proved. But then there is no law against two gentlemen having such a sum of money. It was notorious that Captain Green and Mr. Gilbert Villiers had enriched themselves to this extent by the failure of Prime Minister. But yet nothing was proved!

That the Major had either himself driven in the nail or seen it done, all racing men were agreed. He had been out with the horse in the morning and had been the first to declare that the animal was lame. And he had been with the horse till the farrier had come. But he had concocted a story for himself. He did not dispute that the horse had been lamed by the machinations of Green and Villiers,—with the assistance of the groom. No doubt, he said, these men, who had been afraid to face an inquiry, had contrived and had carried out the iniquity. How the lameness had been caused he could not pretend to say. The groom who was at the horse's head, and who evidently knew how these things were done, might have struck a nerve in the horse's foot with his boot. But when the horse was got into the stable he, Tifto,—so he declared,—at once ran out to send for the farrier. During the minutes so occupied the operation must have been made with the nail. That was Tifto's story,—and as he kept his ground, there were some few who believed it.

But though the story was so far good, he had at moments been imprudent, and had talked when he should have been silent. The whole matter had been a torment to him. In the first place his conscience made him miserable. As long as it had been possible to prevent the evil he had hoped to make a clean breast of it to Lord Silverbridge. Up to this period of his life everything had been "square" with him. He had betted "square," and had ridden "square," and had run horses "square." He had taken a pride in this, as though it had been a great virtue. It was not without great inward grief that he had deprived himself of the consolations of these reflections! But when he had approached his noble partner, his noble partner snubbed him at every turn,—and he did the deed.

His reward was to be £3,000,—and he got his money. The money was very much to him,—would perhaps have been almost enough to comfort him in his misery, had not those other rascals got so much more.   When he heard that the groom's fee was higher than his own, it almost broke his heart.   Green and Villiers, men of infinitely lower standing,—men at whom the Beargarden would not have looked,—had absolutely netted fortunes on which they could live in comfort.   No doubt they had run away while Tifto still stood his ground;—but he soon began to doubt whether to have run away with £20,000 was not better than to remain with such small plunder as had fallen to his lot, among such faces as those which now looked upon him!   Then when he had drunk a few glasses of whiskey and water, he said something very foolish as to his power of punishing that swindler Green.

An attempt had been made to induce Silverbridge to delay the payment of his bets;—but he had been very eager that they should be paid.   Under the joint auspices of Mr. Lupton and Mr. Morton the horses were sold, and the establishment was annihilated,— with considerable loss but with great despatch.   The Duke had been urgent.   The Jockey Club, and the racing world, and the horsey fraternity generally might do what seemed to them good,—so that Silverbridge was extricated from the matter.   Silverbridge was extricated,—and the Duke cared nothing for the rest.

But Silverbridge could not get out of the mess quite so easily as his father wished.   Two questions arose about Major Tifto, outside the racing world, but within the domain of the world of sport and pleasure generally as to one of which it was impossible that Silverbridge should not express an opinion.   The first question had reference to the mastership of the Runnymede hounds. In this our young friend was not bound to concern himself.   The other affected the Beargarden Club;

and as Lord Silverbridge had introduced the Major,
he could hardly forbear from the expression of an
opinion.

. There was a meeting of the subscribers to the hunt
in the last week of October. At that meeting Major
Tifto told his story. There he was, to answer any
charge which might be brought against him. If he
had made money by losing the race,—where was it
and whence had it come? Was it not clear that a conspiracy might have been made without his knowledge;
—and clear also that the real conspirators had levanted?
He had not levanted! The hounds were his own.
He had undertaken to hunt the country for this season,
and they had undertaken to pay him a certain sum of
money. He should expect and demand that sum of
money. If they chose to make any other arrangement
for the year following they could do so. Then he sat
down and the meeting was adjourned,—the secretary
having declared that he would not act in that capactiy
any longer, nor collect the funds. A farmer had also
asserted that he and his friends had resolved that Major
Tifto should not ride over their fields. On the next
day the Major had his hounds out, and some of the
London men, with a few of the neighbours, joined
him. Gates were locked; but the hounds ran, and
those who chose to ride managed to follow them.
There are men who will stick to their sport though
Apollyon himself should carry the horn. Who cares
whether the lady who fills a theatre be or be not a
moral young woman, or whether the bandmaster who
keeps such excellent time in a ball has or has not paid
his debts? There were men of this sort who supported
Major Tifto;—but then there was a general opinion

that the Runnymede hunt would come to an end unless a new master could be found.

Then in the first week in November a special meeting was called at the Beargarden, at which Lord Silverbridge was asked to attend. "It is impossible that he should be allowed to remain in the club." This was said to Lord Silverbridge by Mr. Lupton. "Either he must go or the club must be broken up."

Silverbridge was very unhappy on the occasion. He had at last been reasoned into believing that the horse had been made the victim of foul play; but he persisted in saying that there was no conclusive evidence against Tifto. The matter was argued with him. Tifto had laid bets against the horse; Tifto had been hand and glove with Green; Tifto could not have been absent from the horse above two minutes; the thing could not have been arranged without Tifto. As he had brought Tifto into the club, and had been his partner on the turf, it was his business to look into the matter. "But for all that," said he, "I'm not going to jump on a man when he's down, unless I feel sure that he's guilty."

Then the meeting was held, and Tifto himself appeared. When the accusation was made by Mr. Lupton, who proposed that he should be expelled, he burst into tears. The whole story was repeated,—the nail, and the hammer, and the lameness; and the moments were counted up, and poor Tifto's bets and friendship with Green were made apparent,—and the case was submitted to the club. An old gentleman who had been connected with the turf all his life, and who would not have scrupled, by square betting, to rob his dearest friend of his last shilling, seconded the proposition,—

telling all the story over again. Then Major Tifto was asked whether he wished to say anything.

" I 've got to say that I 'm here," said Tifto, still crying, " and if I 'd done anything of that kind, of course I 'd have gone with the rest of 'em. I put it to Lord Silverbridge to say whether I 'm that sort of fellow." Then he sat down.

Upon this there was a pause, and the club was manifestly of opinion that Lord Silverbridge ought to say something. " I think that Major Tifto should not have betted against the horse," said Silverbridge.

" I can explain that," said the Major. " Let me explain that. Everybody knows that I 'm a man of small means. I wanted to 'edge, I only wanted to 'edge."

Mr. Lupton shook his head. " Why have you not shown me your book? "

" I told you before that it was stolen. Green got hold of it. I did win a little. I never said I did n't. But what has that to do with hammering a nail into a horse's foot? I have always been true to you, Lord Silverbridge, and you ought to stick up for me now."

" I will have nothing further to do with the matter," said Silverbridge, " one way or the other," and he walked out of the room,—and out of the club. The affair was ended by a magnanimous declaration on the part of Major Tifto that he would not remain in a club in which he was suspected, and by a consent on the part of the meeting to receive the Major's instant resignation.

CHAPTER XXIV.

THE DUKE'S ARGUMENTS.

THE Duke, before he left Custins, had an interview with Lady Cantrip, at which that lady found herself called upon to speak her mind freely. "I don't think she cares about Lord Popplecourt," Lady Cantrip said.

"I am sure I don't know why she should," said the Duke, who was often very aggravating even to his friend.

"But as we had thought——"

"She ought to do as she is told," said the Duke, remembering how obedient his Glencora had been. "Has he spoken to her?"

"I think not."

"Then how can we tell?"

"I asked her to see him, but she expressed so much dislike that I could not press it. I am afraid, Duke, that you will find it difficult to deal with her."

"I have found it very difficult!"

"As you have trusted me so much——"

"Yes;—I have trusted you, and do trust you. I hope you understand that I appreciate your kindness."

"Perhaps, then, you will let me say what I think."

"Certainly, Lady Cantrip."

"Mary is a very peculiar girl,—with great gifts,—but——"

"But what?"

"She is obstinate. Perhaps it would be fairer to say

that she has great firmness of character. It is within your power to separate her from Mr. Tregear. It would be foreign to her character to—to—leave you, except with your approbation."

"You mean, she will not run away."

"She will do nothing without your permission. But she will remain unmarried unless she be allowed to marry Mr. Tregear."

"What do you advise then?"

"That you should yield. As regards money, you could give them what they want? Let him go into public life. You could manage that for him."

"He is conservative!"

"What does that matter when the question is one of your daughter's happiness? Everybody tells me that he is clever and well conducted."

He betrayed nothing by his face as this was said to him. But as he got into the carriage he was a miserable man. It is very well to tell a man that he should yield, but there is nothing so wretched to a man as yielding. Young people and women have to yield,—but for such a man as this, to yield is in itself a misery. In this matter the Duke was quite certain of the propriety of his judgment. To yield would be not only to mortify himself, but to do wrong at the same time. He had convinced himself that the Popplecourt arrangement would come to nothing. Nor had he and Lady Cantrip combined been able to exercise over her the sort of power to which Lady Glencora had been subjected. If he persevered,—and he still was sure, almost sure, that he would persevere,—his object must be achieved after a different fashion. There must be infinite suffering,—suffering both to him and to her.

Could she have been made to consent to marry some
one else, terrible as the rupture might have been, she
would have reconciled herself at last to her new life.
So it had been with his Glencora,—after a time.   Now
the misery must go on from day to day beneath his
eyes, with the knowledge on his part that he was
crushing all joy out of her young life, and the conviction on her part that she was being treated with continued cruelty by her father!   It was a terrible pros-
pect!   But if it was manifestly his duty to act after
this fashion, must he not do his duty?

   If he were to find that by persevering in this course
he would doom her to death, or perchance to madness,
—what then?   If it were right, he must still do it.   He
must still do it, if the weakness incident to his human
nature did not rob him of the necessary firmness.   If
every foolish girl were indulged, all restraint would be
lost, and there would be an end to those rules as to
birth and position by which he thought his world was
kept straight.   And then, mixed with all this, was his
feeling of the young man's arrogance in looking for
such a match.   Here was a man without a shilling,
whose manifest duty it was to go to work so that he
might earn his bread, who instead of doing so, had
hoped to raise himself to wealth and position by en-
trapping the heart of an unwary girl!   There was
something to the Duke's thinking base in this, and
much more base because the unwary girl was his own
daughter.   That such a man as Tregear should make
an attack upon him and select his rank, his wealth,
and his child as the stepping-stones by which he intended to rise!   What could be so mean as that a
man should seek to live by looking out for a wife with

money? But what so impudent, so arrogant, so un-
blushingly disregardful of propriety, as that he should
endeavour to select his victim from such a family as
that of the Pallisers, and that he should lay his impious
hand on the very daughter of the Duke of Omnium?

But together with all this there came upon him moments of ineffable tenderness. He felt as though he
longed to take her in his arms and tell her, that if she
were unhappy, so would he be unhappy too,—to make
her understand that a hard necessity had made this
sorrow common to them both. He thought that, if
she would only allow it, he could speak of her love as
a calamity which had befallen them, as from the hand
of fate, and not as a fault. If he could make a partnership in misery with her, so that each might believe
that each was acting for the best, then he could endure
all that might come. But, as he was well aware, she
regarded him as being simply cruel to her. She did
not understand that he was performing an imperative
duty. She had set her heart upon a certain object,
and, having taught herself that in that way happiness
might be reached, had no conception that there should
be something in the world, some idea of personal dignity, more valuable to her than the fruition of her own
desires! And yet every word he spoke to her was
affectionate. He knew that she was bruised, and if it
might be possible, he would pour oil into her wounds,
—even though she would not recognise the hand which
relieved her.

They slept one night in town, where they encountered Silverbridge soon after his retreat from the Beargarden. "I cannot quite make up my mind, sir, about
that fellow Tifto," he said to his father.

"I hope you have made up your mind that he is no fit companion for yourself."

"That 's over. Everybody understands that, sir."

"Is anything more necessary ? "

"I don't like feeling that he has been ill-used. They have made him resign the club, and I fancy they won't have him at the hunt."

"He has lost no money by you! "

"Oh no."

"Then I think you may be indifferent. From all that I hear I think he must have won money,—which will probably be a consolation to him."

"I think they have been hard upon him," continued Silverbridge. "Of course he is not a good man, nor a gentleman, nor possessed of very high feelings. But a man is not to be sacrificed altogether for that. There are so many men who are not gentlemen, and so many gentlemen who are bad fellows."

"I have no doubt Mr. Lupton knew what he was about," replied the Duke.

On the next morning the Duke and Lady Mary went down to Matching, and as they sat together in the carriage after leaving the railway the father endeavoured to make himself pleasant to his daughter. "I suppose we shall stay at Matching now till Christmas," he said.

"I hope so."

"Whom would you like to have here ? "

"I don't want any one, papa."

"You will be very sad without somebody. Would you like the Finns? "

"If you please, papa. I like her. He never talks anything but politics."

"He is none the worse for that, Mary. I wonder whether Lady Mabel Grex would come."

"Lady Mabel Grex!"

"Do you not like her?"

"Oh yes, I like her;—but what made you think of her, papa?"

"Perhaps Silverbridge would come to us then."

Lady Mary thought that she knew a great deal more about that than her father did. "Is he fond of Lady Mabel, papa?"

"Well,—I don't know. There are secrets which should not be told. I think they are very good friends. I would not have her asked unless it would please you."

"I like her very much, papa."

"And perhaps we might get the Boncassens to come to us. I did say a word to him about it." Now, as Mary felt, difficulty was heaping itself upon difficulty. "I have seldom met a man in whose company I could take more pleasure than in that of Mr. Boncassen; and the young lady seems to be worthy of her father." Mary was silent, feeling the complication of the difficulties. "Do you not like her?" asked the Duke.

"Very much indeed," said Mary.

"Then let us fix a day and ask them. If you will come to me after dinner with an almanac we will arrange it. Of course you will invite that Miss Cassewary too?"

The complication seemed to be very bad indeed. In the first place was it not clear that she, Lady Mary, ought not to be a party to asking Miss Boncassen to meet her brother at Matching? Would it not be imperative on her part to tell her father the whole story?

And yet how could she do that? It had been told her in confidence, and she remembered what her own feelings had been when Mrs. Finn had suggested the propriety of telling the story which had been told to her! And how would it be possible to ask Lady Mabel to come to Matching to meet Miss Boncassen in the presence of Silverbridge? If the party could be made up without Silverbridge things might run smoothly.

As she was thinking of this in her own room, thinking also how happy she could be if one other name might be added to the list of guests, the Duke had gone alone into his library. There a pile of letters reached him, among which he found one marked "Private," and addressed in a hand which he did not recognise. This he opened suddenly,—with a conviction that it would contain a thorn,—and, turning over the page, found the signature to it was "Francis Tregear." The man's name was wormwood to him. He at once felt that he would wish to have his dinner, his fragment of a dinner brought to him in that solitary room, and that he might remain secluded for the rest of the evening. But still he must read the letter;—and he read it.

"My dear Lord Duke,—If my mode of addressing your Grace be too familiar I hope you will excuse it. It seems to me that if I were to use one more distant I should myself be detracting something from my right to make the claim which I intend to put forward. You know what my feelings are in reference to your daughter. I do not pretend to suppose that they should have the least weight with you. But you know also what her feelings are for me. A man seems to be vain when he expresses his conviction of a woman's love for him-

self. But this matter is so important to her as well as
to me that I am compelled to lay aside all pretence.
If she do not love me as I love her, then the whole
thing drops to the ground. Then it will be for me to
take myself off from out of your notice,—and from
hers, and to keep to myself whatever heart-breaking I
may have to undergo. But if she be as steadfast in
this matter as I am,—if her happiness be fixed on
marrying me as mine is on marrying her,—then, I
think, I am entitled to ask you whether you are justified in keeping us apart.

"I know well what are the discrepancies. Speaking
from my own feeling I regard very little those of rank.
I believe myself to be as good a gentleman as though
my father's forefathers had sat for centuries past in
the House of Lords. I believe that you would have
thought so also had you and I been brought in contact
on any other subject. The discrepancy in regard to
money is, I own, a great trouble to me. Having no
wealth of my own I wish that your daughter were so
circumstanced that I could go out into the world and
earn bread for her. I know myself so well that I dare
say positively that her money,—if it be that she will
have money,—had no attractions for me when I first
became acquainted with her, and adds nothing now to
the persistency with which I claim her hand.

"But I venture to ask whether you can dare to keep
us apart if her happiness depends on her love for me ?
It is now more than six months since I called upon
you in London and explained my wishes. You will
understand me when I say that I cannot be contented
to sit idle, trusting simply to the assurance which I have
of her affection. Did I doubt it, my way would be

more clear. I should feel in that case that she would yield to your wishes, and I should then, as I have said before, just take myself out of the way. But if it be not so, then I am bound to do something,—on her behalf as well as my own. What am I to do? Any endeavour to meet her clandestinely is against my instincts, and would certainly be rejected by her. A secret correspondence would be equally distasteful to both of us. Whatever I do in this matter, I wish you to know that I do it.

"Yours always,

"Most faithfully, and with the greatest respect,

"FRANCIS TREGEAR."

He read the letter very carefully, and at first was simply astonished by what he considered to be the unparalleled arrogance of the young man. In regard to rank this young gentleman thought himself to be as good as anybody else! In regard to money he did acknowledge some inferiority. But that was a misfortune, and could not be helped! Not only was the letter arrogant; but the fact that he should dare to write any letter on such a subject was proof of most unpardonable arrogance. The Duke walked about the room thinking of it till he was almost in a passion. Then he read the letter again and was gradually pervaded by a feeling of its manliness. Its arrogance remained, but with its arrogance there was a certain boldness which induced respect. Whether I am such a son-in-law as you would like or not, it is your duty to accept me, if by refusing to do so you will render your daughter miserable. That was Mr. Tregear's argument. He himself might be prepared to argue in answer that it was his duty to reject such a son-in-law, even though by rejecting him he might make his daughter miserable. He was not shaken; but with his condemnation of the young man there was mingled something of respect.

He continued to digest the letter before the hour of dinner, and when the almanac was brought to him he fixed on certain days. The Boncassens he knew would be free from engagements in ten days' time. As to Lady Mabel, he seemed to think it almost certain that she would come. "I believe she is always going about from one house to another at this time of the year," said Mary.

"I think she will come to us if it be possible," said the Duke. "And you must write to Silverbridge."

"And what about Mr. and Mrs. Finn?"

"She promised she would come again, you know. They are at their own place in Surrey. They will come unless they have friends with them. They have no shooting, and nothing brings people together now except shooting. I suppose there are things here to be shot. And be sure you write to Silverbridge."

CHAPTER XXV.

"THE Duke of Omnium presents his compliments to Mr. Francis Tregear, and begs to acknowledge the receipt of Mr. Tregear's letter of ——. The Duke has no other communication to make to Mr. Tregear, and must beg to decline any further correspondence." This was the reply which the Duke wrote to the applicant for his daughter's hand. And he wrote it at once. He had acknowledged to himself that Tregear had shown a certain manliness in his appeal; but not on that account was such a man to have all that he demanded! It seemed to the Duke that there was no alternative between such a note as that given above and a total surrender.

But the post did not go out during the night, and the note lay hidden in the Duke's private drawer till the morning. There was still that "locus pœnitentiæ" which should be accorded to all letters written in anger. During the day he thought over it all constantly, not in any spirit of yielding, not descending a single step from that altitude of conviction which made him feel that it might be his duty absolutely to sacrifice his daughter,—but asking himself whether it might not be well that he should explain the whole matter at length to the young man. He thought that he could put the matter strongly. It was not by his own doing that he belonged to an aristocracy which, if all exclusiveness

246

were banished from it, must cease to exist. But being what he was, having been born to such privileges and such limitations, was he not bound in duty to maintain a certain exclusiveness? He would appeal to the young man himself to say whether marriage ought to be free between all classes of the community. And if not between all, who was to maintain the limits but they to whom authority in such matters is given? So much in regard to rank! And then he would ask this young man whether he thought it fitting that a young man, whose duty according to all known principles it must be to earn his bread, should avoid that manifest duty by taking a wife who could maintain him. As he roamed about his park alone he felt that he could write such a letter as would make an impression even upon a lover. But when he had come back to his study, other reflections came to his aid. Though he might write the most appropriate letter in the world, would there not certainly be a reply? As to conviction, had he ever known an instance of a man who had been convinced by an adversary? Of course there would be a reply,—and replies. And to such a correspondence there would be no visible end. Words when once written remain, or may remain, in testimony forever. So at last when the moment came he sent off those three lines, with his uncourteous compliments and his demand that there should be no further correspondence.

At dinner he endeavoured to make up for this harshness by increased tenderness to his daughter,—who was altogether ignorant of the correspondence. "Have you written your letters, dear?" She said she had written them.

"I hope the people will come."

"If it will make you comfortable, papa!"

"It is for your sake I wish them to be here. I think that Lady Mabel and Miss Boncassen are just such girls as you would like."

"I do like them; only——"

"Only what?"

"Miss Boncassen is an American."

"Is that an objection? According to my ideas it is desirable to become acquainted with persons of various nations. I have heard, no doubt, many stories of the awkward manners displayed by American ladies. If you look for them you may probably find American women who are not polished. I do not think I shall calumniate my own country if I say the same of English women. It should be our object to select for our own acquaintances the best we can find of all countries. It seems to me that Miss Boncassen is a young lady with whom any other young lady might be glad to form an acquaintance."

This was a little sermon which Mary was quite contented to endure in silence. She was, in truth, fond of the young American beauty, and had felt a pleasure in the intimacy which the girl had proposed to her. But she thought it inexpedient that Miss Boncassen, Lady Mabel, and Silverbridge, should all be at Matching together. Therefore she made a reply to her father's sermon which hardly seemed to go to the point at issue. "She is so beautiful!" she said.

"Very beautiful," said the Duke. "But what has that to do with it? My girl need not be jealous of any girl's beauty." Mary laughed and shook her head. "What is it, then?"

"Perhaps Silverbridge might admire her."

"I have no doubt he would,—or does, for I am aware that they have met. But why should he not admire her?"

"I don't know," said Lady Mary sheepishly.

"I fancy that there is no danger in that direction. I think Silverbridge understands what is expected from him." Had not Silverbridge plainly shown that he understood what was expected from him when he selected Lady Mabel? Nothing could have been more proper, and the Duke had been altogether satisfied. That in such a matter there should have been a change in so short a time did not occur to him. Poor Mary was now completely silenced. She had been told that Silverbridge understood what was expected from him, and of course could not fail to carry home to herself an accusation that she failed to understand what was expected from her.

She had written her letters, but had not as yet sent them. Those to Mrs. Finn and to the two young ladies had been easy enough. Could Mr. and Mrs. Finn come to Matching on the 20th of November? "Papa says that you promised to return, and thinks this time will perhaps suit you." And then to Lady Mabel: "Do come if you can; and papa particularly says that he hopes Miss Cassewary will come also." To Miss Boncassen she had written a long letter, but that too had been written very easily. "I write to you instead of your mamma, because I know you. You must tell her that, and then she will not be angry. I am only papa's messenger, and I am to say how much he hopes that you will come on the 20th. Mr. Boncassen is to bring the whole British Museum if he wishes." Then there was a little postscript which showed that there was already considerable intimacy between the two young ladies. "We won't have either Mr. L. or Lord P." Not a word was said about Lord Silverbridge. There was not even an initial to indicate his name.

But the letter to her brother was more difficult. In her epistles to those others she had so framed her words as if possible to bring them to Matching. But in writing to her brother, she was anxious so to write as to deter him from coming. She was bound to obey her father's commands. He had desired that Silverbridge should be asked to come,—and he was asked to come. But she craftily endeavoured so to word the invitation that he should be induced to remain away. "It is all papa's doing," she said; "and I am glad that he should like to have people here. I have asked the Finns, with whom papa seems to have made up everything. Mr. Warburton will be here of course, and I think Mr. Morton is coming. He seems to think that a certain amount of shooting ought to be done. Then I have invited Lady Mabel Grex and Miss Cassewary, —all of papa's choosing, and the Boncassens. Now you will know whether the set will suit you. Papa has particularly begged that you will come,—apparently because of Lady Mabel. I don't at all know what that means. Perhaps you do. As I like Lady Mabel, I hope she will come." Surely Silverbridge would not run himself into the jaws of the lion. When he heard that he was specially expected by his father to come to Matching in order that he might make himself agreeable to one young lady, he would hardly venture to come, seeing that he would be bound to make love to another young lady!

To Mary's great horror, all the invitations were ac-

cepted.   Mr. and Mrs. Finn were quite at the Duke's
disposal.   That she had expected.   The Boncassens
would all come.   This was signified in a note from
Isabel, which covered four sides of the paper and was
full of fun.   But under her signature had been written a few words,—not in fun,—words which Lady
Mary perfectly understood.   "I wonder, I wonder, I
wonder!"   Did the Duke when inviting her know
anything of his son's inclinations?   Would he be made
to know them now, during this visit?   And what would
he say when he did know them?

That the Boncassens would come was a matter of
course; but Mary had thought that Lady Mabel would
refuse.   She had told Lady Mabel that the Boncassens
had been asked, and to her thinking it had not been
improbable that the young lady would be unwilling to
meet her rival at Matching.   But the invitation was
accepted.

But it was her brother's ready acquiescence which
troubled Mary chiefly.   He wrote as though there
were no doubt about the matter.   "Of course there is
a deal of shooting to be done," he said, "and I consider myself bound to look after it.   There ought not
to be less than four guns,—particularly if Warburton
is to be one of them.   I like Warburton very much,
but I think he shoots badly to ingratiate himself with
the governor.   I wonder whether the governor would
get leave for Gerald for a week.   He has been sticking
to his work like a brick.   If not, would he mind my
bringing some one?   You ask the governor and let me
know.   I'll be there on the 20th.   I wonder whether
they'll let me hear what goes on among them about
politics.   I'm sure there is not one of them hates Sir

Timothy worse than I do. Lady Mab is a brick, and I'm glad you have asked her. I don't think she'll come, as she likes shutting herself up at Grex. Miss Boncassen is another brick. And if you can manage about Gerald I will say that you are a third."

This would have been all very well had she not known that secret. Could it be that Miss Boncassen had been mistaken? She was forced to write again to say that her father did not think it right that Gerald should be brought away from his studies for the sake of shooting, and that the necessary fourth gun would be there in the person of one Barrington Erle. Then she added: "Lady Mabel Grex is coming, and so is Miss Boncassen." But to this she received no reply.

Though Silverbridge had written to his sister in his usual careless style, he had considered the matter much. The three months were over. He had no idea of any hesitation on his part. He had asked her to be his wife, and he was determined to go on with his suit. Had he ever been enabled to make the same request to Mabel Grex, or had she answered him when he did half make it in a serious manner, he would have been true to her. He had not told his father, or his sister, or his friends, as Isabel had suggested. He would not do so till he should have received some more certain answer from her. But in respect to his love he was prepared to be quite as obstinate as his sister. It was a matter for his own consideration, and he would choose for himself. The three months were over, and it was now his business to present himself to the lady again.

That Lady Mabel should also be at Matching would certainly be a misfortune. He thought it probable that she, knowing that Isabel Boncassen and he would be there together, would refuse the invitation. Surely she ought to do so. That was his opinion when he wrote to his sister. When he heard afterwards that she intended to be there, he could only suppose that she was prepared to accept the circumstances as they stood.

CHAPTER XXVI.

MISS BONCASSEN TELLS THE TRUTH.

On the 20th of the month all the guests came rattling in at Matching one after another. The Boncassens were the first, but Lady Mabel with Miss Cassewary followed them quickly. Then came the Finns, and with them Barrington Erle. Lord Silverbridge was the last. He arrived by a train which reached the station at 7 P. M., and only entered the house as his father was taking Mrs. Boncassen into the dining-room. He dressed himself in ten minutes, and joined the party as they had finished their fish. "I am awfully sorry," he said, rushing up to his father, "but I thought that I should just hit it."

"There is no occasion for awe," said the Duke, "as a sufficiency of dinner is left. But how you should have hit it, as you say,—seeing that the train is not due at Bridstock till 7.5, I do not know."

"I 've done it often, sir," said Silverbridge, taking the seat left vacant for him next to Lady Mabel. "We 've had a political caucus of the party,—all the members who could be got together in London,—at Sir Timothy's, and I was bound to attend."

"We 've all heard of that," said Phineas Finn.

"And we pretty well know all the points of Sir Timothy's eloquence," said Barrington Erle.

"I am not going to tell any of the secrets. I have no doubt that there were reporters present, and you will see the whole of it in the papers to-morrow." Then Silverbridge turned to his neighbour. "Well, Lady Mab, and how are you this long time?"

"But how are you? Think what you have gone through since we were at Killancodlem!"

"Don't talk of it."

"I suppose it is not to be talked of."

"Though upon the whole it has happened very luckily. I have got rid of the accursed horses, and my governor has shown what a brick he can be. I don't think there is another man in England who would have done as he did."

"There are not many who could."

"There are fewer who would. When they came into my bedroom that morning and told me that the horse could not run, I thought I should have broken my heart. Seventy thousand pounds gone!"

"Seventy thousand pounds!"

"And the honour and glory of winning the race! And then the feeling that one had been so awfully swindled! Of course I had to look as though I did not care a straw about it, and to go and see the race, with a jaunty air and a cigar in my mouth. That is what I call hard work."

"But you did it?"

"I tried. I wish I could explain to you my state of mind that day. In the first place the money had to be got. Though it was to go into the hands of swindlers, still it had to be paid. I don't know how your father and Percival get on together;—but I felt very like the prodigal son."

"It is very different with papa."

"I suppose so. I felt very like hanging myself

when I was alone that evening.   And now everything is right again."

" I am glad that everything is right," she said, with a strong emphasis on the everything.

" I have done with racing, at any rate.   The feeling of being in the power of a lot of low blackguards is so terrible!   I did love the poor brute so dearly.   And now what have you been doing?"

" Just nothing;—and have seen nobody.   I went back to Grex after leaving Killancodlem, and shut myself up in my misery."

" Why misery?"

" Why misery!   What a question for you to ask! Though I love Grex, I am not altogether fond of living alone; and though Grex has its charms, they are of a melancholy kind.   And when I think of the state of our family affairs, that is not reassuring.   Your father has just paid £70,000 for you.   My father has been good enough to take something less than a quarter of that sum from me;—but still it was all that I was ever to have."

" Girls don't want money."

" Don't they?   When I look forward it seems to me that a time will come when I shall want it very much."

" You will marry," he said.   She turned round for a moment and looked at him, full in the face, after such a fashion that he did not dare to promise her further comfort in that direction.   " Things always do come right, somehow."

" Let us hope so.   Only nothing has ever come right with me yet.   What is Frank doing?"

" I have n't seen him since he left Crummie-Toddie."

" And your sister?" she whispered.

" I know nothing about it at all."

" And you? I have told you everything about my·self."

" As for me, I think of nothing but politics now. I have told you about my racing experiences. Just at present shooting is up. Before Christmas I shall go into Chiltern's country for a little hunting."

" You can hunt here."

" I shan't stay long enough to make it worth while to have my horses down. If Tregear will go with me to the Brake, I can mount him for a day or two. But I dare say you know more of his plans than I do. He went to see you at Grex."

" And you did not."

" I was not asked."

" Nor was he."

" Then all I can say is," replied Silverbridge, speaking in a low voice, but with considerable energy, " that he can use a freedom with Lady Mabel Grex upon which I cannot venture."

" I believe you begrudge me his friendship. If you had no one else belonging to you with whom you could have any sympathy, would not you find comfort in a relation who could be almost as near to you as a brother? "

" I do not grudge him to you."

" Yes, you do. And what business have you to interfere? "

" None at all ;—certainly. I will never do it again."

" Don't say that, Lord Silverbridge. You ought to have more mercy on me. You ought to put up with anything from me,—knowing how much I suffer."

" I will put up with anything," said he.

"Do, do. And now I will try to talk to Mr. Erle."

Miss Boncassen was sitting on the other side of the table, between Mr. Monk and Phineas Finn, and throughout the dinner talked mock politics with the greatest liveliness. Silverbridge when he entered the room had gone round the table and had shaken hands with every one. But there had been no other greeting between him and Isabel, nor had any sign passed from one to the other. No such greeting or sign had been possible. Nothing had been left undone which she had expected, or hoped. But, though she was lively, nevertheless she kept her eye upon her lover and Lady Mabel. Lady Mary had said that she thought her brother was in love with Lady Mabel. Could it be possible? In her own land she had heard absurd stories,—stories which had seemed to her to be absurd, —of the treachery of lords and countesses, of the baseness of aristocrats, of the iniquities of high life in London. But her father had told her that, go where she might, she would find people in the main to be very like each other. It had seemed to her that nothing could be more ingenuous than this young man had been in the declaration of his love. No simplest republican could have spoken more plainly. But now, at this moment, she could not doubt but that her lover was very intimate with this other girl. Of course he was free. When she had refused to say a word to him of her own love or want of love, she had necessarily left him his liberty. When she had put him off for three months, of course he was to be his own master. But what must she think of him if it were so? And how could he have the courage to face her in his father's house if he intended to treat her in such a fashion?

But of all this she showed nothing, nor was there a tone in her voice which betrayed her. She said her last word to Mr. Monk with so sweet a smile that that old bachelor wished he were younger for her sake.

In the evening after dinner there was music. It was discovered that Miss Boncassen sang divinely, and both Lady Mabel and Lady Mary accompanied her. Mr. Erle, and Mr. Warburton, and Mr. Monk, all of whom were unmarried, stood by enraptured. But Lord Silverbridge kept himself apart, and interested himself in a description which Mrs. Boncassen gave him of their young men and their young ladies in the States. He had hardly spoken to Miss Boncassen,— till he offered her sherry or soda-water before she retired for the night. She refused his courtesy with her usual smile, but showed no more emotion than though they two had now met for the first time in their lives.

He had quite made up his mind as to what he would do. When the opportunity should come in his way he would simply remind her that the three months were passed. But he was shy of talking to her in the presence of Lady Mabel and his father. He was quite determined that the thing should be done at once, but he certainly wished that Lady Mabel had not been there. In what she had said to him at the dinner-table she had made him understand that she would be a trouble to him. He remembered her look when he told her she would marry. It was as though she had declared to him that it was he who ought to be her husband. It referred back to that proffer of love which he had once made to her. Of course all this was disagreeable. Of course it made things difficult for him. But not the less was it a thing quite assured that he would press his suit to Miss Boncassen. When he was talking to Mrs. Boncassen he was thinking of nothing else. When he was offering Isabel the glass of sherry he was telling himself that he would find his opportunity on the morrow,—though now, at that moment, it was impossible that he should make a sign. She, as she went to her bed, asked herself whether it were possible that there should be such treachery;— whether it were possible that he should pass it all by as though he had never said a word to her!

During the whole of the next day, which was Sunday, he was equally silent. Immediately after breakfast on the Monday shooting commenced, and he could not find a moment in which to speak. It seemed to him that she purposely kept out of his way. With Mabel he did find himself for a few minutes alone, and was then interrupted by his sister and Isabel. "I hope you have killed a lot of things," said Miss Boncassen.

"Pretty well, among us all."

"What an odd amusement it seems, going out to commit wholesale slaughter. However, it is the proper thing, no doubt."

"Quite the proper thing," said Lord Silverbridge, and that was all.

On the next morning he dressed himself for shooting,—and then sent out the party without him. He had heard, he said, of a young horse for sale in the neighbourhood, and had sent to desire that it might be brought to him. And now he found his occasion. "Come and play a game of billiards," he said to Isabel, as the three girls with the other ladies were together in the drawing-room. She got up very slowly from her seat, and very slowly crept away to the door. Then

she looked round as though expecting the others to
follow her.   None of them did follow her.   Mary felt
that she ought to do so; but, knowing all that she
knew, did not dare.   And what good could she have
done by one such interruption?   Lady Mabel would
fain have gone too;—but neither did she quite dare.
Had there been no special reason why she should or
should not have gone with them, the thing would have
been easy enough.   When two people go to play billiards, a third may surely accompany them.   But now
Lady Mabel found that she could not stir.   Mrs. Finn,
Mrs. Boncassen, and Miss Cassewary were all in the
room, but none of them moved.   Silverbridge led the
way quickly across the hall, and Isabel Boncassen followed him very slowly.   When she entered the room
she found him standing with a cue in his hand.   He
at once shut the door, and walking up to her dropped
the butt of the cue on the floor and spoke one word.
"Well!" he said.

"What does 'well' mean?"

"The three months are over."

"Certainly they are 'over.'"

"And I have been a model of patience."

"Perhaps your patience is more remarkable than
your constancy.   Is not Lady Mabel Grex in the as-
cendant just now?"

"What do you mean by that?   Why do you ask
that?   You told me to wait for three months.   I have
waited, and here I am."

"How very—very—downright you are."

"Is not that the proper thing?"

"I thought I was downright,—but you beat me
hollow.   Yes, the three months are over.   And now

what have you got to say?" He put down his cue, and stretched out his arms as though he were going to take her and hold her to his heart. "No;—no; not that," she said, laughing. "But if you will speak, I will hear you."

"You know what I said before. Will you love me, Isabel?"

"And you know what I said before. Do they know that you love me? Does your father know it, and your sister? Why did they ask me to come here?"

"Nobody knows it. But say that you love me, and every one shall know it at once. Yes;—one person knows it. Why did you mention Lady Mabel's name? She knows it."

"Did you tell her?"

"Yes. I went again to Killancodlem after you were gone, and then I told her."

"But why her? Come, Lord Silverbridge. You are straightforward with me, and I will be the same with you. You have told Lady Mabel; I have told Lady Mary."

"My sister!"

"Yes;—your sister. And I am sure she disapprove. it. She did not say so; but I am sure it is so. And then she told me something."

"What did she tell you?"

"Has there never been reason to think that you intended to offer your hand to Lady Mabel Grex?"

"Did she tell you so?"

"You should answer my question, Lord Silverbridge. It is surely one which I have a right to ask." Then she stood waiting for his reply, keeping herself at some little distance from him as though she were afraid that

he would fly upon her.   And indeed there seemed to
be cause for such fear from the frequent gestures of
his hands.   " Why do you not answer me?   Has there
been reason for such expectations? "

" Yes ;—there has."

" There has! "

" I thought of it,—not knowing myself ; before I
had seen you.   You shall know it all if you will only
say that you love me."

" I should like to know it all first."

" You do know it all ;—almost.   I have told you
that she knows what I said to you at Killancodlem.   Is
not that enough? "

" And she approves! "

" What has that to do with it?   Lady Mabel is my
friend, but not my guardian."

" Has she a right to expect that she should be your
wife? "

" No ;—certainly not.   Why should you ask all this?
Do you love me?   Come, Isabel ; say that you love
me.   Will you call me vain if I say that I almost think
you do?   You cannot doubt about my love ;—not
now."

" No ;—not now."

" You need n't.   Why won't you be as honest to
me ?   If you hate me, say so ;—but if you love
me—— "

" I do not hate you, Lord Silverbridge."

" And is that all? "

" You asked me the question."

" But you do love me?   By George, I thought you
would be more honest and straightforward."

Then she dropped her badinage and answered him

seriously. "I thought I had been honest and straight-forward. When I found that you were in earnest at Killancodlem——"

"Why did you ever doubt me?"

"When I felt that you were in earnest, then I had to be in earnest too. And I thought so much about it that I lay awake nearly all that night. Shall I tell you what I thought?"

"Tell me something that I should like to hear."

"I will tell you the truth. 'Is it possible,' I said to myself, 'that such a man as that can want me to be his wife; he an Englishman of the highest rank and the greatest wealth, and one that any girl in the world would love?'"

"Psha!" he exclaimed.

"That is what I said to myself." Then she paused, and looking into his face she saw that there was a glimmer of a tear in each eye. "One that any girl must love when asked for her love;—because he is so sweet, so good, and so pleasant."

"I know that you are chaffing."

"Then I went on asking myself questions. 'And is it possible that I, who by all his friends will be regarded as a nobody, who am an American,—with merely human work-a-day blood in my veins,—that such a one as I should become his wife?' Then I told myself that it was not possible. It was not in accordance with the fitness of things. All the dukes in England would rise up against it, and especially that Duke whose good-will would be imperative."

"Why should he rise up against it?"

"You know he will. But I will go on with my story of myself. When I had settled that in my mind, I just cried myself to sleep. It had been a dream. I had come across one who in his own self seemed to combine all that I had ever thought of as being lovable in a man——"

"Isabel!"

"And in his outward circumstances soared as much above my thoughts as the heaven is above the earth. And he had whispered to me soft, loving, heavenly words. No;—no, you shall not touch me. But you shall listen to me. In my sleep I could be happy again and not see the barriers. But when I woke I made up my mind. 'If he comes to me again,' I said —'if it should be that he should come to me again, I will tell him that he shall be my heaven on earth,—if, —if,—if the ill-will of his friends would not make that heaven a hell to both of us.' I did not tell you quite all that."

"You told me nothing but that I was to come again in three months."

"I said more than that. I bade you ask your father. Now you have come again. You cannot understand a girl's fears and doubts. How should you? I thought perhaps you would not come. When I saw you whispering to that highly born well-bred beauty, and remembered what I was myself, I thought that—you would not come."

"Then you must love me."

"Love you! Oh, my darling!—No, no, no," she said, as she retreated from him round the corner of the billiard-table, and stood guarding herself from him with her little hands. "You ask if I love you. You are entitled to know the truth. From the sole of your foot to the crown of your head I love you as I think

a man would wish to be loved by the girl he loves.
You have come across my life, and have swallowed
me up, and made me all your own. But I will not
marry you to be rejected by your people. No;—nor
shall there be a kiss between us till I know that it will
not be so."

"May I speak to your father?"

"For what good? I have not spoken to father or
mother because I have known that it must depend
upon your father. Lord Silverbridge, if he will tell me
that I shall be his daughter I will become your wife.
—oh, with such perfect joy, with such perfect truth!
If it can never be so, then let us be torn apart,—with
whatever struggle, still at once. In that case I will
get myself back to my own country as best I may, and
will pray to God that all this may in time be forgotten."
Then she made her way round to the door, leaving
him fixed to the spot in which she had been standing.
But as she went she made a little prayer to him. "Do
not delay my fate. It is all in all to me." And so he
was left alone in the billiard-room.

CHAPTER XXVII.

"THEN I AM AS PROUD AS A QUEEN."

DURING the next day or two the shooting went on without much interruption from love-making. The love-making was not prosperous all round. Poor Lady Mary had nothing to comfort her. Could she have been allowed to see the letter which her lover had written to her father, the comfort would have been, if not ample, still very great. Mary told herself again and again that she was quite sure of Tregear;—but it was hard upon her that she could not be made certain that her certainty was well grounded. Had she known that Tregear had written, though she had not seen a word of his letter, it would have comforted her. But she had heard nothing of the letter. In June last she had seen him, by chance, for a few minutes, in Lady Mabel's drawing-room. Since that she had not heard from him or of him. That was now more than five months since. How could her love serve her,—how could her very life serve her, if things were to go on like that? How was she to bear it? Thinking of this she resolved, she almost resolved, that she would go boldly to her father and desire that she might be given up to her lover.

Her brother, though more triumphant,—for how could he fail to triumph after such words as Isabel had spoken to him,—still felt his difficulties very seriously. She had imbued him with a strong sense of her own firmness, and she had declared that she would go away and leave him altogether if the Duke should be unwilling to receive her. He knew that the Duke would be unwilling. The Duke, who certainly was not handy in those duties of match-making which seemed to have fallen upon him at the death of his wife, showed by a hundred little signs his anxiety that his son and heir should arrange his affairs with Lady Mabel. These signs were manifest to Mary,—were disagreeably manifest to Silverbridge,—were unfortunately manifest to Lady Mabel herself. They were manifest to Mrs. Finn, who was clever enough to perceive that the inclinations of the young heir were turned in another direction. And gradually they became manifest to Isabel Boncassen. The host himself, as host, was courteous to all his guests. They had been of his own selection, and he did his best to make himself pleasant to them all. But he selected two for his peculiar notice, —and those two were Miss Boncassen and Lady Mabel. While he would himself walk, and talk, and argue after his own peculiar fashion with the American beauty,—explaining to her matters political and social, till he persuaded her to promise to read his pamphlet upon decimal coinage,—he was always making awkward efforts to throw Silverbridge and Lady Mabel together. The two girls saw it all and knew well how the matter was,—knew that they were rivals, and knew each the ground on which she herself and on which the other stood. But neither was satisfied with her advantage, or nearly satisfied. Isabel would not take the prize without the Duke's consent;—and Mabel could not have it without that other consent. "If you want to marry an English duke," she once said to Isabel in that anger which she was unable to restrain, "there is the Duke himself. I never saw a man more absolutely in love." "But I do not want to marry an English duke," said Isabel, "and I pity any girl who has any idea of marriage except that which comes from a wish to give back love for love."

Through it all the father never suspected the real state of his son's mind. He was too simple to think it possible that the purpose which Silverbridge had declared to him as they walked together from the Beargarden had already been thrown to the winds. He did not like to ask why the thing was not settled. Young men, he thought, were sometimes shy, and young ladies not always ready to give immediate encouragement. But when he saw them together he concluded that matters were going in the right direction. It was, however, an opinion which he had all to himself.

During the three or four days which followed the scene in the billiard-room Isabel kept herself out of her lover's way. She had explained to him that which she wished him to do, and she left him to do it. Day by day she watched the circumstances of the life around her, and knew that it had not been done. She was sure that it could not have been done while the Duke was explaining to her the beauty of quints, and expatiating on the horrors of twelve pennies and twelve inches and twelve ounces,—variegated in some matters by sixteen and fourteen! He could not know that she was ambitious of becoming his daughter-in-law, while he was opening out to her the mysteries of the House of Lords, and explaining how it came to pass that while he was a memebr of one House of Parlia-

ment, his son should be sitting as a member of another;
—how it was that a nobleman could be a commoner,
and how a peer of one part of the Empire could sit as
the representative of a borough in another part. She
was an apt scholar. Had there been a question of any
other young man marrying her, he would probably have
thought that no other young man could have done
better.

Silverbridge was discontented with himself. The
greatest misfortune was that Lady Mabel should be
there. While she was present to his father's eyes he
did not know how to declare his altered wishes. Every
now and then she would say to him some little word
indicating her feelings of the absurdity of his passion.
" I declare, I don't know whether it is you or your
father that Miss Boncassen most affects," she said. But
to this and to other similar speeches he would make
no answer. She had extracted his secret from him
at Killancodlem, and might use it against him if she
pleased. In his present frame of mind he was not disposed to joke with her upon the subject.

On that second Sunday,—the Boncassens were to
return to London on the following Tuesday,—he found
himself alone with Isabel's father. The American had
been brought out at his own request to see the stables,
and had been accompanied round the premises by
Silverbridge, Mr. Warburton, by Isabel, and by Lady
Mary. As they got out into the park the party were
divided, and Silverbridge found himself with Mr. Boncassen. Then it occurred to him that the proper thing
for a young man in love was to go, not to his own
father, but to the lady's father. Why should not he
do as others always did? Isabel, no doubt, had sug-

gested a different course. But that which Isabel had suggested was at the present moment impossible to him. Now, at this instant, without a moment's forethought, he determined to tell his story to Isabel's father,—as any other lover might tell it to any other father.

"I am very glad to find ourselves alone, Mr. Boncassen," he said. Mr. Boncassen bowed and showed himself prepared to listen. Though so many at Matching had seen the whole play, Mr. Boncassen had seen nothing of it. "I don't know whether you are aware of what I have got to say."

"I cannot quite say that I am, my lord. But whatever it is, I am sure I shall be delighted to hear it."

"I want to marry your daughter," said Silverbridge. Isabel had told him that he was downright, and in such a matter he had hardly as yet learned how to express himself with those paraphrases in which the world delights. Mr. Boncassen stood stockstill, and in the excitement of the moment pulled off his hat. "The proper thing is to ask your permission to go on with it."

"You want to marry my daughter!"

"Yes. That is what I have got to say."

"Is she aware of your—intention?"

"Quite aware. I believe I may say that if other things go straight, she will consent."

"And your father—the Duke?"

"He knows nothing about it,—as yet."

"Really, this takes me quite by surprise. I am afraid you have not given enough thought to the matter."

"I have been thinking about it for the last three months," said Lord Silverbridge.

"Marriage is a very serious thing."

"Of course it is."

"And men generally like to marry their equals."

"I don't know about that.   I don't think that counts for much.   People don't always know who are their equals."

"That is quite true.   If I were speaking to you or to your father theoretically I should perhaps be unwilling to admit superiority on your side because of your rank and wealth.   I could make an argument in favour of any equality with the best Briton that ever lived,— as would become a true-born republican."

"That is just what I mean."

"But when the question becomes one of practising, —a question for our lives, for our happiness, for our own conduct, then, knowing what must be the feelings of an aristocracy in such a country as this, I am prepared to admit that your father would be as well justified in objecting to a marriage between a child of his and a child of mine, as I should be in objecting to one between my child and the son of some mechanic in our native city."

"He would n't be a gentleman," said Silverbridge.

"That is a word of which I don't quite know the meaning."

"I do," said Silverbridge confidently.

"But you could not define it.   If a man be well educated, and can keep a good house over his head, perhaps you may call him a gentleman.   But there are many such with whom your father would not wish to be so closely connected as you propose."

"But I may have your sanction?"   Mr. Boncassen again took off his hat and walked along thoughtfully. "I hope you don't object to me personally."

"My dear young lord, your father has gone out of his way to be civil to me. Am I to return his courtesy by bringing a great trouble upon him?"

"He seems to be very fond of Miss Boncassen."

"Will he continue to be fond of her when he has heard this? What does Isabel say?"

"She says the same as you, of course."

"Why of course?—except that it is evident to you as it is to me that she could not with propriety say anything else."

"I think she would,—would like it, you know."

"She would like to be your wife!"

"Well;—yes. If it were all serene, I think she would consent."

"I dare say she would consent,—if it were all serene. Why should she not? Do not try her too hard, Lord Silverbridge. You say you love her."

"I do indeed."

"Then think of the position in which you are placing her. You are struggling to win her heart." Silverbridge as he heard this assured himself that there was no need for any further struggling in that direction. "Perhaps you have won it. Yet she may feel that she cannot become your wife. She may well say to herself that this which is offered to her is so great that she does not know how to refuse it; and may yet have to say, at the same time, that she cannot accept it without disgrace. You would not put one that you love into such a position?"

"As for disgrace,—that is,—that is nonsense. I beg your pardon, Mr. Boncassen."

"Would it be no disgrace that she should be known here in England to be your wife, and that none of those of your rank,—of what would then be her own rank,—should welcome her into her new world ? "

" That would be out of the question."

" If your own father refused to welcome her, would not others follow suit ? "

" You don't know my father."

" You seem to know him well enough to fear that he would object."

" Yes ;—that is true."

" What more do I want to know ? "

" If she were once my wife he would not reject her. Of all human beings he is in truth the kindest and most affectionate."

" And therefore you would try him after this fashion? No, my lord ; I cannot see my way through these difficulties. You can say what you please to him as to your own wishes. But you must not tell him that you have any sanction from me."

That evening the story was told to Mrs. Boncassen, and the matter was discussed among the family. Isabel in talking to them made no scruple of declaring her own feelings ; and though in speaking to Lord Silverbridge she had spoken very much as her father had done afterwards, yet in this family conclave she took her lover's part. " That is all very well, father," she said ; " I told him the same thing myself. But if he is man enough to be firm I shall not throw him over,—not for all the dukes in Europe. I shall not stay here to be pointed at. I will go back home. If he follows me then I shall choose to forget all about his rank. If he loves me well enough to show that he is in earnest, I shall not disappoint him for the sake of pleasing his father." To this neither Mr. nor Mrs.

Boncassen were able to make any efficient answer.
Mrs. Boncassen, dear good woman, could see no reason
why two young people who loved each other should
not be married at once. Dukes and duchesses were
nothing to her. If they could n't be happy in England, then let them come and live in New York. She
did n't understand that anybody could be too good for
her daughter. Was there not an idea that Mr. Boncassen would be the next president? And was not
the President of the United States as good as the
Queen of England?

Lord Silverbridge when he left Mr. Boncassen wandered about the park by himself. King Cophetua
married the beggar's daughter. He was sure of that.
King Cophetua probably had not a father; and the
beggar, probably, was not high-minded. But the discrepancy in that case was much greater. He intended
to persevere, trusting much to a belief that when once
he was married his father would " come round." His
father always did come round. But the more he
thought of it the more impossible it seemed to him
that he should ask his father's consent at the present
moment. Lady Mabel's presence in the house was
an insuperable obstacle. He thought that he could
do it if he and his father were alone together, or com-
paratively alone. He must be prepared for an opposition, at any rate of some days, which opposition would
make his father quite unable to entertain his guests
while it lasted.

But as he could not declare his wishes to his father,
and was thus disobeying Isabel's behests, he must explain the difficulty to her. He felt already that she
would despise him for his cowardice,—that she would

not perceive the difficulties in his way, or understand that he might injure his cause by precipitation. Then he considered whether he might not possibly make some bargain with his father. How would it be if he should consent to go back to the liberal party on being allowed to marry the girl he loved? As far as his political feelings were concerned he did not think that he would much object to make the change. There was only one thing certain,—that he must explain his condition to Miss Boncassen before she went.

He found no difficulty now in getting the opportunity. She was equally anxious, and as well disposed to acknowledge her anxiety. After what had passed between them she was not desirous of pretending that the matter was one of small moment to herself. She had told him that it was all the world to her, and had begged him to let her know her fate as quickly as possible. On that last Monday morning they were in the grounds together, and Lady Mabel, who was walking with Mrs. Finn, saw them pass through a little gate which led from the gardens into the Priory ruins. " It all means nothing," Mabel said with a little laugh to her companion.

" If so, I am sorry for the young lady," said Mrs. Finn.

" Don't you think that one always has to be sorry for the young lady? Young ladies generally have a bad time of it. Did you ever hear of a gentleman who had always to roll a stone to the top of a hill, but it would always come back upon him ? "

" That gentleman, I believe, never succeeded," said Mrs. Finn. " The young ladies, I suppose, do sometimes."

In the meantime Isabel and Silverbridge were among the ruins together. "This is where the old Pallisers used to be buried," he said.

"Oh, indeed. And married, I suppose."

"I dare say. They had a priest of their own, no doubt, which must have been convenient. This block of a fellow without any legs left is supposed to represent Sir Guy. He ran away with half-a-dozen heiresses, they say. I wish things were as easily done now."

"Nobody should have run away with me. I have no idea of going on such a journey except on terms of equality,—just step and step alike." Then she took hold of his arm and put out one foot. "Are you ready?"

"I am very willing."

"But are you ready,—for a straightforward walk off to church before all the world? None of your private chaplains, such as Sir Guy had at his command. Just the registrar, if there is nothing better,—so that it be public, before all the world."

"I wish we could start this instant."

"But we can't,—can we?"

"No, dear. So many things have to be settled."

"And what have you settled on since you last spoke to me?"

"I have told your father everything."

"Yes;—I know that. What good does that do? Father is not a Duke of Omnium. No one supposed that he would object."

"But he did," said Silverbridge.

"Yes;—as I do,—for the same reason; because he would not have his daughter creep in at a hole. But to your own father you have not ventured to speak." Then he told his story, as best he knew how. It was not that he feared his father, but that he felt that the present moment was not fit. "He wishes you to marry that Lady Mabel Grex," she said. He nodded his head. "And you will marry her?"

"Never! I might have done so, had I not seen you. I should have done so, if she had been willing. But now I never can,—never, never." Her hand had dropped from his arm, but now she put it up again for a moment, so that he might feel the pressure of her fingers. "Say that you believe me."

"I think I do."

"You know I love you."

"I think you do. I am sure I hope you do. If you don't, then I am—a miserable wretch."

"With all my heart I do."

"Then I am as proud as a queen. You will tell him soon?"

"As soon as you are gone. As soon as we are alone together. I will;—and then I will follow you to London. Now shall we not say good-bye?"

"Good-bye, my own," she whispered.

"You will let me have one kiss."

Her hand was in his, and she looked about as though to see that no eyes were watching them. But then, as the thoughts came rushing to her mind, she changed her purpose. "No," she said. "What is it but a trifle! It is nothing in itself. But I have bound myself to myself by certain promises, and you must not ask me to break them. You are as sweet to me as I can be to you, but there shall be no kissing till I know that I shall be your wife. Now take me back."

END OF VOL. II.

+163 = 50

164 [illegible]

Lines

88–90

Few

141

250